Praise for

SANCTUARY

A *TEEN VOGUE* BOOK CLUB PICK
A YALSA BEST FICTION BOOK FOR YOUNG ADULTS
A *SCHOOL LIBRARY JOURNAL* BEST BOOK OF THE YEAR
A *KIRKUS REVIEWS* BEST BOOK OF THE YEAR

"A story of survival and hope, *Sanctuary* is a gripping work of
fiction with a message about xenophobia that's rooted in a scarily
real world." —*New York Times*

"Like classic dystopian novels *1984* and *Fahrenheit 451* . . .
Sanctuary feels all too real in today's oddly apocalyptic world."
—*Teen Vogue*

★ "This searing near-future dystopian novel . . . [uses] a specu-
lative lens to lay bare the trauma and anguish that migrants
to the U.S. can experience as well as the human capacity for
survival. . . . Its message of hope and resilience will carry readers
through." —*Publishers Weekly*, starred review

★ "Beautifully mirror[s] the treacherous, painful, and terrifying treks involving natural and human threats that migrants to
the U.S. undertake as they traverse continents and oceans . . .
Wrenching and unmissable." —*Kirkus Reviews*, starred review

★ "[This] stunning work of YA dystopian fiction . . . is a triumph
in its genre and so politically astute that it sears."
—*School Library Journal*, starred review

SANCTUARY

PAOLA MENDOZA & ABBY SHER

putnam

G. P. PUTNAM'S SONS

G. P. PUTNAM'S SONS
An imprint of Penguin Random House LLC, New York

First published in the United States of America by G. P. Putnam's Sons,
an imprint of Penguin Random House LLC, 2020
First paperback edition published 2021

Visit us online at penguinrandomhouse.com

THE LIBRARY OF CONGRESS HAS CATALOGED THE HARDCOVER EDITION AS FOLLOWS:
Names: Mendoza, Paola, author. | Sher, Abby, author.
Title: Sanctuary / Paola Mendoza & Abby Sher.
Description: New York: G. P. Putnam's Sons, [2020] | Summary: In 2032, when sixteen-year-
old Vali's mother is detained by the Deportation Forces, Vali must flee Vermont with her little
brother, Ernie, hoping to reach their Tía Luna in the sanctuary state of California.
Identifiers: LCCN 2020015279 (print) | LCCN 2020015280 (ebook)
ISBN 9781984815712 (hardcover) | ISBN 9781984815729 (ebook)
Subjects: CYAC: Voyages and travels—Fiction. | Brothers and sisters—Fiction.
Illegal aliens—Fiction. | Hispanic Americans—Fiction. | Science fiction.
Classification: LCC PZ7.1.M47147 San 2020 (print) |
LCC PZ7.1.M47147 (ebook) | DDC [Fic]—dc23
LC record available at https://lccn.loc.gov/2020015279
LC ebook record available at https://lccn.loc.gov/2020015280

Printed in the United States of America

ISBN 9781984815736

5 7 9 10 8 6 4

SKY

Design by Suki Boynton
Text set in Laurentian Std

To the migrants, refugees, and undocumented immigrants who over the years entrusted me with their stories, this book is for you. The power of your love, courage, and dignity lives in these pages.

To my son, Mateo Ali, you are my light, my guide, my hope.

—PAOLA

×

To Sonya, Zev, and Samson. You are remarkable, bright, and brave, and I'm so excited to watch you charge forward into this world with love.

—ABBY

CHAPTER 1

It took fifteen steps for her to die.

Fifteen—one for each year of her life before they snuffed it out.

I was supposed to be doing homework. I actually *was* doing homework, but my phone kept buzzing, so I tapped on the notifications, and there she was.

I never did learn her name. In the reports they would call her "an illegal fifteen-year-old" or "a fifteen-year-old immigrant." It depended on who was talking.

The underground reporters would also call her *brave, defiant, fearless.*

And the government news would call her *disease-ridden, illegal, criminal.*

✖

BUT AS I watched it with my own eyes, I saw that she was just a girl my age. Wearing a faded Mickey Mouse T-shirt and jean shorts that were rolled over on top but still looked like they might fall off her skinny waist. She had somehow gotten over a line of concrete ballasts and the chain-link fence stretching across the burnt-out field between Tijuana and San Diego. That rusty, mangled barricade that was supposed to keep people on the Tijuana side. It stood there as a scar. A reminder. A warning. Its sole purpose was to say

STAY OUT. YOU DON'T BELONG HERE.

That girl in the Mickey Mouse shirt had no time for warnings. She had no interest in being intimidated. She looked completely unafraid as she stepped away from the fence, entering the no-man's-land between Mexico and the United States. The girl was alone, unarmed. Her dark hair was tied back in a bouncy ponytail, and she had a bright red scratch under her left eye. Besides that, her face looked clear, even calm, as she made her way across the dusty strip of scrubland between Tijuana and the wall.

Or really, the Wall. The Great American Wall.

There was nothing great about it. More like grotesque. It blocked out the sky, with fifty-foot-tall reinforced steel slats and thick metal mesh in between. Every few feet there were coils of barbed wire strung across, and on top there was a maze of cables spitting out electricity. The government had spent gazillions of dollars and called in all the Reserves to help build this monstrosity. Sealing us off from the rest of the Americas.

2

Stop where you are! snarled a voice through a speaker by the Wall.

Technically, that girl wasn't even on United States soil. But as the President loved to say, America was the greatest nation in the history of greatness, and we needed to do whatever it took to protect our sacred borders. That was why there was a platoon of Border Patrol officers lined up on top of the Wall. Green zombies, I called them. Standing at attention in their olive-colored uniforms with pale, expressionless faces. They had the newest AK-87s strapped to their backs and German shepherds circling at their feet as they stared down that girl.

Because this was their land.

Because it was their duty to preserve and defend the United States of America.

Because whatever this fifteen-year-old intended, walking across in her flip-flops and saggy shorts, she had now become a national threat.

✖

I WAS SO scared and awestruck by that girl's slow, deliberate steps forward. I could even hear myself panting for her as I watched.

"Mi'ja, what are you doing?" Mami asked me. "If you're done with your homework, get ready for bed."

"Wait. You have to see this."

"No, I don't."

"Yes, Mami, you do," my little brother, Ernie, said, padding in from the bathroom in his pj's. Last I knew, he was watching soccer on his phone, but he must've gotten the same alerts as me. "Something weird is going on at the Wall," he reported.

Mami hated all the notifications and interruptions from our phones, even if we had saved up and paid for them with our own money. But when Ernie came in and made that announcement, Mami stopped wiping the kitchen counter and marched over to stand behind me at the table.

"¿Qué es eso? I can't even see. The screen is too small," she sighed.

Mami loved to tell us how when our family first came to this country, we watched the same show, all together, on a single television. Of course, that was before the government took over the broadcasting system. Before they censored any newscasters who disagreed or said too much, any movies or shows that seemed unpatriotic. If we wanted to see anything honest or original these days, we had to watch someone's livestream on the dark web. Which is what we were doing now. The three of us pressed our heads together, watching the image blink in and out because of the poor connection. The camera panned around, showing faces caught between hope and panic.

"I don't like this," Ernie said. I didn't either, but we couldn't turn away from the screen. We couldn't move. We could only gape at this staticky footage as that gutsy girl planted each foot down—one, two, three.

There were shouts from the crowd of people in Tijuana gathering behind the barricade:

¿Qué estás haciendo? ¡Cuidado!

An airhorn blasted. Another green zombie shouted through the speakers:

Get back behind the fence! he bellowed. *You are not permitted on US soil. We repeat, you are not permitted on US soil!*

The girl paused and raised both of her hands in the air to show that she meant no harm. She squinted into the bright West Coast sun with a sort of half grin. Her arms were loose and gawky. I wondered if she was born with this kind of wild bravery or if she'd just already lost too much to care.

She stepped forward again.

"Why's she doing that?" whispered Ernie. "Why isn't she listening to them?"

I tried to mumble some sort of response, but my tongue felt too big for my mouth. I flipped to another livestream in Tijuana—they were all filming this girl now. Some from so far away, she looked like a speck creeping across the frame, in between the concrete posts. Others zoomed in so close, I swear I could see the hairs in that girl's nose. Yes, we were watching her on a screen from thousands of miles away, in the safety of a dusky Vermont evening. But my whole body was trembling for her. I wished I had even a smidge of her courage.

There is no trespassing in the demilitarized zone! the zombies ordered again. *We repeat, no trespassing in the demilitarized zone!*

"Dios mío," Mami said in a low voice, clicking her tongue. She made the sign of the cross, and I swallowed hard. Mami was as tough as they came, the creases around her eyes holding on to all her worry and pain so that she could always face the world with composure. If she was asking God for help, then this was definitely a moment of truth.

Meanwhile, the girl took another step forward. And another. She looked like she was full-on smiling now. At least, that's how I want to remember her.

This is your last warning! roared the zombies.

¡Eres un héroe! ¡Cuidado! yelled the crowd behind her in Tijuana. I could hear people chanting from behind the Wall in San Diego. It sounded like they were saying, *Let her through! Let her through!*

The voices on all sides swelled and lifted her up so she looked like she was floating those last few steps. Eleven, twelve.

I was counting in my head.

She had just put down her flip-flop for the fifteenth time when the ground exploded underneath her. The sudden flares of orange, yellow, and red slashing through her. Blowing her into bits. Turning her into dust.

Everything shuddered around me. I felt like that bomb had just detonated inside my gut, the shock waves rumbling through me. The fierce blast of flames was the sharpest color

I'd ever known. And scariest of all, there was no sound. Or, really, there was only the *absence* of sound. Like the whole world had just been punctured and we had to suck in whatever air was left in one giant gasp, holding it all in for as long as we could.

Ernie was the first one to lose it. "What happened? Where'd she go? How come we can't see her?" he said, panicking.

"She's . . . she's," I stammered. I didn't know how to explain what had just happened—to him or to myself. "Mami?"

Mami just stood there, watching the screen, as Ernie and I let a thousand unanswerable questions dribble out of our mouths. We needed to fill all the space between us. To keep talking, because talking was breathing, and breathing was living, and living meant we still existed even if it was in some crazy effed-up world where a fifteen-year-old girl was blown up because she tried to cross the border.

"Mami, did you see what happened?" I begged. When I couldn't take Mami's silence anymore, I grabbed her warm wrist and squeezed.

"Sí, claro que sí," Mami murmured. Seeing Mami this disturbed only made it more horrible, more real. She exhaled slowly, the air whistling through her teeth. Then she clenched her eyes shut, like she was trying to erase what she'd just seen on my screen. "It is a land mine, mi'ja. Like in Colombia."

"What?" I shouted. As if my anger could change what had just occurred. Although maybe it did, because the picture of the girl in flames went dark. The connection severed.

I flipped to a different livestream again. The first one I found was from someone standing on the San Diego side of the Wall. I heard people wailing and shouting, *They killed her! They killed her!*

Then I saw a mad rush of bodies, pushing and shoving their way toward the Wall. Hurling themselves at the steel slats, scraping and kicking at the mesh in between.

A stampede of green zombies charged into the fray. It looked like there were just as many of them on the ground in San Diego as there were on top of the Wall. Maybe more. Now they were unleashing their German shepherds on the American side. The canines grunting and snapping.

There was a blast of white.

Whoever was filming our livestream started shaking and running. Shouting, *Cover your mouths! Run!*

It sounded like the Border Patrol officers on the American side were now launching tear gas canisters at the scrambling crowd in San Diego.

"Dios mío," Mami gasped again.

There were bodies writhing and twisting on the ground. They clawed at each other, desperate for pockets of fresh air. Then there was a thud. All we could see on my phone was the dusty ground—a flood of sneakers, flip-flops, and bare feet running by.

"No!" I pleaded. I wanted to reach through the screen and save whoever had just gone down, but I had to find another feed to see what was happening. I scrolled through image after image. The crowds on both sides of the Wall were multiplying by the second now. Surging with rage and heartache. Shouting into their screens or at the Border Patrol helicopters swooping in and circling overhead.

In Tijuana, there were people scaling the chain-link fence. Tripping over themselves as they charged toward the bits of that broken girl.

¡Era una niña! they wailed. Mothers clutched their children, tears coursing down their cheeks.

In San Diego, there were people banging rocks on the Great Grotesque Wall. Pounding and hammering at the ballasts, like a growing thunder.

No more walls! No more deaths! they yelled. There were thousands of hands grabbing, scratching. Trying to rip apart the steel, the barbed wire, the hatred that went into building the Wall. The green helicopters hovered over them like a venomous cloud.

"What are the helicopters for? Are they gonna hurt more people?" Ernie asked in a tiny voice.

"I don't think so. No, they cannot," Mami said, reaching for my phone, maybe to shut it off and protect us from seeing any more. Only, as she did, a new and horrifying sound belted out from my screen.

Tet-tet-tet-tet-tet-tet-tet!

The helicopters were shooting into the crowds on both sides.

"No!" I screamed.

"Dios mío santísimo . . ."

The shrieks and moans were piling on top of each other. It didn't matter what language they spoke; they were all crying *Help!* Ernie buried his head in Mami's chest.

"Wait! What if . . . what if Tía Luna's there?" I sputtered.

Mami lunged at the kitchen counter to get her phone.

"Todo va estar bien. Tranquilos," was all she'd say as she dialed her sister's number.

"Call Tía Luna!" I screamed at my phone. It couldn't recognize my voice when I was this frantic and screechy, though. So I tried to type in her name, my fingers jerking and stuttering from key to key.

A stale recording came on at the other end of the phone:

Your request cannot be processed at this time. Please hang up and try again.

Mami was pacing across the linoleum, hanging up and trying again. Hanging up and trying again.

"Do you think she's there?" I asked. "She wouldn't go there, would she?"

"No. No creo," Mami said, her face a knot of pain and anger. She put down her phone for a brief moment and clasped her hands together in front of our kitchen window like she was begging the sky to tell her something else.

"I don't get it," Ernie whimpered. "What's going on?"

There were so many shots coming from my screen now. I couldn't count them anymore. I couldn't do anything. The gap between us and whatever was going on at the border widening like a giant hole.

Dividing us into here and there.

Before and after.

"We know nothing," Mami told us. "We don't know if Tía Luna is there or if . . ."

And then it was all cut off.

Our phones went dark. There was no sound, no image. No connection to whatever was unraveling on the other side of the country. Just a blank screen. We held our breath and waited, pinched with fear.

And then, a few moments later, a new, haunting image flickered on. I'd never seen anything like this being broadcast before. It was a large desk in the middle of a bare room. There were stark gray cinder-block walls behind it, interrupted only by a portrait of the President and an empty wooden chair.

I flipped to another feed, and another. But they were all showing the same thing. The same desk, the same wall, the same portrait.

As if to wipe away everything that had just happened.

As if to wipe *us* all away.

CHAPTER 2

Mami didn't even pretend to sleep that night. I could feel her next to me on the pullout couch, rolling around, getting up, and lying back down. By three in the morning, I went to get a drink of water and found her in the kitchen making a big pot of ajiaco. Her long, wavy hair was slipping out of its usually tight bun. She was chopping and stirring so slowly as she stared out our palm-sized window. The sky outside was cool and steely, with just a scoop of fading moon.

"Mami? Why are you cooking?" I asked.

"¡Mi'ja!" she said, spinning around. She blinked quickly to wipe away any signs of being frightened or even surprised by my voice. Then she came over and squished my cheeks hard between her thick palms. "Vali, vete a dormir," she told me.

"I can't sleep," I said.

"You have to," she insisted.

Mami was fiery and tough as nails. Even at five foot one, I was sure she could hold up the world, or carry me and Ernie through the apocalypse—whichever came first. She had broad shoulders, a barrel-shaped middle, and weathered café con leche skin; her dark eyes were always sparking with determination. Mami worked on McAuley's Dairy Farm just outside of our town of Southboro, Vermont. A few weeks before, she helped birth a calf that was breech. She tried to tell me about the thrill of catching its placenta, but I gagged. Absolutely nothing made Mami squeamish or scared. Her rules for survival were:

1. Love all creatures, great and small.
2. Quit your worrying, and praise God you're alive.
3. Protect your family at all costs.

"Mi'ja, a dormir," she said, her voice low and husky. Her thick lips only worked their way into a smile if she truly meant it. Now they were pursed into a tight frown.

I frowned back, our faces almost identical. I loved that I looked so much like my mami. We had the same skin color, the same long dark hair, even the same hips. We got to share bras, lip liners, and an obsession with old-school reggaeton. Most of all, I felt like Mami could see straight inside me, tunnel through all my confusion and fear, and hold on to my heart for safekeeping.

On any other day, I wouldn't have dared argue with my mami. I'd just have gone back to bed like she told me to. I was a pretty respectful kid. But I couldn't ignore what I was feeling and go lie down. No matter what Mami said, this wasn't a normal day. This was only a few hours since we'd witnessed that girl being blown to bits in front of the Mexican/United States border, since we'd seen people in San Diego charging toward the Wall and then heard shots tear through the crowds. This was the morning after, or maybe just a continuation of that terrifying instant when we were here and the West Coast was on fire, and nobody was telling us what was going on.

I knew that if I tried to lie down for another minute, all I would see when I closed my eyes was that girl's ponytail—so bouncy and full, and then swallowed in flames in the same breath. Or I would fall into another nightmare about her stepping on a land mine and her body exploding into guts and eyeballs and shreds of Mickey Mouse shirt.

And me, running across that field, desperate to put her back together, knowing I never could.

"¿Mi'ja?" Mami squeezed my cheeks. "Go."

"But what about Tía Luna? Have you talked to her yet?"

Mami shook her head, turning back to her pot on the stove.

"Is everything still down?" I asked. Mami didn't answer. One glance at my phone said it all. The government had shut everything off—internet, cell service. Nothing to see here; nothing to be done. Feeding us only that empty chair and portrait in a cinder-block room.

This was where we were now: in the utter darkness.

"We still have the National News report," Mami said, resigned. "They tell about same thing over and over. The econ-

14

omy so good, trade wars we win. And did you know there is a new sandal with a . . . cremallera? It is very popular this season," she reported.

"What are you talking about?" I shot back—a little too loudly for Mami.

"Shhh. Por favor, Ernie's still sleeping," she whispered. "This is all they tell us. This is all the news I have for you."

I reached for Mami's phone on the counter. It was hot in my hand. I saw she'd dialed Tía Luna's number fifty-three times since last night. I tried for a fifty-fourth time, but all I got was that meaningless message again: *Your request cannot be processed at this time.*

"Vali, por favor," Mami said, taking the phone from me before I could dial again.

"I wanna know what's going on!"

"Me too, mi'ja. Pero they tell us nothing right now. So just go to sleep," she said. She smushed me into her chest for a brisk hug, then pushed me out the kitchen door. And that was that.

I tried to go to sleep. I really did. I went into the living room and lay down, first on my side of the bed, then on Mami's side, then horizontally. There was just too much tumbling inside of me. Bright flashes of that girl stepping forward. The earth erupting, the livestream falling, the stampede of feet and dust. The gunshots going wild.

I grabbed my phone and searched for any possible pictures or reports about last night. There was nothing. Or really, there was the National News morning show, with hosts in chalky makeup, pointing to weather maps and sipping fake coffee from their empty mugs. Putting on this government-sponsored charade about the US waking up to a brand-new, fantabulous day, even though I knew for a fact that we were in the middle of the worst economic downfall in American history. Nothing was growing here. The drought was killing off all vegetation and livestock, we had strict water rations, and we were lucky that Mami even had a job.

The TV hosts' teeth were so white and straight as they yammered on about made-up facts, like

The US economy is soaring!

The drought is almost over!

And look at these adorable new sandals!

I got it. I got how Americans could become mesmerized and hypnotized by these vapid talking heads. I wanted to get lulled into believing them too. It probably would've been so much easier that way.

Only, I knew what it meant to live a lie. A lie that made me awkward and shy around people I didn't know. A lie that made me skittish when I heard sirens or got assigned a project in school that involved personal family narratives. A lie that thrived off of all my fear.

For me, the lie started when we left Colombia.

My name is Valentina González Ramirez, but people who really know me call me Vali. I was born in a town called Suárez, wedged between mountains in el Norte del Cauca. I lived there

16

until I was four years old, so I only remember it in blips of color and sound . . .

The orange glow of the sun seeping through our wooden door frame.

The quick panting of Papi as he hiked up a steep, muddy path, with me on his back.

The dust below me turning dark red after I tripped over a mining excavator and sliced open my lower lip.

The sweetness of Mami cooking plantains over our stove.

I didn't understand all the threads connecting these details, though. I didn't know that there were big corporations trying to take over our town when I was little. That people were getting death threats and being murdered as they tried to stop the corporations from taking the gold under our mountains. I certainly didn't know that my abuela and abuelo had burned to death in their own home or that five girls had been tortured and drowned in the river where I first learned how to swim.

They were all casualties of this undeclared armed conflict in Colombia. It was no longer the fifty-two-year civil war, but instead it was a quieter war. Almost deadlier, because it was so stealthy and cruel. A war camouflaged inside the shadows of peace.

Mami only told me all this after we'd come to the United States. She said she missed Colombia every second of every day, but that the mountains and rivers were covered in blood. That was why we had to leave our home and make a new one here.

Tú naciste en Colombia pero también eres de acá, Mami told me every night before I went to sleep.

And I said it back to her: *Naci en Colombia pero también soy de acá*.

It was like my prayer, my plea. I would always be Colombian. Just like I would always be American. At least, I felt like I was American after living here for twelve years now.

Mami, Papi, and I crossed into San Diego two weeks after my fourth birthday. I remember that day because I saw Mami crying for the first time, and she couldn't tell me whether she was happy or sad. We had to sleep in a homeless shelter for a while, and they separated me and Mami from Papi, which made me angry and scared. So Mami decided we would sleep in the parks instead; that way we could be together. Papi found a farm where he and Mami could pick tomatoes during the day. I had to sit behind a shed and be very quiet so no one got mad. My tummy hurt from too many tomatoes, and I got stung by bees a lot.

San Diego was beautiful and horrible all at once. The roads were wide and paved. The sun turned pink before it set every night. There was an amusement park with jumping dolphins and roller coasters. But even after I started going to kindergarten and hanging out with kids my age, I had this lonely feeling that wouldn't go away. I knew that I was different. I knew that most families didn't have to plan for if Mami or Papi didn't come home from work because ICE took them away. I knew it wasn't normal that I jumped if there was an unexpected knock on the classroom door.

I memorized the Pledge of Allegiance and tried to recite it very loudly every day in class. On the school playground, I made friends with a blond-haired girl named Rosie. She said we should be besties and that I could sleep over at her house anytime. Only, when I tried to, her dad asked me where I was from and I got so nervous, I said, "Nowhere!" and ran home. Rosie stopped talking to me after that.

Mami, Papi, and I moved into an apartment of our own. It was really an office above a car dealership, so it smelled like gasoline and we had a cooler instead of a refrigerator. But it was ours. I remember that when I started the first grade, I got a laminated notebook and wrote my new address across the top of it—just in case it got lost. And because I was so proud.

I kept begging Mami to buy me zippered jeans and stretchy headbands so I could look like all the popular girls in my class. But I didn't look like them. I never would. I was wider and darker. One girl said I was the color of her favorite kind of caramel. Another asked me why my arm hair was so long and if I could teach her to roll her *r*'s.

I just wanted to be done with school. I wanted to go to work like Mami and Papi. I told them that one day I would be a heart doctor or a famous singer, and I'd make enough money to buy them a fancy car from the dealership below us—at the full price. Mami laughed, and Papi said he couldn't wait to drive it. I figured a car was the thing they needed most. They were both working their asses off at two and three jobs apiece, trying to pay for things like food, and rent, and saving up for the new baby. Mami was pregnant with my little brother, Ernesto, who was born the same day the President replaced California's governor with a cabinet member to promote "unity and integrity."

By this point, the deportation raids were getting more and more intense. There were daily riots and protests. The night after the President won reelection for his third term, Mami and Papi let me stay up and watch television with them. We stared at the red, white, and blue fireworks going off as the first steel columns were drilled into the ground just north of the border.

It was really happening. The Great American Wall was going up between Mexico and California.

The censorship laws went into effect soon after that. Papi threw out our TV and said from now on we only listened to independent, real news sources. But the government invaded our space any way it could. The President started broadcasting his vision through gigantic holograms, flashing and flickering like some intergalactic prophet. He talked about "cleaning up" this country so there would be no more homelessness, no more infestations, no more opioids or threats to our democracy.

What he really meant was, no more immigrants without papers. No more us.

From now on, he explained, everyone living in the US had to get an identification chip implanted in their wrist. The chips would have all of our information on them—ID number, birthplace, blood type, medical history, even allergies. The chips would make everything so much easier, the President told us. With just a simple scan, we would know who belonged here once and for all.

If you didn't have a chip, clearly you were "illegal."

Getting a chip put in was free and painless, but mandatory. All we had to do was show up at a clinic with our birth certificates or proof of citizenship. Each chip was small enough that it could be injected using a little numbing spray and a syringe. I watched Ernie get his when he was just a baby, and he barely squeaked. It was easy, since he was born in the US.

Mami, Papi, and I were a different story, of course.

While the President was still yammering in front of those fireworks, Mami started reaching out to everyone she knew in San Diego for help. She managed to connect with some guy who was implanting fake ID chips in his kitchen. He was charging five thousand dollars each, which was way beyond what my parents had, even if we paid in installments. Papi said he would get one later; it was most important for me and Mami to have them. He promised he would be careful; he would be fine.

I remember the chip was no bigger than a grain of rice, but it hurt so much when the man cut into my skin—anesthesia was extra—that I passed out. I was trying with all my might to be brave for Mami. Squeezing her hand and boring my eyes into her steady gaze for strength. She'd given this guy literally every penny we had. When I woke up, I was now

Amelia Catherine Davis
ID number 072-54-3998
Born on July 22, 2016, in Arcata, CA
Blood type: A+, brown eyes, no allergies

I didn't know who Amelia Catherine Davis really was. I didn't know whether she was even alive or dead. I just knew that she had given me a new identity, a new chance at being safe. I recited these facts over and over again. I said them to my parents, to baby Ernie, to the walls, to the sky. I said them ten times before going to bed, ten times before brushing my teeth, and ten times for each shoe I put on in the morning. I rubbed that tiny lump of scar tissue on my right wrist until it was red and raw. Because I had to reassure myself it was still there, and I was still here.

The government installed the first ID scanners in California soon after. They looked like those devices used to pick up the barcodes off groceries. Only instead of cashiers using them, there were ICE officers in full combat gear, waiting to see that we all made it through. When I got stopped for my first scan at school, I watched the thin blue light wash over my lumpy wrist and thought I might shatter into a million pieces.

I am Amelia Catherine Davis. 072-54-3998, I repeated in my brain. *I was born in the United States.*

When the scan was done, I heard a quiet click, and the ICE officer nodded, sending me on my way. I was so sick from holding in all my nerves that I had to go to the bathroom and press my cheek against the cold tile to calm down. But when I told my parents about it that night at dinner, they nodded with pride. Papi even called me his little guerrera.

"I'm not little," I told him, puffing out my chest. He laughed and tugged at his beard. He was always doing that.

Until they shaved it off.

On my last day of third grade before winter break, while I was hanging up my backpack and braiding my friend's hair at school, my papi was taken by ICE. He was handcuffed and herded onto a cattle truck. Everyone working on the tomato farm—over three hundred total—was rounded up and carted off to a detention facility in some undisclosed location. Mami was actually home that day because Ernie had a fever. But as soon as she heard about the raid, she strapped my brother to her chest and ran to the schoolyard to get me at recess.

I remember that instead of greeting her with a smile or even noticing the circles of worry under her eyes, the only thing I said to her was "What are you doing here? I'm playing tag!"

Papi was in that detention center for the next six months. He was stripped of all his possessions and shaved bald. I bit my cheeks to stop from crying every time he called us on a videophone. He tried us at random times every few days and asked us questions about all the silly details of our lives. I told him that Ernie was crawling and eating a ton of avocados. I made sure he knew I was the only nine-year-old soprano in the school choir, and that I got 92 percent on my spelling test. It felt so stupid to be saying all these things to him, but he acted like he wanted to hear it. Like he wanted to know we were all getting on without him.

We weren't, though. At least, I wasn't. This was the hardest part of those long months—pretending we were all fine and happy and smiling at my teachers in school or the guy who owned the deli near us and wondering, *Do you want me gone too?*

I was scared of everything and everyone. Of scanning stations and empty trucks and the question *What's up?* or *You okay?*

I got quiet and angry and small as a clenched fist. I flinched if I thought someone was looking at me funny—if I thought someone was looking at me at all. I just wanted to punch the world and grab my papi and run, run, run.

We had to leave the car dealership and live in the shelters again. Mami couldn't go back to work. Both farms where she'd been a day laborer were hiring again, but it felt too risky, even with a fake chip. She heard about a network of nannies who got paid well, but that seemed dangerous too. We had no idea where the "cleanups" would happen next or who could be trusted. Every time we talked to Papi, he told us he would be home soon. Only, his voice was getting so tired and unconvincing.

And then, he stopped calling. We waited for days that turned into a week and then two weeks and then a month. Even the lawyer Mami paid with whatever she could pawn couldn't answer our pleas. We never got to learn when or how or why the detention center was emptied out, forcing all of the immigrants onto planes for deportation. We never found out where Papi was when the war caught up with him in Colombia.

Had he made it back to our home in Suárez?

Was he just stepping off the plane?

Did he see who shot him in the back nine times?

Mami never intended for me to see that picture of my father's remains. No nine-year-old should ever have to see something like that. But one of our cousins, who was still living in Suárez, texted Mami one night as we were eating dinner. She dropped her phone and let out such a gut-wrenching wail. As I went to pick it up, she tried to grab it from me, only, for once in her life, she was too weak.

The photo was of Papi's body lying on the side of a steep path through the mountains. Maybe the same one he used to climb with me on his back when I was too little to appreciate it. His face was beaten into a purplish mess, and his eyes were frozen in pain. There was blood everywhere.

When we got that picture, I kept staring at it. Trying to rearrange it or turn it upside down or inside out so it could be someone else. But there was no denying it was him. He was wearing the same pale yellow T-shirt I'd last seen him in almost a year before. His new chin hairs poking out in thin tufts.

I saw that image of Papi constantly, twisted and cold in all his deadness. I saw him when I closed my eyes at night and when I opened them again in the morning, when I brushed my hair or heard a guitar on the radio or smelled fried onions or walked, talked, laughed, breathed.

The Sunday after we got that picture, Mami took us to church to pray for him. I wanted to scream at everyone there, *My papi is dead! They took him away, and you don't care!*

Instead, I sat there not even crying.

Just waiting for all the candles to go out.

✖

"¡NIÑOS, VALI, ERNESTO!" Mami shouted from the kitchen, pulling me out of my dream as I sobbed for Papi all over again. This was why I didn't want to even try to sleep, especially without Mami lying next to me. It was too easy to get sucked into any of those brutal memories. "¡Vengan! ¡Rápido!"

Ernie stumbled out of the closet Mami had repurposed as a little bedroom for him. It was tight quarters, but at least it was his own. Which was a blessing, even if it stank of old socks in there.

"What's wrong?" he asked. His long eyelashes blinking fast as he tried to figure out why I was in tears. He was hugging Señor Cebra—the purple-and-white-striped stuffed zebra that he'd been sleeping with since he was born. I sometimes forgot my little brother was only eight years old. It was easy to do, since he had Papi's genes and was already up to my chin. Ernesto Palmero, Mami called him, because he towered like a palm tree.

"Nothing. It's okay," I told him.

It wasn't okay. Nothing about this world was okay.

But maybe I was just too used to living a lie to say anything else.

CHAPTER 3

Ángel de Dios, mi querido Guardián, me presento hoy ante ti para agradecerte y pedirte que siempre estés a mi lado, para que guies, ilumines y gobiernes mi vida.

It was just a few minutes past dawn now. Mami's ajiaco was still simmering on the stove, and I was still smoldering with questions, but we had to keep going. Somehow, it was a weekday and I could hear people in our apartment building turning off alarms and opening doors, and we had to do that too, to keep up with the charade of our lives here.

Ernie and I stood next to Mami as she offered a morning prayer in front of her altar. It wasn't so much an altar as a wooden shelf that she'd nailed to the wall above our kitchen table. On it were all the people Mami treasured most—a yellowing photograph of my abuela and abuelo, some ridiculously awkward school pics of me and Ernie, a palm-sized portrait of la Virgen.

My favorite picture was in a smaller oval frame—the one tucked behind an ivory crucifix. It was of me and Papi at the beach, just after we'd arrived in California. Papi loved going to the ocean, howling into the wind. The photo was a little blurred, but I could still make out his fingernails, wide and flat like weathered seashells. His shaggy beard was just giving way to a hint of a smile, and his T-shirt clung to his chest with sweat. I looked like I couldn't have been more than five at the time, decked out in my blue-and-white polka-dotted bathing suit. Papi was holding me up on his shoulder like a trophy. But really, he was the prize.

Today as I stared at that picture, everything in me shook. Mami's votive flames looked too close to Papi's beard, and la Virgen wasn't even watching over him.

"What if San Diego is still under attack? Or all of California?" I whispered. Mami ignored me, continuing with her prayers. But maybe I did have a sense of defiance in me after all. Or just a searing, unstoppable pain from having my papi stolen from me and murdered all those years ago. "They could deport Tía Luna," I said louder. "They could come here next."

"Shhh. Tenemos que tener fe," Mami said.

Te imploro desde el fondo de mi corazón que por favor protejas a nuestra querida Tía Luna. En tu dulce nombre, Amen.

As she finished her prayers, she dug her worn knuckles into the tops of my shoulders, trying to knead out all my knotted worries. I had to squirm away from her, though. I felt like if she pressed too hard, she would unleash a storm of tears and terror that I'd never be able to overcome.

"It is okay," she told us. "We eat breakfast."

She started cooking a pan of huevos pericos. I had to admit, it did smell comforting. And I knew we were very lucky to have eggs, tomatoes, onions and the occasional hunk of cheese from McAuley's farm, especially when there was no fresh produce or dairy for sale around here. The three of us sat down and tore into our food. It was like we were filling up all those holes and unanswerable questions with this meal. As Mami chewed, I saw the muscles in her cheeks clenching and releasing; her eyes focused only on her food. I didn't know how she kept it all together. How she fed and clothed us while our world was being demolished. I couldn't decide whether this was resilience, or foolishness.

"Okay, al colegio!" Mami said as she swallowed a last bite of egg. She blew out her candles, scooted back from the table, and watched us eat a few more forkfuls before giving us our orders for the day.

"Dishes dried before you leave. Make sure the door is locked. Stand up straight, respect your teachers." As she spoke, she planted kisses on the top of both our heads and then pulled three different bags over her shoulders. They were filled with her uniform, her lunch, her hairbrush, and probably another crucifix.

"You're going to work?" I asked, totally confused.

"Sí, and you are going to school," Mami instructed. "We're safe. We going to be okay. Oh! And Ernesto, after school, you go to fútbol and wait until Vali comes to pick you up, yes?"

"Soccer, Mami," he corrected her.

"Fútbol," she insisted. "¡Adiós! Y tranquilos que todo va estar bien."

I think she really believed that too. She enunciated everything in her imperfect English, her voice clear and firm so I could hear her resolve.

"Love you, Mami!" Ernie called after her, even though she was already out the door. Then he turned to me and said, "The bathroom's mine."

With water rations, every drop counted. The person who took the first shower got the longest shower. On any other day I would have fought my little brother for those extra drops, but again, this wasn't any other day. I was still sitting at the table, stunned by Mami's blind optimism.

"Go for it," I told him.

Though after waiting ten minutes for Ernie to finish up in the bathroom, my bladder and I regretted that decision. Through a crack in the bathroom door frame, I could see my little brother posing in front of the mirror, staring at his reflection.

"Hey!" he yelped as I pushed open the door. "A little privacy?"

I had to glue my lips together so I didn't bust out laughing. He was trying to tame his crazy hair with a wet comb, some gel, and what looked like a squirt of toothpaste. Ernie definitely had Papi's mane—dark, wild, and unmanageable. It now had a minty sheen to it too, with some of his curls shellacked down, but most of the back still sticking up in tufts.

"Wow. Someone special you want to take to snack time?" I teased. As if anyone in his second-grade classroom would notice.

"Whatever," Ernie shot back. "Your face looks like snack time." Which didn't make sense at all. But on this day after, or day before, or whatever we were now calling this darkness disguised as a school day morning, I was grateful for my little brother getting me to laugh.

✖

OUTSIDE, THE AIR felt charged and hot. It was only the first week of May, but I was already sweating buckets in my itchy school uniform. Before we moved up to Vermont, I'd always heard that the winters here were bone-chilling and the only hope of summer was a few weeks in August. Maybe those were just stories, though. I still had yet to experience a real blizzard or build a snowman. We'd had a few ice storms and some flash floods up here, followed by our current drought, which was in its second sweltering year. Even today as we walked to school, it had to be eighty-five degrees, and the wind was so strong it stung my eyes. The streets and sidewalks were splintering; the forests that used to cover the mountains around us were singed from all the wildfires. It was like a town built out of shadows.

Nothing to see here. Nothing to say or do or change.

Not that Southboro, Vermont, had ever promised to be some great metropolis or even have more than one street that could be called "downtown." That was the whole reason Mami had relocated us up here from San Diego almost seven years ago. Everything we had was gone. Papi was gone. Our home was gone. Our sense of security and promise were gone.

Mami's little sister, Tía Luna, didn't want us to leave California. She found a man who for the right price married her and gave her papers. She told us to come stay with her a few miles away in Imperial Beach, where she was a housekeeper. And we did for a while. But we still felt the "cleanups" and riots amping up around us. I was a mess—peeing my bed and beating my fists into the floor. Trying to knock out that image of Papi on the ground, purple and lifeless.

When we lived in Imperial Beach, every day there were new Presidential proclamations about how "illegals" were trying to ransack and ravage the country. The economy was in danger. The land was in danger. Everybody's taxes had to triple because there were evil foreigners lurking everywhere, ready to pounce on innocent Americans and take everything they'd worked so hard to achieve. The Great Wall, which had started in San Diego, now had to be extended across all the southern states that touched the border—Arizona, New Mexico, Texas.

Still, the President reminded America, nobody was safe from "the immigrant infestation."

So Mami did the thing that Colombia had taught her to do—

Run.

When they are coming for you, run.

Run faster than them. Run smarter than them. Just run.

She looked up agricultural towns as far away from San Diego and the border as possible, and found McAuley's Dairy Farm near Southboro, Vermont. With the help of Tía Luna's savings, Ernie, Mami, and I got on a plane to the other side of the country. We said goodbye to the amusement park with the dolphins and the lemons in Tía Luna's yard. To the last places we had been when Papi was still alive.

I remember Ernie being so excited about our first trip in an airplane. We shared a bag of cheese crackers and I pretended not to notice the motorcades of tanks and cranes down below as we flew over the expanding Wall construction.

I knew Mami had moved us up here to protect us and hopefully start over. I knew she thought that here, in this pocket of quiet she had created and prayed for, we could find some peace. Colombia couldn't give it to us. California couldn't either. Maybe a ho-hum unextraordinary town like Southboro, Vermont, could. As soon as we got here, there was a new rule from Mami: we could only speak to each other in English. Even though there were ID scans in schools and government buildings, the public parks and stores were left alone. For the most part, we were able to live here without feeling afraid.

But would that still be true after what we'd seen last night?

"Vali," Ernie said now, elbowing me as we approached his school's gates. "I said *bye!*"

"What? Wait." I felt the overwhelming urge to hug him and hold him, but I knew he wouldn't abide by that this close to his school, where his friends could see him. Or maybe I could impart some wisdom or warning about being aware and alert and the frailty of our existence. I couldn't form any of these frantic feelings into a sentence, though. So instead I said something random just to keep him there a moment longer.

"Um, did you pack your lunch?"

"Yeah. You watched me do it," he answered, rolling his eyes.

"Did you brush your teeth?"

Instead of answering, he just breathed on me so I could smell his breath. "Anything else?" he asked. "Or can I go now?" I couldn't tell if he was amused or annoyed by my stalling. Either way, I was going to make us both late for school, and that wouldn't help either of us stay under the radar.

"Nah . . . that's it," I said, trying to sound nonchalant. "Just . . . go straight to the soccer field after school and . . . yeah. I'll meet you there!"

"Okay. Bye!" he yelled over his shoulder as he ran toward Southboro Elementary's entrance.

I watched him step through the first gate and get his wrist scanned without a single glance back. Then he showed his school ID to the nearest security guard and skipped through an open door. I felt myself wincing as I stood there. I was grateful Ernie could sail into school without fearing he'd get stopped or questioned. I really was. But I was also incredibly jealous. I rubbed my finger over that lump in my right wrist. I could still remember my first few years of elementary school, in California, when there were no guards outside of schools. Also, teachers weren't armed at all, and students could read whatever they wanted. I could also remember when I first got my fake chip and Mami said, "These won't last forever, but . . ."

That dot-dot-dot at the end of her sentence hounded and haunted me every day. The government still hadn't figured out a way to track down all these counterfeit chips, but it was only a matter of time. If someone had taken on the identity of a dead person, the death records caught up with them. Or if there was a real, live Amelia Davis out there, scanning her wrist at the same time as me, what then? We'd heard about people being taken away by ICE because their fake chips got detected or somehow malfunctioned. When that happened, the scanner made this horrible chirping noise, like a carbon monoxide detector that had run out of batteries.

I knew that noise all too well, because I heard it one day last year. It was the worst day of my life since Papi disappeared.

Mami was going into Town Hall to pay our water bill. Ernie and I usually just waited outside because it smelled like hot floor wax in that building. But we heard Mami say good morning to the ICE officer in the doorway, followed by the scanner chirping once, then twice, then over and over again in rapid fire.

We ran toward the front steps of the building, but he was already escorting her into a back alley behind the parking garage.

"Wait!" I called out after them. The officer turned around and glared at me. He looked like he'd just woken up, his face sagging with a bushy mustache and thick jowls. Mami refused to make eye contact with me, though. Instead, she raised her pointer finger ever so slightly at me. As if to say, *Stop. Do not cause a scene.*

The officer had my mami behind that parking garage for at least a half hour. It was agonizing waiting for her to come back. Ernie and I just sat behind a parked car. We couldn't move a muscle. We couldn't ask questions or look concerned, and we certainly couldn't shout and plead, *Give us back our mami!*

Even though that's exactly what we both wanted to do.

Mami did come back. Only, when she emerged from that back alley, she looked a thousand years older. Her jeans were scuffed at the knees and had bits of gravel flaking off. Ernie and I both ran to her and wrapped our arms around her so tight.

"Mami! I thought you weren't coming back!" Ernie wailed into her chest. She told him of course she was coming back and everything was okay, but I could see that the edges of her eyes were wet as she ushered us away from the building. Ernie was only seven at the time, so I wasn't about to explain

37

what I thought that man had done to our mami in the alley-way. Instead, I clung to Mami's side, desperate to get us home. Mami didn't speak for the rest of that day. I tried to make her an arepa and some coffee, even though I knew she didn't want it. She was stuck in a horror I couldn't pull her out of. I made sure Ernie and I gave her some quiet. We swept the floors and carried our trash to the dump and turned on the lights when it got late. Because otherwise, I think Mami would have just sat in the dark until the next morning.

We never discussed what had happened. From that day on, Mami delivered our water payments after hours so no one would be scanning at Town Hall. She lived carefully, vigilantly. Never looking back; only forward. This is what it took to survive.

I, on the other hand, felt like I was suffocating just remembering that day. As I headed toward my bus for school, I kept looking around to see if I was being watched. I had this image of my family being in some sort of bubble or snow globe while the world—or at least California—was catching fire. As I got on the bus, my fears swirled around me so fast, I forgot to breathe. My legs buckled.

"You okay?" asked my best friend, Kenna. She always got on at the stop before me and saved me a seat.

"Yeah. No. I mean . . . how about you?"

"Same."

Kenna was tall and skinny, with the most gorgeous ebony skin and a smile that took over her entire face when she was happy. But she was barely opening her mouth to speak this morning. Her arched eyebrows were taut with worry.

I was so thankful for Kenna. She and I had been best friends since I moved to Southboro. We were also both juniors at Morrow Magnet High School, across town. Even though Kenna was born in the States, she *got* me. Her parents were both from Nigeria and undocumented. Kenna was the only one outside my family who knew my status. She was brilliant at coding and told me she was going to design a foolproof fake chip one day. I just needed her to do it soon. Like, today.

As we sat side by side, I wanted to grill her on what footage she'd seen of the border last night or if she had possibly heard any updates. But I wasn't about to ask her anything while we were on public transportation. I just had to keep moving forward.

"Everything's fine," I said, trying to sound as cool and impenetrable as Mami.

The buses that stopped in our neighborhood were small, with just a handful of benches for seating. Ernie called them R2-D2s because they were from the first fleet of driverless commuter vehicles and they scuttled along the outer loop of Southboro, making creaky noises when they turned too fast.

It was such a weird experience, driving through these different sections of Southboro. Like we were gliding through some alternate universe. While our side of town had been on water rations and electricity curfews for close to a year now, most of the homes closer to Morrow had drone irrigation, freshly painted storefronts, and real meats and vegetables in the grocery windows. The people strolling by were so clearly wealthy and white. Their homes looked sturdier; their grass looked thicker. They *belonged* here.

We did not. The only reason Kenna and I were on this bus heading to Morrow was because of blind admission exams and our kickass test scores. But I was sure the government would find a way to put an end to blind admissions soon too.

We were just a few blocks from our high school when the bus slowed down to pick up a group of exhausted-looking farmhands. They'd probably been spraying pesticides all night; their faces were slick with sweat, and their clothes reeked of burnt chemicals.

"Hold up!" called a sharp male voice.

"Comin' through," boomed another.

Two men dressed in gray combat gear—bulletproof vests, helmets, and everything—cut past the workers and boarded our bus.

"Good morning to you all," the taller one said to us passengers. "This won't take more than a minute." He had some sort of protective shield covering his eyes, but I could see a gleaming smile that made me feel nauseous. There was a sudden, cold hush.

He pulled a handheld scanning device from one of his holsters and started grabbing people's wrists for inspection. This had never happened before. Scanning whoever they wanted, whenever they wanted, wherever they wanted. I couldn't watch the tired, terrified faces of everyone on the bus as the officers charged through. When one of them approached me, I tried to look interested in a broken branch outside the bus window. It was the only thing I could do to hide my terror. The gray monster stood in the aisle right next to me, waiting for me to stick out my wrist. My skin was clammy and trembling, no matter how much I willed myself to be still.

I heard it. The sweet relief of the scanner clicking, registering my data. Then the click as it registered Kenna's data too. A warm sigh escaped through my lips. I heard the scanners clicking up and down the aisles, until . . .

That hideous chirping sound cut through the quiet. There was a dreadful pause before one of the officers shouted, "Illegal!"

Illegal! Illegal! the other officers joined in.

Kenna and I squeezed each other's hands, and I tasted my breakfast at the back of my throat. One of the workers was cuffed and shoved off the bus. He was a thin, stooped man. He didn't protest. He didn't even cringe as both officers shouted at him about the integrity of this nation and all the diseases and drugs that people like him had brought into our society. I wondered what he was thinking or feeling or wishing he'd said to his family the last time he saw them. The last time he'd probably ever see them.

I thought of Papi sleeping on the floor of that detention center for months. His voice on the phone sounding more like echoes than actual words. The overworked lawyer who'd taken our life savings and tried her best to help but, in the end, stopped answering our phone calls. The ICE officer glaring at me over his mustache as he took my mami toward a back alley.

Why did all these people hate us so much?

Kenna and I watched as the man was shoved into a windowless gray patrol car, practically folded in half so he'd fit. Then the taller of the two gray officers turned around with a sickening smile on his face.

And as he got into the passenger seat, I saw bright yellow letters splashed across the back of his bulletproof vest.

They read **DEPORTATION FORCE**. The same words were now visible across the back bumper of that car too.

I didn't know what they meant yet exactly. I just knew it was bad.

CHAPTER 4

Morrow Magnet High School was the whitest place on earth. Every day I came to school, I felt like all the color had been sucked out of my life. The entire building was just so freaking sterile and bare. It was constructed entirely of transparent walls and bulletproof glass and had a massive metal fence surrounding it. Inside, not a single poster or piece of art was allowed to be hung, and every inch of furniture was painted white. Even though it was almost the end of my junior year, I still got lost all the time in this white maze of blah.

The design was supposed to keep us calm and compliant. Apparently, the founders were two psychologists who did some research about teenage angst and decided that we could only be safe in a world as pale as skim milk. All teachers were required to carry a gun, and Morrow had three mandatory checkpoints—a wrist scan, a fingerprint test, and a voice recognition gate.

"Amelia Davis," I said into the VR speaker. "072-54-3998."

Though I could hear the hum of the speaker digesting and processing my words and then the click of the gate catch releasing, I still quaked as I walked through. I was sure at any minute, someone would pop out from behind an aluminum column and shout, *STOP!* just like I'd seen this morning with Kenna.

Nobody did, though. At least not at that moment.

The student population at Morrow looked like a tide of ghosts roaming through the halls, all of us in these insanely itchy white tunics that smelled like institutional soap. Maybe this was what made Morrow still feel so foreign and frightening to me. Morrow claimed to provide "equal educational opportunities for all," but I was one of only eight nonwhite students in a class of two hundred. Even though the principal always touted Morrow's great math department, someone had obviously forgotten to calculate that imbalance. Plus, I was the only girl in my grade to have curves front and back. I kept my hair down so it fell over my chest because the principal had even called me in once for being "too provocative."

"Ah, cutting it a little close, aren't we?" said my history teacher, Ms. Marsh. (For the record, the first bell hadn't rung yet, but that didn't matter. Kenna and I were still the last ones in our seats.) "I will give you exactly two minutes to copy down the morning assignment. The rest of the class is already preparing for our test."

Ms. Marsh was pacing the front of the classroom, hunched over in her white teacher's cloak. She was either thirty or sixty;

it was too hard to tell her age because she was just so saggy and sour-looking, always finding a reason to scowl. Most of my classmates were scared of her. This morning, they were fidgeting and reciting important dates to themselves to prepare for the test. But I really couldn't get too concerned. There was a test of some sort at least once a day at Morrow. Besides, everything we learned in history was just the government's official version of the facts.

The only subject in school that felt close to exciting was math, since two plus two would always equal four, and Kenna told me daily that creating code and deciphering algorithms was the only way we'd survive in this world of artificial intelligence. Sometimes I wondered if we should just hand everything over to the robots now, since it was pretty clear that we humans were destroying the earth and each other.

I didn't have time to figure out how a world run by artificial intelligence would work at this very moment, though, because everyone was getting up on their feet for the morning prayer, followed by the Pledge of Allegiance. Morrow had smart surfaces on almost every wall, which meant we were surrounded by projections of the American flag as we recited the pledge, and I was pretty sure we were being filmed, so I always spoke up and plastered a fake patriotic smile on for this part of school. Kenna and I constantly drilled each other on flattening our vowels and pronouncing every consonant precisely so we could blend in with the rest of Morrow's white kids. Most of the students in my grade were too self-absorbed or stressed out about test scores to suspect or even notice me. But it did feel like on this morning—more than any other, really—I had a target on my back. Or actually, embedded in that chip on my wrist.

Once we sat back down, Ms. Marsh ordered us to log in to our testing site and wait until she unlocked the exam. But as she was plugging in her teacher code, a low rumbling sound started coming from the front of the room.

The classroom lights dimmed, and the national anthem blared through our intercom. I could feel the floor vibrating underneath us, the whole building throbbing. Then a swath of air at the front of the classroom started shimmering in a giant hologram. A floating oval orb hovered and shifted along the front wall, until the President's large, disembodied face appeared. His bare, gleaming forehead pulsated and his eyes looked squinty, like he was searching for something. Or someone. He was so big, my desk could easily fit into one of his nostrils.

"Good morning, Citizens," the President thundered.

Everyone scrambled back up to stand at attention.

"Good morning, Mr. President," we answered in unison.

"I come before you today with some very urgent news," he said. "Last night, an act of treason was perpetrated upon the United States in the state of California."

"Treason?" whispered Kenna. "What the—"

"Shhh!" Ms. Marsh hissed.

I loved Kenna so much. She said all the things I was thinking. I knew even without asking that she had seen what happened with that girl at the border last night. But I didn't dare look her way or show her how terrified I was. My skin was already hot and tight, and I had to force myself to keep my breaths steady.

The President continued.

"I am hereby declaring a state of federal emergency and deploying our newest and most advanced team of tactical operatives. They are the United States Deportation Force, and they are tasked with arresting and detaining all illegal aliens. They may arrest suspects without a warrant. They may also enter private property without a warrant. They will also have absolute discretion to forgo deportation trials should they deem it appropriate in order to protect our country."

Ms. Marsh started clapping and nodded at us all to do the same. At least it was something to do with my sweaty, shaking hands.

"Let me assure you," the President continued, "we are and will continue to be the strongest, most prosperous nation on the planet. As such, it is my duty as President of these United States and commander in chief of the armed forces to also enforce mandatory curfews and accelerated monitorization in accordance with the newly enacted Alien Registration Act of 2032. Failure to comply will result in arrest, detainment, and/ or prolonged internment."

More forced applause, led by Ms. Marsh.

"All travel to and from California is strictly prohibited, and all government-issued ID chips will be analyzed and submitted for a national system upgrade to find and terminate any rebellions. We will wipe out this scourge of migrant invasion in a strong, decisive campaign. Thank you, may God bless you, and may God bless these United States of America."

As soon as the President signed off, there was a roar of cheering outside our classroom, and I remembered that his face was flickering in homes and buildings all over town. His ominous message about deportation forces, curfews, and "wiping out this scourge of migrant invasion" was being broadcast nationwide. Ringing from sea to shining sea. I wanted to drop down into a hole or blast myself into outer space and never come back.

"This is insane," Kenna said as we waited to fill up our cafeteria trays two hours later.

"What does it even mean?" I asked.

"I don't know," moaned a girl named Vivian from my statistics class. "But I do know that because of it we only had twenty-five minutes for our morning quiz instead of thirty-five, and if I fail statistics, I will literally have no future."

Vivian was a whisper of a girl. About half my width and always skulking around in a frown. I wanted to tell her that she had no idea what having no future could feel like, but of course I didn't. Vivian's sidekick, Naomi, was equally wispy and self-centered, only I guess she had actually listened to the President's announcement. Or at least tried.

"Yeah, I couldn't follow anything he said," Naomi whined.

"I mean, I guess it's sad for some people. I'm just glad we don't live in California."

"Um, sad for who?" said Maddie Fitz, sliding in line between us, eager to get in on the discussion. Maddie was one of those rare species of teenager who was all confidence. She was already the debate team captain and the starter on most of our track-and-field events. She was the freckle-faced, clear-eyed, all-American girl who was now very excited to tell us her opinion.

"I mean, it's a pain in the ass for us, because everyone's gonna have to be inside by nine P.M. for this annoying curfew, and they're putting up, like, a ton of checkpoints. But it's totally necessary. There are sooooo many illegals, even in Vermont. It's really scary."

Vivian and Naomi nodded their heads, but I was too angry to move. I felt my stomach cramp and the back of my neck bristle.

"Illegals?" rumbled Kenna.

"Like, hundreds of thousands. Maybe even millions," said Maddie, bugging out her bright green eyes. "My dad is on one of the Preservation of America Advisory Committees, so . . . yeah, I get the inside scoop."

Her smug look was so horrifying, I wanted to throttle her. I also wanted to hurl myself at the triple-bolted cafeteria exit or even jump over the bulletproof glass separating us from the kitchen so I could hide in a refrigerator.

I knew I couldn't do either of those things for real. But I also couldn't just stand there gaping at Maddie Fitz while she basically told me how I was going to be hunted. I could feel Kenna seething next to me too, her breath sharp and fast.

Luckily, one of the cafeteria proctors took that moment to come over and pull us out of the hungry procession. "Enough talking! Go to your seats, or I'm taking your student numbers and writing you up."

Even the cafeteria was supposed to be silent and sterile at Morrow. We had exactly nine minutes to "mindfully" ingest whatever patty they put in front of us before heading back to class. It was so chewy and salty, reeking of its plastic packaging after it had been reheated.

But I didn't complain. I didn't say a single word again until the end of the school day, when I found Kenna by the 3:38 bus back home. Actually, I didn't even talk then, because there were too many people coming on and off the bus and too many things that I wanted to say. Slowly, the seats emptied as we wound our way back toward Southboro. I saw Ernie on the soccer field and literally blurted out, "He's there!"

That wasn't exactly a recognizable command for the bus, so Kenna said into the speaker, "Stop. Southboro Park," and we climbed out.

Ernie was not as thrilled to see me as I was to see him. He was passing the ball back and forth with his friend Pete and barely slowed down to say hi.

"Please, can I play just a few more minutes?" he whined.

"Coach never showed up, so Pete's teaching me how to do rollbacks."

"What do you mean, Coach never showed up? Did he message you about practice being canceled, or . . . ?"

Ernie gave me a blank stare, waiting for me to finish that sentence. All I knew was that his coach was a Korean guy named Tony who was just twenty years old. I couldn't remember him ever canceling or missing practice before.

"There's a curfew, you know. Did you watch the Presidential announcement?"

"Yeah." Ernie shrugged. "We had to. I don't get it, though. What's it mean for Tía Luna?"

"Nothing!" I cut him off with a sharp voice and an even sharper glare. "She's totally fine and doesn't live anywhere near that mess."

"Oh . . . right," said Ernie, looking down. I knew he'd gotten my message to shut up, though, because he added, "Sorry, I forgot."

"Don't be sorry. Doesn't really affect us," I said for whoever was listening, even though the soccer field was pretty empty besides Ernie and Pete. "Just annoying because I only had twenty-five minutes to finish my quiz instead of thirty-five," I added, imitating that anemic-looking girl, Vivian.

"C'mon," said Kenna. "Let's go get something to eat at Uncle Jimi's. We can watch Ernie from there. I'm super hungry."

"Okay."

"Bye!" Ernie called, already tearing off to practice more drills with his friend. We did have an hour before Mami would get home from work, anyway.

"It's okay," Kenna said, looping her long arm in mine. "I mean, what else can we do?"

It was a good question. And I had no answer for her. As we walked around the soccer field, I tried calling Mami just to hear her voice, but her phone was turned off. That was normal for her when she was at the farm, I told myself. Completely normal. Nothing to worry about or twist into some dark what-if.

"Are you coming?" asked Kenna, pulling me out of the way of a flying soccer ball.

"Yeah."

Uncle Jimi's was just past the stone bridge at the edge of Southboro Park. Most days, when Kenna and I got off the bus, we went straight there to dig into our homework and a plate of fries. We were always greeted by one of Kenna's little cousins. She had a ton of them. At least three of the little girls liked to run over right after school and start sifting through the bins of candy. By the time Kenna and I walked in, they were usually bouncing off the walls with a sugar high, begging to play with my hair or to climb on the red-and-white-striped awning.

Only today, there was no awning over Uncle Jimi's door.

There was just the bare aluminum scaffolding that used to hold it up.

"What's that about?" I asked.

"Dunno," Kenna answered. Her voice was low and far away. She made a beeline toward the shop, and I followed close behind, even though all I wanted to do was turn around and go home. It was like walking toward the scene of a crime, being drawn in by a dizzying, magnetic pull.

As I watched Kenna reach for the screen door, I saw there was a new white plastic frame in place of Uncle Jimi's red wooden one. Kenna pulled too hard, and it swung open and shut with a loud clatter behind us. The shop was empty and still, the air so cold, I shuddered.

"Hello?" Kenna called. "Uncle Jimi?"

It was too quiet in there. Too clean. The jars of gumballs and jawbreakers were wiped down so there was not a single fingerprint or smudge. The grill behind the cash register was spotless, and the refrigerator for sweet drinks was open, puffing out cool, lemon-scented disinfectant. The rest of the room was still, too still. As if frozen in time.

I wanted this all to be just a dream, but there were too many real sensations as we moved farther into the store. The divot from a broken piece of linoleum on the floor, the brown stain on the far wall from a long-ago soda spill, the sound of Kenna muttering to herself.

"Hello!" she tried again, more forcefully now.

Past the candy counter and stools, Uncle Jimi had a couple of shelves he kept stocked with crackers, canned soups, and random toiletries, and behind that was a door leading to a loading dock. The door opened now, and a long, bony man dressed in gray combat gear came barreling into the room.

"Can I help you?" he barked. There was nothing in his voice that hinted at help. His skin was pasty white and drawn so tight across his cheekbones, I could see blue wormy veins crisscrossing underneath.

"Where's Jimi?" Kenna said. I tried to breathe for her, with her, to keep us both from losing it.

"Don't know who you're talking about," the man replied.

"This is his shop," I said. "We come here all the time."

The man squinted and gave me a snort. "Is that so?" he said.

A female officer, dressed in matching gear, came through the screen door now. "None in the back," she reported to the bony man. "But I have the team circling."

She stood in front of me and Kenna and pulled out a scanning device from her holster, waiting for us to comply. As she grabbed my wrist, I tried to look straight ahead, to count to eight as I inhaled and exhaled, just as Mami had once coached me. But I kept imagining Kenna rushing back to the soccer field and telling Ernie, *They got your sister! They got your sister!*

The scanner clicked, and the woman let me go.

Kenna's scan clicked too. I shivered with relief.

"So, what did you come in here for, girls?" asked the female officer. Her voice dripped with saccharine, and her pink eye shadow sparkled.

"Nothing, thank you. Come on," Kenna mumbled, tugging me toward the door.

"Yeah, thank you," I echoed.

I had the feeling that Kenna and I were walking back down the hill toward the soccer field, but I couldn't be sure. The ground felt like it could dissolve under me, or maybe I was the one dissolving.

"What do we do now?" I whispered at Kenna, but she wouldn't answer me until we were past the bridge. At which point she turned to me, her eyes flashing hot and wide. She was quivering as she spoke through clenched teeth.

"I'm going home, and I think you should too," she said. Then she spun around and charged up the hill toward her apartment complex.

There were helicopters circling overhead now—the thwap of their blades growing more and more deafening. Stirring up funnels of dry leaves from whatever trees were trying to bloom in this dry heat.

"Ernie! Let's go!" I called from the edge of the soccer field.

"What? It's only been, like, ten minutes!" he protested.

"We have to go! Now!"

He blasted the ball into a tree trunk and said something

to Pete, which I'm sure was not flattering about me. Then he grabbed his backpack and met me on the sidewalk.

"Why do we have to go?" He sulked, struggling to keep up as I race-walked toward home. There were sirens now too. Red, white, and blue lights spinning a few blocks ahead. The road next to ours was blocked off completely by a row of gray trucks with the words **DEPORTATION FORCE** splattered across them.

"I don't know," I whispered to my little brother.

Which I knew was no answer at all. But for once in our lives, he didn't argue with me.

CHAPTER 5

Mami rushed at us before we'd even fully opened the apartment door. She squeezed us so tight, I felt like I might snap into pieces. Her body was jittery and damp with sweat.

"El pájaro," she said. "It saves me."

"What?" I asked.

"Why is it so dark in here?" Ernie added.

Mami had shut all the windows and put up sheets and towels to act as shades. The only light was from Mami's Virgin Mary candle on her altar, so it felt like we were stepping from day into sudden night. The single flame lapped at the shadow of Mary's tragically tilted head.

"El pájaro," Mami repeated. "Ven, let me show you."

She double bolted the front door and then led me and Ernie over to her altar. In between the pictures and crosses was an orange saucer no bigger than my palm. Once my eyes adjusted to this gloomy dusk, I could see the saucer had on it some dry twigs, a clod of dirt, and a crushed turquoise egg. Mami picked up the saucer and hovered over it. Her face looked swollen and eerie, her lower lip puffy and misshapen.

"Mami, what happened to you?"

I reached out to flip the kitchen switch on, but Mami stopped me with a sharp "No."

"But—"

"Just look at this beautiful nest, mi'ja. It's incredible. And they leave it behind because we have that second frost, so late."

"Mami, what are you talking about? You don't make sense," said Ernie. I elbowed him in the gut to tell him to shut up. Even though I was thinking the exact same thing.

"Every year, there's less animals," Mami said. "Y las vacas. Las pobres vacas."

"Mami, please sit down." I pulled a chair from the table, but she ignored me. "What's going on?"

"The farm. The farm."

"What happened to the farm?" Ernie and I said almost in unison. Mami's eyes glittered. She chewed on the inside of her cheek like she did when she had too much to say and couldn't decide where to begin. When she did speak, her voice was low and gravelly. She focused solely on the image of Mary in her votive.

"I go to the farm this morning, and it is so strange because Mr. McAuley, he stand at the wooden gate. He not normally do that. He is looking so sad. *Liliana, it is very good to see you,* he say. Maybe he already know. But I don't think so."

"Already knows what?" Ernie pounced.

I shushed him as Mami continued. She told us that she went to her workstation and got busy. She was just starting to flush the dairy pipelines with cleaning solution when she heard a loud bird squawking from outside the barn. It was angry or hurt—she couldn't tell exactly. She just knew it was in trouble, so she followed its call down the hill to a dry riverbed at the edge of McAuley's property. That's where she found this nest with the broken egg inside. She even held out the saucer to us so we could understand better while she let out a sad, deep sigh.

"Mami," Ernie whispered, "I'm scared."

Mami's eyes glistened with tears.

"No!" she whispered, looking straight at Ernie. She put down the dish with the nest in it and faced us both. "What does this do, to be scared? They want us to be scared."

"Who is they?" I demanded.

"They," Mami said, as if that explained anything. "They. The men, you know? They have the yellow letters on their backs. I see them on top of the hill, next to the barn. They all come in with big cars. They drive so fast, they make dust into clouds. And then they scream at everyone to line up, and they hold the big rifles. They don't scan. They shoot into the air."

Mami had watched from behind a tree as the Deportation Force shoved the day laborers onto the ground—Esteban, Nicola, all the people she'd worked with for the past six years. There were over forty women and men working there on any

59

given day. Mr. McAuley came out of the house and tried to say something. He was a good man, Mami kept repeating. An older man with a stuttery limp and leathery white skin from all his own years out in the fields. Whatever he was trying to tell the Deportation Force officers was not working, though. The officers beat him to the ground. Kicking him in the head over and over again. That was when Mami started running.

"I run, and I run," Mami said. She stared at la Virgen's flame again now, her face hardening as she spoke. "I run into the next farm. I go right through the animals, then I go into the hills again. And I fall on the rock." Here, she pointed to her left cheek, which was not only puffy but was caked with dried blood under her jaw.

"Mami, I'll clean you up." I could barely get the words out.

She waved me away. "Estoy bien."

"No, you're not." I reached over to touch her gently, but instead, she took my hand in hers. Ernie burrowed his head into her side and started whimpering.

"Come here, mi vida," she said. She steered us both closer to the altar. Closer to that abandoned nest and its trampled egg inside. I could smell the dirt and dried buttermilk in Mami's trembling skin. The bitter taste of too much coffee on her breath.

"El pájaro, it is ready to fly in just the few weeks after it is born," Mami told us. "And it sings . . . hermoso. So the whole forest can hear."

The three of us stood in front of that saucer for what felt like forever. I didn't know if Mami was listening to the bird's song in her head or expecting us to hear it somehow or what. All I could make out was the thrumming of the helicopters, still overhead outside. And Ernie sniffling into Mami's shoulder as she rocked forward and back ever so slightly. I needed to rock with her. It was the only way to keep up with the world spinning this furiously.

"Gracias por cuidarme, pájarito," Mami prayed.

Her voice was half whisper, half sob. But she was here. I had to keep reminding myself of that. The rest of the farmworkers had been taken, but our mami somehow made it through. Even though I wasn't big on praying or lighting candles, I had to admit that was a miracle.

"En el nombre del Padre y del Hijo y del Espíritu Santo. Amen," finished Mami.

"Amen," Ernie and I chimed in after her.

"A comer. Wash your hands. I will heat up the ajiaco and, Vali, get the arepas."

Ernie wiped his nose on his sleeve and nodded his head obediently. But I couldn't do the same.

"Mami, wait. How do we know they didn't follow you home?"

Mami looked at me as if I'd just slapped her across the face with my words.

"They took Uncle Jimi. And Ernie's soccer coach," I pressed.

Mami tipped her head toward Ernie. "¿Verdad, mi'jo?"

Ernie just shrugged.

"We have to get out of here," I told her. "They're coming for us! And what's going on with California? Have you heard from Tía Luna? We have to find her and go . . . somewhere!"

"Shhhh, mi'ja!" Mami gripped my arms. Her lips twitched as she tried to hold back whatever pain was now too close to ignore. Then she forced out a long exhale and pressed one of her callused palms into my chest. "Mi'ja," she tried again in a more measured tone, "I call Tía as soon as I get home. It is still no answer."

"So then what do we do?" I pleaded.

"What do we do? We be grateful that we are here and that we are together. And we eat. We cannot do anything with the empty stomach."

I had no appetite, but I couldn't argue with her anymore. We were all silent as I reheated the arepas and she stirred the ajiaco. It smelled amazing, though I had a hard time putting anything in my mouth. My stomach was too knotted; my thoughts were too scrambled. Mami didn't really eat either. She lit two more candles so we could see our meal. Then she pushed her food around her plate for a bit, got up, poured herself a shot of aguardiente, and lit a cigarette, which she rarely did.

I hated that she was hurting so much and that she couldn't bring herself to say it out loud. My mami was a force to be reckoned with. She kept us clothed and fed; worked the land and protected all the animals. She got shit done. Maybe that was what made this night so terrifying to me—watching her dish out soup and pray to a broken bird's nest, struggling to make everything or anything seem okay again. She drained her shot of aguardiente and lit up a second cigarette, taking a long, slow drag. The embers got brighter as our apartment sank into a hazy dark. At least the smoke from her cigarette helped put some distance between us. Otherwise, it was too spooky catching her eyes roam around our apartment, dull and distracted.

Ernie had at least three portions of ajiaco. I swear that boy could have eaten even if he was being chased by a pack of ravenous wolves. When he finally pushed back his plate, Mami said, "Bueno," and started clearing the dishes. She washed, and I dried. Ernie was in charge of sweeping up the stray crumbs on the floor. These were our everyday chores before homework and bed. Because I guess that was our plan—to just keep going as if this were every other day.

Though it so clearly wasn't.

I was drying the last of the spoons and putting them away when Ernie opened the back door by the fire escape to dump out his dustpan. The beating of helicopter wings got so loud, I gasped.

"Mi'jo! Mi'jo! No!" Mami yelled. She lurched at Ernie, pulling him back from the door like she was saving him from the edge of a cliff. Then she slammed the door shut and pressed her body against it.

Ernie's small face dissolved into tears. "I'm sorry, Mami. I'm sorry!" he repeated over and over.

63

"Shhh . . . it's okay, mi'jo," she said, hugging him. "We just have to be even more careful now."

My eyes flooded with tears. I fought hard to push them back down. I didn't want Ernie to see me cry. He didn't need to be more scared than he already was. He was just eight years old, after all. He'd already lost his papi, and now he was facing the idea of losing me and Mami too.

"We're going to be okay," Mami repeated. "We just have to . . ."

It sounded like Mami didn't know how to complete that thought.

"We just have to what?" I asked.

"We have to remember . . . Ven." Mami led us into the living room, and we all sat on the couch together. She pulled us in close, so I could feel all our hearts thumping in stereo, her voice vibrating through me as she traveled back in time.

"Let me tell you about how we first come here. When Papi and I live in Suárez, it is so green everywhere. The mountains so big, the trees so tall. Because they have been there for hundreds of years. The flowers are all colors. The chivas, remember what those are, Vali?"

I had to shake my head no.

"They are buses, but so beautiful. They are painted all different colors. And inside the bus is like a rainbow. Color everywhere. Artists paint them. They take people from town to town. And we ride on them to see family, to go to work. So much beautiful things in Suárez. But then it was not safe. You understand?"

Mami told us about the violence and the threats. She told us about getting off a chiva and smelling the charred remains of her house. Walking, then running, searching for her parents. Next to her, I heard Ernie sniffling, trying to hold back more tears.

"It's okay, it's okay," Mami said, pulling Ernie in and rubbing his back, as if he'd gotten some of her grief stuck in his throat. "This is why Papi and I come to the United States. Because the mountains in Colombia have más sangre que agua, and we want to be here, safe with our family. We walk through Panama, Costa Rica, Guatemala, Honduras, Mexico. All for both of you. Vali, you remember when we go to the beach and el parque de atracciones in San Diego?"

"Yeah!"

"And I was in your belly, right, Mami?" asked Ernie.

"Not quite yet, mi'jo. Not until after we are living in California for some years."

Ernie still confused time a lot. He could always remember exactly when the next World Cup was going to start and, of course, his birthday and Christmas, but he couldn't really fathom that a whole world existed before he was alive.

"But you are always in my heart," Mami explained. "This is why we have to come here, and this is why I know we will be okay. Because you are a strong boy. A smart boy. This is your home!"

"Tell me about when we lived in California," Ernie said.

"It was awesome!" I jumped in.

"It is nice for the first years," Mami said. "Muy tranquilo, pero then the President keeps getting elected, and there is many changes. The raids and detentions . . . Everybody so angry. Teniamos mucho miedo."

I remembered moving into Tía Luna's one-room apartment after Papi was killed. Mami kept begging her sister to come east with us. "Luna, aquí no es seguro."

I remembered getting on that plane to come to Vermont. Holding Mami's hand as she told me and Ernie that we were going on an aventura.

"It is good that we come here," Mami told us now. "We live here with not much troubles for many years. And now, if we have to go on another aventura, we will. Together. But first, we wait and plan. And rest. ¿Bueno?"

The three of us brushed our teeth side by side. Usually, we all fought for our own space in the bathroom, but that night, we must have known. We must have felt the whirring of the helicopters outside, the terrifying uncertainty inside. And so we stood in front of that one sink, leaning into each other even as we spat out our toothpaste. Then Ernie climbed into bed with me and Mami, and the pull-out couch springs moaned with the weight of all of us, but I couldn't imagine asking him to go into his own bed instead.

"Mami, are we going to school tomorrow?" Ernie asked.

Mami squinted at me and pressed her lips together. She looked like she had so many answers to that question, and didn't know which one to choose.

She decided on "No sé. No sé."

"Will the people from the farm today ever get to come home?" he said.

"Mi'jo . . ." Mami said. I knew she wanted to protect him, but I didn't know if that was even possible anymore. "No sé," she whispered again. Sounding so tired.

"Do they get to call home?"

"No sé."

"Or maybe write letters?"

"No sé."

Ernie kept firing out unanswerable questions and Mami kept repeating, *No sé, no sé, no sé.* She didn't know. How could she? How could any of us prepare for all the unknowns that loomed around us now?

"But where do they go?" Ernie pleaded. "What do the officers do to them?"

"They send them back to their countries," Mami said.

The silence of what that had meant for our family filled the room. How many other families would be torn apart tonight, tomorrow, and in the days to come? How many of them would get pictures of their murdered loved ones?

"Well, if they try to take you and Vali, I'm going too," Ernie whimpered.

"Shh, shh," Mami answered. Even putting her hand over his mouth so those words couldn't linger in the air. Though I still felt them, and again had to fight back tears.

"Duérmete, niño chiquito, que tengo que hacer . . ."

Go to sleep, little boy, Mami sang. Her lullaby was more of a command tonight than anything else. Directing us to close our eyes and trust. To just give in to our obvious exhaustion. And it worked, I guess. For me too. I didn't even make it to the end of the song before I sank into unconsciousness.

"Este niño hermoso . . ."

Her voice held us both, protected us, at least for this night.

CHAPTER 6

I didn't wake up until after seven the next morning, and that was only because Ernie was kicking me in the shins while he snored next to me. Mami was already in the kitchen, of course, this time mopping the floor. The window over the sink was covered in one of her floral pillowcases, letting in just slivers of whatever this morning sun had. The only other light in here was a small blue flame on the stove, warming her morning coffee.

"Mami, what's going on? Why'd you let me sleep so late?" I asked.

Mami rested her mop against the fridge and kissed my cheek. Her skin felt clammy from however long she'd been up cleaning. "Today we all stay inside, todos juntos," she told me. "Until we know . . ." She smiled at me, or at least she tried to smile. But her lips barely parted, and her eyes were moist. "Ven."

She led me to the sink and lifted just a small triangle of the pillowcase's edge so I could see the scene outside. Our apartment was on the second floor of a pretty dilapidated brick building. Our fire escape led into a parking lot that was usually full of malt liquor bottles or the people who'd been drinking them before they fell asleep on the ground. At the other end of the lot, there was a hardware store that was never open, a pub that was always open, and an electronics repair shop that shouldn't have been open for another half hour or so, but all the lights were on and the door had been smashed. The glass counters and display cases were shattered too.

There were two officers, dressed in gray combat uniforms, circling the debris. I didn't even need to see the yellow lettering on their backs to know who they were and why they were here. The electronics shop was run by an older Indian man named Mr. Rashid. He never spoke much, but he'd always nodded to me and Ernie as we walked by.

Mami tucked the pillowcase back in so it covered the entire window again.

"They are there waiting for him this morning. I see him get taken away and put into the truck."

I couldn't find any words that made sense in this moment. But Mami could.

"I am okay. You are okay. We will all be okay," she said, pulling me in to her chest. I wanted to stay there in the crook of her neck for the rest of my life. It was the only place that felt close to safe right now. "Ven. Help me to clean. It is good to stay busy."

She kissed me again and handed me the mop. I started pushing it around the linoleum, just to have something to do besides going back to that window. After I finished mopping, Mami handed me a duster and had me clean off all her pictures and the altar while she scoured the sink.

When Ernie woke up, it was after eight o'clock, and Mami and I were rewashing and drying the pots and pans from last night. We'd also tried calling Tía Luna a dozen times each, and I had fielded a bunch of frantic messages from Kenna:

Are you coming? The bus is leaving.

Where are you?

Please answer!

It's ok. Staying home.

Holy shit. Scared the crap out of me. You ok?

No. You?

No.

"No school?" Ernie croaked, his voice still thick with sleep. The creases from our sheets zigzagged across his cheeks.

"No," Mami and I answered in unison.

71

"We will just play the hooky together, yes?" Mami said. Ernie and I both giggled at that one. "Ven. You hungry?"

Over breakfast, Mami pulled up a picture of the United States on her phone and started quizzing us on everything we knew about its geography. At first, she seemed interested in just the names of state capitals. But then she started asking more complicated questions like *Tú sabes which state has the most inmigrantes?* Or *What do you learn in school about Atlanta?*

I knew most of the answers. But I wasn't sure what she was getting at, testing us like this.

"Wait, Mami," said Ernie. "Does this mean you're gonna be our teacher from now on?"

Mami almost cracked a real smile at that one. "No, no, no, mi'jo. We just are learning together to see what we do next."

That first day of hiding in our apartment felt awful and endless. It was like we were trapped inside the walls of our building while everyone else around us went about their daily activities. I could hear our neighbors making coffee, flushing their toilets, listening to music, or chatting about the possibility of a storm. They were just walking through their days and their lives, knowing they were safe and secure, because somehow, that was their birthright. Meanwhile, Mami forbade us to play any music or speak above a mumble for most of the day. We had to scuttle around on tiptoes. I wiped down the kitchen counter five times, even though it was already clean. I ate cold arepas just to stop the angry aching in my jaw. Still, I couldn't look at the clock on our stove; it only made the hours pass slower.

That night, Kenna called.

"Hello?" Her voice rushed at me, shrill and frantic. "Are you okay? Where are you? I thought maybe they . . . got you!"

"I'm here. I'm hiding. I'm . . ." I was tripping over my own words, trying to tell her all the things that had happened since yesterday afternoon at Uncle Jimi's. "They got everyone on the farm except my mami. They got Mr. Rashid too. And now we're stuck inside, with all the lights off."

Kenna moaned with me. She also told me about more people who'd been taken from our town. When she'd gotten off the bus this morning, she could see two gray DF trucks parked in front of Morrow Magnet's gates, and she wanted to turn around and run the four miles back to Southboro, but she'd already made eye contact with enough people that she didn't dare. Two of the Morrow janitors and our beloved math teacher, Ms. Kochiyama, were led out of the school with their arms bound behind their backs.

"It was disgusting," Kenna reported. "They tied their arms with this thick wire and walked them past the entire school." I could just imagine all those white walls and white faces staring at their deportation march. "And the worst part was seeing that Maddie girl. Standing there with her hands on her hips. I swear she looked like she was smiling. I wanted to kick her in the throat."

"I'm glad you didn't," I told Kenna.

"Yeah." Kenna half laughed. "Guess that wouldn't go over too well. But still . . . I wish I did something besides just stand there and watch."

I wished she had too. But what? What could any of us do?

Kenna continued. "I just stared . . ." Her voice began trailing off. "I love you so much, Val."

"I love you too."

A long, heavy silence lay thick between us. Until she said, "I gotta go. My mom is freaking out. She thinks they're listening in."

"Can they actually do that?" I said, feeling my pulse quicken.

"No. Or, I don't know. Maybe? I'm sorry, I really have to go. Talk mañana?"

"Yeah. Mañana."

✖

IF MY MAMI had heard any theories about the phones being bugged, she chose to ignore them. The next morning, she was busy making a ton of calls in the kitchen. First she called Morrow and Southboro Elementary to report that we'd be absent again. Then she tried a few friends, I guess, and told them everything. I didn't know who was on the other end; I just heard Mami speaking in rapid Spanish. She was asking about what cities were safest or any news on how we could possibly travel. I stayed in bed past eight. Not because I was sleeping, though. I just had nothing else to do but listen and wonder what our next move was going to be.

When Ernie and I did get up, Mami had laid out all of our savings on the kitchen table. She was bustling around the kitchen, reaching into cabinets and shaking empty cracker boxes, unearthing little wads of cash like a magician. It was mostly ones and fives of course, but every little bit counted.

"¡Buenos días!" she said. She gave us both brisk kisses and charged into the living room so she could unzip couch cushions and reach into the springs of the pull-out mattress. There was another clump of bills there to add to the pile. All in all, it came to almost twelve hundred dollars.

Mami saw my shock and said, "Don't get too excited, mi'ja. That barely pays for bus tickets out of this mierdero."

"Where are we going?"

"I trying to figure that out."

"And how do we know when to leave?"

"No sé," Mami answered. "We just know when it is too dangerous to stay."

She told me and Ernie how she'd been trying to reach everyone she knew from San Diego—some were friends from the farms where she and Papi had worked, some from the church they took us to where Ernie got baptized. She still couldn't get through to anyone in California. Most of the people she'd spoken to were asking the same questions that were eating away at me:

What is this system upgrade?

Do you know where the DF are taking all these people?

Is it safer to go or stay?

And if we go, go where?

Mami did know one person who gave her hope, though.

"Her name is Sister Lottie," Mami told me and Ernie. "She is so good to us when we live in San Diego, and now she live in New York City. So, if I can talk to her, maybe we go there . . ."

"So we're going to live in a church?" asked Ernie, blinking fast.

Mami kissed the top of his head. "No sé, mi'jo. But this is what we do. We find our way through together."

After another breakfast of reheated arepas, Ernie and I wiped down inside the refrigerator and kitchen cabinets even though they were already spotless. When we were done with that, Mami had us each pick out two sets of clothes and fold them into tight bundles. We were also allowed to take a bar of soap and whatever toiletries could fit into a sandwich bag. I stuffed in my toothbrush, makeup, and deodorant. I didn't know how many tampons to throw in there, and I wanted to take my zit cream, only the cap was missing.

"Did you do something stupid with it, like throw it out or something?" I grilled Ernie. I knew I was being obnoxious and vain, but it was all I could control. I just felt this angry restlessness heating up and burning inside me. I was itchy and edgy and needed to do something.

Ernie went to tell Mami that I was being a pain in the ass,

76

but she didn't have time for our bickering. She was too busy crouching under the shaded window in our living room, peeking through the seam of daylight still visible. Ernie and I squatted down on either side of her, squinting at the scene outside, listening to the gut-wrenching screams.

A gray truck was idling on the corner by Southboro Park. Two officers in combat gear were pulling away a young woman, her hair falling over her face. I couldn't see who it was. I could only see her two little girls running after her. They had matching pigtails, and they were shrieking, their mouths so wide. And yet, they could never be big enough to hold all this pain.

Ernie and I pressed our bodies to Mami's, the tears pouring down our cheeks. I didn't know how we could possibly continue like this, just watching all these horrors play out in front of us. These weren't gory, made-up tales. These were our friends and neighbors being rounded up and carted away. It had to be just a matter of time before we were dragged away too.

But Mami kept promising us that we would leave as soon as possible. When we had a place to go and a safe way to get there and all the pieces were in place. Otherwise, she warned, we wouldn't even make it to that corner.

✖

BY OUR THIRD day inside, I felt like the air was a hundred degrees and the walls were closing in on us. Maybe they were.

I wanted to punch a hole through them all. I wanted to rip the window shade to shreds. But I also knew these were the only things possibly keeping us protected, holding us in.

"We will be okay," Mami told us. "I tell you, we will be okay." She sounded more fed-up than convincing. She also had run out of chores for us to do, so Ernie pulled out a deck of cards and asked if I'd play crazy eights with him. It was distracting enough until he started switching up the rules, or maybe he was actually forgetting how to play. Either way, I had no patience.

"Forget it. I'm done," I told him.

"You can't just be done," he whined. "We're in the middle of a game!"

"Well, I don't want to play anymore."

"You're a quitter."

"A what?"

"A quitter!"

"No, I'm not!"

"¡Niños, niños, por favor!" Mami whisper-shouted.

I shot Ernie the harshest glare I had and stormed off to the bathroom to rage by myself. Yes, I knew little brothers were supposed to be annoying, and "quitter" was a stupid, childish put-down. But somehow it had unleashed a tornado of fury, fear, and self-doubt.

I did want to quit—I wanted to run away from all of this as fast as possible. What were we waiting for, anyway? Could it possibly get any worse for us? Would we stay here until someone pounded on our door or took a bat to our windows?

In this life, though, there was no option to quit. Even if we did leave Southboro, there was no guarantee that anywhere else could be safer. Mami's chip was unreliable; mine could start beeping too. How long could we run before we got caught?

"Mi'ja," Mami rumbled through the door, "come, please. We need to be together."

I looked at myself in the mirror and tried to put on a calmer face. I tucked my hair behind my ears, threw back my shoulders, and set my lips in a tight line. Kenna called this my SuperVali stance. She said I could take on anyone when I wore that expression.

Only, that's when I realized Kenna hadn't called me back since that first night. Didn't she say she was going to call me the next day? Or was I supposed to call her?

I tried her now, even though it was ten thirty in the morning and she'd be making her way to third period at Morrow, so I knew her phone would be off.

We're sorry. The subscriber you are trying to reach no longer exists.

"What?" I yelped.

"Are you talking to your imaginary friends again?" Ernie teased on the other side of the bathroom door.

"Shut up," I snapped.

"Mami, Vali's saying mean things to me!" I heard as I dialed Kenna's number again and again.

"Valentina," Mami said, knocking on the door. "This is enough. You come out and apologize to Ernesto."

I flung the door open and crumpled. "I can't . . . I can't . . . get through to Kenna!"

I pushed my phone at her so she could hear that ominous message.

The subscriber you are trying to reach no longer exists.

I felt like someone was strangling me, forcing all the oxygen out of my system. I felt tears tipping over my bottom lids and didn't even try to swipe them away.

"What does that mean?" Ernie asked as he watched Mami and me hug. I couldn't answer him. Neither could Mami. But he must have known it was our worst fear, because I felt him clinging to my shoulders a moment later, crying too. I didn't know for sure whether Kenna and her family had been taken, but it felt too possible, too probable. And every time I thought of Kenna now, I thought of Maddie Fitz standing in that cafeteria line, explaining how scary it was to have "illegals" in this city.

"Mami, please," I wept. "When can we go?"

Mami blew her nose and pulled up the map on her phone again for us. She looked like she'd had enough of this waiting now too.

"Bueno. We get on the bus from Southboro to New York City, and this will be the three hundred dollars," she said, counting out the bills we would need. "We meet Sister Lottie, and we stay at her church for some time. If it is safe, we maybe go to Papi's cousin in the Indiana." She drew her finger across the screen, westward.

"What about up through Canada?" I offered.

"I hear there is DF on that border too."

"Why?"

"No sé . . . we go where we know it is safe . . ." Mami instructed.

There was no option to quit.

"We do not know when they coming next, so we keep moving. We stay together."

"I don't get it," Ernie moaned. "Why don't we just go back to Colombia?"

Mami opened her mouth to speak and then had to shut it again. Her eyes were already brimming as she shook her head.

"This is not . . . this is not possible, mi'jo," she whispered. I knew she had lost too much there—her parents, her sister, my papi. Instead of explaining any more, Mami stood up and went to her altar, lighting the Virgin Mary and saying la bendición. She asked la Virgen to watch over us and guide us, to have mercy on her children.

Then she spent most of the afternoon giving me and Ernie a lesson on how to be careful and conserve energy when we were traveling. She made us swear that at every checkpoint we stay cool and composed. If we got separated, we were to just keep going toward Sister Lottie's in New York City. She wrote down Sister Lottie's address on three slips of paper and gave us each one. Then we cleaned out our backpacks and put in our clothes, toiletries, and whatever snacks were left in the cupboard.

"That is all," Mami said. Although she did add to her pack a copy of the Bible, my abuela's silver spoon, a set of rosary beads, a flashlight, and a kitchen knife—the sharpest one we owned.

"What if we run out of food? Are we gonna have to hunt?" asked Ernie. I wanted to be annoyed with him again, but I knew we actually had to figure these things out.

"Mi'jo, we are going to take a bus. Qué tal, hunt for food," Mami said, smiling. But Mami wasn't talking like we were going to take a bus. She started giving us detailed instructions on how to survive on the road. "Agua. Es lo más importante."

She opened the refrigerator and gave us each three bottles of water to pack too. She said when she and Papi were fleeing, they learned how to follow animals to their water sources, because they had a better sense of smell than humans. Also, how to identify broadleaf plants and dig into their root structure since they could only survive near water. She showed us photos of different bodies of water throughout the US, from the Great Lakes to the Colorado River. I wanted to record everything Mami was saying, or at least write it down. But of course, she was talking too fast and barely took a pause for breath. She was also tucking dollar bills into different pockets of our backpacks.

"So when do we leave?" I asked, feeling exhausted and jittery at the same time.

"At nighttime," she promised.

Only, once again, the President had another plan for us.

We could feel a low rumbling throughout the building, and then all our phones jolted to life with a holographic announcement from the National News. The anthem sounded ten decibels too loud as the President's floating face took shape in front of us. His narrow, pasty face leering.

"Good afternoon, Citizens," he commanded. "I come before you once again with some very urgent news. As you may be aware, the state formerly known as California refuses to cooperate with our initiatives to keep America's borders safe and secure. Therefore, I have no choice but to order the building of a new Great American Wall between our region and California. I have also deployed twenty-five hundred specialized emissaries to not only safeguard this process, but all of the surrounding populace. Anyone attempting to enter this rogue state will be subject to arrest, detainment, and all measures of martial law. We are a nation built on trust and loyalty. It is our duty as American citizens to keep this country safe and strong. Thank you, may God bless you, and may God bless these United States of America."

As the President's hologram started fading, I saw Mami trying to parse out exactly what he was saying.

"It means they're trying to wall off California now too," I told her. "It means we have to—"

But Sister Lottie explained it better than me. Mami's

phone now lit up with a message from Sister Lottie in all caps that read

CALIFORNIA SECEDING TO FORM SANCTUARY.

ALL ARE WELCOME.

FOLLOW PLAN AND I WILL FIND YOU PASSAGE.

CHAPTER 7

To leave is to die a little.
To arrive is never to arrive.

—Immigrants' Prayer

We waited until just after four A.M. to leave. Not that we could count on it being any safer then; it was just the first time we put our ears to the door and did not hear stomping, yelling, or replays of that Presidential announcement seeping into the hallways.

"Okay, vámonos," Mami whispered.

"Wait!" I gulped. I looked back at our tiny apartment, suddenly paralyzed with fright. Or maybe it was more like an intense sense of grief. There were so many things we were losing when we walked out of this door. I had no idea how to say goodbye to all the pieces we were leaving behind. There were things in here that could never fit into a backpack—like the dent in the side of our fridge from when Ernie first learned how to make a goal, the fog of Mami's garlic and onions seeping into our skin, even Miss Nichols, the homeless woman who had eyelashes thicker than tar and always slept by our back fire escape with her cats and screamed at us about life on Mars. All the sounds, smells, and sights that made this our home.

Then again, if we stayed here another day, or even another hour, I was sure we'd get the telltale knock at our door. Or at this point, they'd probably just tear it off its hinges and pull us apart, like they'd most likely done to Mr. Rashid and that woman in the park. I was even envisioning a line of DF in our hallway, waiting for us to step out so they could haul us away. I squeezed my eyes shut as Mami put her weathered hand on the knob and turned.

"Vali . . ." she urged, tugging my elbow. The hallway was empty. It was just as I remembered it—murky and smelling of mold. Ernie, Mami, and I tried to be as silent as possible, but I guess even the swish of our backpacks and our tiptoed steps were enough to draw attention. We were almost at the strip of carpet that passed for a lobby downstairs when Ms. Murphy from 1C opened her door and scowled at us.

"Go! Get!" she ordered. As if we were a pack of stray dogs or mangy cats rifling through her trash. Mami used to pay Ms. Murphy ten bucks an hour to babysit me and Ernie after school. She always let us watch shows about housewives and millionaires, and she fed us caramel candies until our teeth were slick.

"Bye, Ms. Murphy," said Ernie. He was just trying to be polite, I guess. But Mami had to shoot him a hot glare so he knew not to say anything else. Ms. Murphy, on the other hand, didn't acknowledge in any way that she'd heard Ernie.

She wouldn't let her eyes come anywhere near to resting on us either. To her, we were already gone.

"No talking. To anyone," Mami said when we got to the sidewalk. "If someone asks, we are going to the bus to New York City to see our cousins," she said with rehearsed precision.

✖

THE SOUTHBORO BUS hub was just a half mile away, but it took us almost an hour to get there since Mami insisted that we walk in the most roundabout way, sticking to the darkest pools of shadow between streetlights. Mami wouldn't let us go too fast or too slow either. We had to be as unnoticeable as possible. When a swarm of gray trucks tore past us, we kept walking. When the thrum of helicopter blades swelled overhead, we kept walking.

We are going to New York City to see our cousins, I repeated under my breath.

To see our cousins, I heard Ernie echo.

I had no idea the Southboro bus terminal was this big or this busy, though I guess luckily for us, it was filled with college kids already finished with their spring semester at the University of Vermont. They were rowdy and thoroughly confused by all the new levels of security.

"I just got scanned again," I heard one of them complain.

"Me too. Pain in the ass," added his friend.

Ernie gripped my hand tight, and I nodded at him, as if to

87

say, *Yup. This is totally fine. We are totally fine.* Before we got any further, Mami explained that me and Ernie were going to go in first and she would follow up in a few minutes.

"What? No! Why?" I blurted. "We have to go in together."

"Shhh. Remember, my chip. It doesn't always work . . ."

Mami's eyes narrowed and I flashed to the gravel on her knees as she came back from that alley behind Town Hall last year.

"But . . . but . . ." I didn't have a way out of that memory. A way to keep us all together.

"Todo va estar bien," Mami assured us. "If something happen to me, you to go to Sister Lottie's. She'll know what to do. Que Dios los bendiga." She pushed her backpack into my hands and steered me and Ernie into the scanning line.

"But, Mami!" Ernie yelped. I jabbed him in the side to shut him up. She was right, even if I didn't want her to be.

By the time we wove our way through the college-aged crowds to the first checkpoint, the DF officer manning the machine looked pissed off and tired. He let all the blond-haired, blue-eyed students in front of us just stick out their wrists and walk through without a second glance. But when we came up, he stood in front of us like a human blockade and let a creepy grin ooze across his lips.

"Where you going?" he asked.

"Going to New York City to see our cousins!" Ernie and I said in almost perfect unison.

"Sorry," I added. "Just excited is all."

I stuck out my wrist and tried to ignore my trembling legs. The light danced over my skin as I stared into the distance. I heard the scanner click and practically swooned with relief. After Ernie went through, the officer looked mad. Then he raised his handheld scanner toward Mami, and I tucked my head down. Boring my eyes into her wrist as I tried to pray. It was more of a demand, actually. And I didn't know who exactly I was addressing.

Please let it work. Please.

Call it faith. Call it a miracle. Call it five thousand dollars well spent. All I know is, the infrared beams washed her wrist in a pale blue light, slowly inching its way up and down her skin. Then we heard the scanner make a clicking noise. The click of acceptance. The click of possibility. The click that hushed all the shrieks lodged in my throat and got us onto that bus to New York City.

"Move it!" the officer ordered. There was no trace of that ugly smile anymore. I guess he'd wanted some new capture to brag about. Another medal for his patriotism.

"Thanks. Let's go!" said Ernie with a little skip. As if we were headed out on some magical journey, instead of fleeing for our lives. My heart was hammering as Mami charged forward.

"Okay. Three tickets for the first bus leaving for New York. One way," she said, making a beeline through the station.

There were only a handful of ticket machines still in working condition here, and most of them used Bitcoin or e-cash. Everybody else was buying tickets on their phones or screens.

There was no way for us to do either of those things with only paper money, though. I just had to hope we didn't stick out too much as Mami fed her bills into the little metal teeth and pressed the buttons for our destination.

"Ugh, be careful. This machine just stole my last twenty-dollar bill," grumbled a woman with doughy cheeks and a helmet of hair the color of carrots. "Are you going to New York City? Do you know which gate that bus leaves from?"

None of us answered her, so she stuck her wallet back into a little fanny pack and wandered off toward the information teller, which was also automated. I doubted she'd have any luck complaining about one machine to another. I was just grateful she left us alone as Mami fished out our tickets from the slot. With seven minutes to spare, we choked back our terror, located our bus, and climbed on board.

It was already pretty packed inside. Ernie and Mami got seats together, but I had to sit across the aisle and a row behind them. The woman I'd seen by the ticket machines was actually next to me. I wondered how she'd made it on faster than us. She looked up and waved.

"Never got my twenty bucks back," she said with a shrug.

I was about to say sorry to her when Mami turned around and squeezed my arm so hard that I yelped, "Ow!"

Mami didn't apologize, though. She just said, "You need to switch seats?"

"No."

Mami gazed at the carrot-haired lady and then back at me,

drawing a line across her lips, as if to zip them up. The message was clear. I was not to talk to anyone. Not even nice old ladies in fanny packs.

The woman didn't look too upset. She got on her phone and started telling someone else about her lost twenty dollars.

A dormir, Mami mouthed at me. And even though I didn't want to trust this quiet, my body was too worn out to resist. As the bus glided out of the station, my eyelids sagged until I couldn't keep them open any more.

✖

"LET'S GO! LET'S GO!"

I awoke to people scurrying and climbing over each other. People pushed into single file and marched off the bus into to a hot, stuffy corridor.

"What's happening?" I whimpered.

"It's okay," answered Mami. "Sorry to not wake you up sooner. They have to make fuel stop. But it's okay. We get back on in a few minutes and just three more hours to New York."

The air in the terminal was hot hitting my face. According to the large clock on the wood-paneled wall, it was almost noon; an orange haze hung over all the snack kiosks.

"Where are we?" asked Ernie.

"I think somewhere near Boston, Massachusetts," Mami answered. "So many nice trees," she added, gazing at one of the floor-to-ceiling windows near the front of the building. Or maybe she was looking at the flanks of fully armed DF officers fanning out in every direction, pulling handheld scanners from their holsters.

"Wrists out!" one barked.

Mami pushed me and Ernie ahead of her. She also shoved her backpack at me. "Just in case," she murmured. "Go go go." We moved ahead, letting a bunch of people fill in the space between us and Mami. The officer closest to us gripped Ernie's wrist so tight, I could see his skin blanch.

Click.

"Get back on the bus!" the officer ordered.

He took mine and clamped down. I tried not to wince. I tried to just stare straight ahead, like I'd been taught.

Click.

"Keep it moving. Keep it moving!"

From behind me, I heard another officer yell, "Wrists!" and Mami answer quickly, "Yes, of course."

And then, a chirping noise.

"I'm sorry, officers," Mami said.

It chirped again.

"My chip, it works before. I do not know—"

And againandagainandagain.

In a hot second, there was a mob of DF officers lurching and tripping over each other. Their watches crackling with emergency procedure instructions:

Alien apprehended! Alien apprehended! Secure all entrances and exits for possible conspirators.

"Get on the ground!" I heard a male voice bellow at Mami. "Hands behind your back!"

"Please!" Mami cried.

I pulled Ernie away from the growing crowd and tucked him close as we both shuddered, trying to make out what was happening from behind the flood of people.

"It is okay!" Mami called again. I knew she was talking to us. She needed us to keep going. But I couldn't get my body to move any farther.

"Wait. Isn't that your mom?" The woman with the orange hair and fanny pack was standing right next to me and Ernie. Her hands were on her hips and she was squinting at us, as if we were some riddle she needed to solve.

"What?" I croaked. "Who?"

"There," she said, pointing at Mami.

That's when I had to look. I had to see my mami, lying facedown on the dirty floor. One DF officer was pinning her with a thick knee and handcuffing her. Another hovered close, his boot just next to her ribs. Ready to kick or stomp on her if she misbehaved.

But Mami did neither. She lifted her head and tilted it just enough that I could catch sight of her face.

And when I did, she mouthed one single word:

GO!

CHAPTER 8

We slammed through the double glass doors. The taste of panic filled my mouth, my nose, my lungs. There was no air to breathe and no time to gasp. Only the sudden clutch of everything falling away. We were running, running, running away from our mother's shrieks.

I had to trust that was what she wanted. What she told us to do.

I pushed Ernie toward one of the buses lined up outside. As if this was the most ordinary thing to do—two unaccompanied minors on a little adventure. Going to visit our cousins in New York City!

Only we could know it was the end of our world. A dark stain seeped down Ernie's pants leg; he was pissing himself.

About a yard away from the bus's entrance, I spotted two DF officers. One was pacing in between the bus's headlights, talking into his earpiece. The other was going from bus to bus, checking under the vehicles with a glaring flashlight. Searching for stowaways.

. . . claims she was traveling alone, but a witness reports she had two children with her at the time of arrest . . . sputtered one of the officers' phones. That was all I needed to hear. I squeezed Ernie's hand and forced out a grim smile, even as my insides were churning, convulsing. There were passengers behind us, in front of us, jostling us toward the officers. I stepped to the side and whispered to Ernie, "Follow me."

I led him away from the line and toward an abandoned-looking gas station.

"Where's Mami?"

"Shhh!" I slapped a hand over Ernie's mouth so hard his eyes pooled with tears.

"I'm sorry, I'm sorry," I whispered. "We just have to . . . Come on!"

Past the station, there was a mangled chain-link fence, and beyond that, a clump of charred-looking trees. I shoved Ernie under the fence and slid after him.

And then we ran.

We ran and ran and ran. Hurling our bodies forward, tripping over crooked branches and tufts of dried brush. The ground below us was hard and unpredictable. Ernie stumbled and went down with a groan. I pulled him back up and tried to ignore his tears. We had to brush it off and keep going. Sprinting as fast and as hard as we could. Stealing through knotty tree limbs and wading through wretched-smelling marshes.

Eventually the trees thinned out and the scrub emptied into a dried-out aqueduct. We crawled through a cobwebbed tunnel that was slick with sewage. I heard Ernie gag behind me but kept on pressing forward. When we got to the other side, there was a deserted parking lot. Instead of cars, it was filled with choke weeds and trash. Four concrete beams came up out of the ground in front of us. There was a row of rusted dumpsters, mountains of burnt lumber, and shattered glass in between the beams. Holding a cracked pane together was an orange neon sign that read **EVERYTHING MUST GO!**

I pitched forward into a run at full speed again.

"Vali, wait!" Ernie pleaded.

We couldn't stop. I had no idea how far we'd run, but it could never be far enough. I pulled my little brother harder. My eyes getting so thick and blurry with tears. A scream clawing its way up, making my whole body sting.

"Please, Vali, please!"

This time I yanked him so forcefully that he fell forward, taking us both down to the ground. My chin jammed into a rock and snapped my jaw shut. Blood filled my mouth and dripped down my chin.

"No!" Ernie screamed. He stared at me with wide, watery eyes. They looked almost golden now, they were so light and pleading.

"We can't stop," I said, swallowing hard and swiping at my bloody chin.

"Where's Mami?" he wheezed. I didn't have the words or the breath to answer him, but he kept pressing me. "Where'd they take her? When can we see her? How are we gonna get her back?" he wailed.

"I . . . I . . . I don't know," I managed. I needed to find something brave to say to him, but everything was crowding inside me, blaring and spinning. "We just have to keep going. That's what she told us to do, right?"

I kept seeing Mami's mouth, stuck in that jagged O as she mouthed the word *GO!*

Only now I felt tortured by the question—what if she didn't say *GO* at all? What if she was screaming *NO*? Or moaning *OH*?

Begging me to save her?

I couldn't stop replaying that scene in the bus terminal, the guilt and grief swelling in my chest.

"Ernie, you saw what Mami said. You saw, right?" I asked.

He didn't answer.

"Ernie, answer me!" I demanded. He couldn't help me, though. He was racked with grief too.

"I want Mami!" he bleated over and over. "Mami! Mami! Mami!"

"Stop!"

Yes, we were collapsed in the middle of a deserted lot and his voice was small and scratchy, but I didn't know who or what could hear us. The sky was made of a billion eyes; the earth was simmering with hate. Over Ernie's sobs I could make out a rumbling noise that I was sure was DF helicopters and the yowling of some feral-sounding animal. I tried to clap a hand over Ernie's mouth again so I could hear better, only he elbowed me in the side. Our heads clonked together, and the world turned hot pink for a second, the pain bouncing between my ears.

Then everything inside me came undone. It was like a vicious storm erupting out of me, raining tears and terror. The misery and shame were too big, pushing me to the ground. Drowning me.

I heard Ernie next to me. "I want Mami . . . I want Mami!"

This time, instead of trying to shut him up or make any attempt at answering him, I took his hands and molded them into fists, ramming them into my chest. I wanted him to crack my ribs open. What good were they, anyway? Protecting a heart that didn't even know how to save our mother?

We stayed there in between two hulking dumpsters on that deserted parking lot for hours. Shrieking and crying until our cheeks were chapped and swollen, until our throats were too hoarse to make any sound and the only thing I could hear was my pulse throbbing in my ears. And then we lay there some more. Just panting and moaning for everything that was now gone.

Sad but true: part of me believed that if I cried long enough or loud enough, my mami would hear me and come back. She always had before. But there was no way for her to hear us or piece us back together now. And if I was honest with myself, I had to admit that I was mad at her. Because when she was here, Mami had me convinced she was a superhero. And now I saw how terribly human she was.

✖

AT SOME POINT, I realized that Ernie and I were both shivering. I felt the sky shutting down, and the chill of dusk hollowing out whatever was left to call a day.

"Hungry?" I asked Ernie. He shrugged. I opened up Mami's backpack and took out some of her supplies. She'd packed us a stack of arepas, three water bottles, a box of crackers, some cans of mini hot dogs, and toilet paper. I handed Ernie a bottle of water first and watched him guzzle it in one gulp.

"Slow," I mumbled, then drained one of the other bottles just as fast.

I opened Ernie's backpack next, searching for any sort of hidden message of hope. But of course, there were none. Ernie's soccer ball and Mami's Bible were both wedged into the bottom with the flashlight. The kitchen knife was tucked inside a knife guard, with Mami's rosary knotted around its handle. The wooden beads were warm and smooth. I wondered how long they could hold on to her oniony scent and her unspoken prayers.

"What now?" Ernie asked, his face looking so drawn and drained.

I made a little nest for us between the dumpsters. The crusty, rusty bins were hardly going to protect us if we were really attacked, but then again, I had no idea where the enemy was anymore. The night was inky and mostly quiet, except for the skittering of some rodents in and out of the trash.

I put a backpack on my lap and had Ernie lay his head there.

"It's gonna be okay," I told him. I said it over and over. Even though we both knew it was a lie. We were utterly lost. They'd already taken our papi, and now our mami. With one hand clenching Mami's knife and the other on Ernie's head, I sat up straight and tipped my eyes to the sky.

"*Please,*" I said. Begging whoever or whatever was there to take care of my mami. To tell her that I loved her and I missed her and I would get us to Sister Lottie's.

CHAPTER 9

The sky was just inching toward dawn when I heard a rustling sound next to me. I tried to pull Mami's knife out from its hiding place without waking Ernie. He didn't stir. Whatever was coming for us did, though. It was scraping and rasping so close now. There were scratching noises too, the grating of fingernails or talons against metal. I didn't know which to fear more—being devoured by some sort of ravenous animal or coming face-to-face with a bloodthirsty DF officer. As if there was a difference. My heart was hammering so hard now, I could feel it behind my eyes.

I got the knife up above my head and held it there, poised to stab.

And then, scuttling out from under the dumpster to my right, I saw a bloated raccoon. It paused in front of my feet, the edge of a corn chip bag dangling from its mouth. I swear, it was sizing up whether to eat me too, with its tiny black-hole eyes. But I was so relieved that it was walking on four legs, I felt almost giddy.

"Shoo!" I ordered, baring my teeth and hissing.

The raccoon was totally unfazed, so I stamped my foot, waking Ernie.

"What was . . . ? Who was . . . ?" Ernie sputtered. He unfolded himself from my lap and tried to blink himself into understanding this picture.

"It's okay," I told him. "You can go back to sleep."

I was so exhausted physically and emotionally, I just wanted us both to sleep for a year and wake up in some new reality.

I knew we couldn't, though. As the raccoon trudged away, I got to take in more of our surroundings. It was bleaker than bleak. In with the mounds of burnt wood and shattered glass, there were also metal shelving units and mannequin limbs, twisted and mangled. I peered around the side of our dumpster hideout and saw there was a whole strip mall full of gutted buildings that had been ransacked and looted too.

"We're not staying here, are we?" Ernie asked, probably reading the haunted look on my face.

"No," I said. "But we have to figure out . . ."

I looked up at the open sky and felt trapped. There were too many unknowns to name. Where were we exactly? And where was Mami? Should we try to find Sister Lottie in New York City like Mami told us? How were we supposed to do that? How could this world possibly keep spinning without Mami to hold it up?

"I'm hungry," Ernie said, refocusing me at least for the moment.

"Me too."

I reached into Mami's backpack and started digging through the food. I got out the cold arepas, handing one to Ernie and taking another for myself. I opened a can of mini hot dogs and watched Ernie chomping away on the cold, oily meat. I couldn't believe we were here, huddled together in this dump. Consigned to the shadows, with barely enough food and water to keep us alive, hiding from officers who only wanted to hurt us because of where we were from.

"You want some?" Ernie asked, passing me the hot dogs midbite.

"No, thanks." I was so hungry and nauseous at the same time. My stomach, my throat, my whole body was cramped in anger. I could still hear Mami's cries echoing inside me. I ached with guilt, knowing she'd sacrificed herself for us.

"How we gonna find Mami?" Ernie asked in a broken voice. His lips were glistening from the mini hot dogs, and his eyelids were pink and puffy from all the hours we'd spent crying yesterday.

I just looked at him, trying to figure out how to respond.

"Hello?" Ernie was getting frustrated with my silence.

"You're right," I told him. "We need to find Mami."

I knew that was impossible, but I didn't have any other way to keep us going. I couldn't tell him that I had no idea where Mami was, no idea where we should head next, no idea how we would survive with one more can of hot dogs, some crackers, water, and a Bible. I couldn't do that to him, or to me.

At least I didn't tell my little brother about the horrific visions I'd been wrestling with all night—Mami being dragged to a windowless van and then thrown into a jail with hundreds of other people. Piles of bodies twisted together on frigid concrete floors. People keening and coughing, maybe a hole in the middle to serve as a toilet. Everything swarming with flies and vomit and urine and shit.

These were the reports I'd read about, the images I'd seen back when we had access to the dark web and independent news. Back when I was idiotic enough to think this only happened to other people, not us.

"Mami wanted us to go to Sister Lottie's. So that's what we're gonna do," I announced. I didn't know this was my plan until those words fell out of my mouth. Ernie's forehead scrunched together with worry.

"But what about Mami?"

"She knows where Sister Lottie is," I said. "Maybe she told us to go there because that's where she's gonna go." I didn't mean to make up these false hopes. I just needed to focus on the closest thing we had to a direction. Ernie listened and nodded, not totally convinced but willing to give it a try. "We just have to figure out where she lives and how to get there," I added.

El pájaro . . . It saves me.

Maybe it was divine intervention. Maybe it was a coincidence. Whatever it was that made a scrawny-looking pigeon swoop down and swipe at my last bite of arepa, it was a gift. Or really, whatever it was that made me check in Mami's bag for another snack was a gift. Because I did not uncover anything more than those crackers and canned hot dogs, but in the bottom of the bag, I now felt a square of paper, no bigger than my palm. I pulled it out to inspect. It was folded like a piece of mysterious origami. As I laid the paper out, I saw it was a map of America.

"What's that?" asked Ernie over my shoulder. The map was obviously old—from before GPS had been invented, probably. The states were all colored in powdery pastels and labeled in boxy block letters. There was still a strip of pink labeled LONG ISLAND and a whole section of Florida, even though I'd watched the footage of those places being destroyed in hurricanes years ago. Also, there were all these bodies of water drawn up near Southboro, which must've dried up long before, because I'd never heard of them. And a river winding its way down from Southboro to New York.

"I don't get it," said Ernie.

"Well, it's old," I explained. "So here's where we started, and now we must be—"

I stopped, my finger pointing at that winding "river" on the map. Only now I could tell it wasn't a river at all, but a line drawn in Mami's ballpoint pen.

"Ernie!" I gulped. "Mami must have done this!"

"Mami must have done what?"

"She drew this route for us to take! This is how we get to Sister Lottie's!"

Ernie was more confused than excited. He leaned in to look—the line was definitely thicker and wobblier than the other blue lines on the paper. It wound down from Southboro, through Massachusetts and Connecticut, until it wove across the state line to a star that was labeled NEW YORK CITY.

"This is what Mami wanted us to do, so we're gonna do it, okay?" I pointed to the end of her blue line and even tapped it for emphasis.

"Okay, but how are we gonna get there?"

"We're gonna walk," I said, as if it were the most natural thing in the world.

"Walk?" Ernie said.

I had no idea where we were. I was scared of turning on my phone to check our location—who knew if they were tracking us just like Kenna's mom had suspected? At the same time, I didn't even know if we were still in Boston. How could we even locate Mami's ballpoint route without our starting point?

I held my breath and turned on my phone. It told me that we were about four miles southwest of Boston. Also, that I had no new messages. I tried dialing Tía Luna's number one more time, just to see if there was some way to connect. Now, instead of the recorded message, there were high-pitched chirping noises that reminded me of the DF scanners. I dropped my phone on the ground as if it had just stung me.

Then I turned the phone off and buried it in the bottom of my backpack again.

"We shouldn't turn the phone on anyways," I told Ernie, trying to blot out that chirping noise in my head. As I leaned in to consult Mami's map, I saw another set of markings on the back. I flipped over those pastel states and read Mami's slanted cursive:

81 Street
37 Ave
Queens, NY

"Eighty-one Street. Thirty-seven Avenue. Queens, New York," I said aloud.

"What?"

I read the numbers and words again, wishing they made more sense or spelled out some sort of instruction to me. But all I could offer was a guess.

"This is where we need to go," I told my little brother.

"You sure?" he murmured.

"I'm pretty sure."

"And that's where Mami's gonna meet us?"

"I . . . hope so," I said. Desperately willing it to be true.

CHAPTER 10

We only made it about ten miles that day, but I told Ernie that was "Amazing! Awesome! Probably farther than James Rodríguez ever ran in an entire tournament!"

James Rodríguez was Ernie's favorite old-time soccer player from Colombia. I thought Ernie would be at least a little impressed that I'd paid enough attention to remember that name. But my little brother was too miserable and tired to give me more than a sigh. As the sun sank and our second night alone engulfed us, I found a small bunch of sagging trees where we could, hopefully, get some rest. So far, I'd been careful to keep us away from any main roads that might have new scanning stations. I convinced myself we were somehow safer if we could travel between the trees or even overgrown weeds and scrub. Only now, with darkness closing in, I felt more lost and disconnected than ever.

I gave Ernie the last can of mini hot dogs while I forced a handful of crackers into my mouth. We only had a half bottle of water left to wash it all down, which made me hungrier and thirstier. Ernie did fall asleep practically midbite, though, so I had to be grateful for at least that.

I wanted to sleep too, but my head was too busy again. Or really, my heart. I didn't know where or how she was, but I needed to "talk" to Mami. I told her how petrified I was. How I hadn't meant to leave her at the bus station, but I thought she wanted us to get out of there. How I didn't know if we could possibly walk over two hundred miles with a box of crackers between us, but I was going to do my best, and would she please, somehow, some way, be able to meet us?

She couldn't answer me, of course. Which only made me ask more questions. *Is it safe to go into a town and buy more water? Will Sister Lottie even still be there if we make it to Queens?* And the most horrible, unspeakable question of all: *Mami, what are they doing to you?*

✖

THE WORST PART was seeing dawn the next day and feeling my breath stutter in disbelief. Because this was still happening and we were still here, wherever here was exactly. Ernie woke up begging for that last gulp of water. Of course, I gave it to him. Whether it was safe or not, we would have to find some new supplies.

"Let's go," I urged.

We walked through the woods in silence. Already so drained

and sore. Already so scared and uncertain. We kept going until the sun screamed at the top of the sky. At which point, Ernie flopped on the ground, crying, "I can't, Vali. I can't!"

I tried carrying him on my back, but it was brutal. I wasn't just carrying the fifty-seven pounds of my brother. I was also carrying the kitchen knife, the Bible, the flashlight, the map, the rosary beads, and the soccer ball. I was carrying the three empty water bottles, some toilet paper, twenty-five tampons, and two bras that once upon a time seemed so important, I couldn't possibly live without them.

I was carrying all of Mami's instructions and directions inside the folds of my brain.

I was carrying those palm-treed visions of California in my heart.

It was too much for me or any one person to carry. I made it maybe a half mile before I tripped over a rock and fell. Taking all of it with me.

When we went down, Ernie howled louder than I did. He ripped off his sneakers and showed me how the backs of his ankles were rubbed raw. The new skin underneath a gooey red. He tried to wipe them with the edge of his dirty T-shirt, but I could tell from his shudders that it stung too much.

"How about we change your socks?" I suggested.

"Didn't bring any more," he said.

"Okay. Let's cut the back of your shoes so you can slip them on?"

I had him sit in the dirt while I went to work on his sneakers.

Mami's knife cut through easily; the worn pleather was thin and spongy from all his blood and sweat. I felt a sort of weary pride for coming up with this solution, but when I handed the sneakers back to Ernie, he could barely muster a smile. I felt like there was something broken in him that I would never be able to soothe or fix. I couldn't even reach his pain.

"What if we pretend we're in the World Cup?" I tried. "Except instead of playing soccer, we're walking. And we have to keep walking because this is just the first quarter of the first game and we have, like, twelve more games, and at any moment, we could get eliminated . . ." My analogy was getting darker and darker. Ernie chewed on his bottom lip and sniffed a little, which I knew meant he was working hard to push back more tears.

I started over.

"Okay, scratch that. What if we try heading a little closer to the highway or into a town, and if it looks empty enough, we can stop for some food?"

Ernie nodded, though I could see the glint of new tears in his eyes.

As we started out again, even the air felt so heavy. Or maybe we were just moving in slow motion through this maze of rotting foliage and broken rock. Ernie was hobbling and moaning. I kept plodding forward, humming his favorite song for motivation. My legs felt like they were made of lead, and I was getting bitten by tiny gnats. My tongue shriveling from being so dry.

Somewhere in the world, though, it was "a blessed day of harmony."

That's what some preacher was bellowing from the pulpit as Ernie and I stumbled into this little New England town. The church doors were wide open, and we could hear the congregation echoing *Amen!* after every blessed proclamation. I knew if Mami were here, she would probably march in and offer up some prayer of protection to keep us alive. But I was too nervous to go anywhere near that white clapboard building. I didn't know who was inside. I could guess they didn't look like us, though.

Ernie was more mesmerized by what was going on across the street from the church. There was a scrubby-looking field with two soccer goals set up and about a dozen kids practicing. I swore I could see Ernie's shoulders clench; he looked like he might drool with jealousy. The kids playing were smaller than him and, of course, white. Along the edge of the field there were parents and grandparents sitting on camping chairs, cheering for winners and losers, and yelling things like "Keep your eye on the ball!" and "Run! Pass it!"

I wanted to tear onto that field and yell, *Don't you see how crazy this is? You're running after a ball while we're running for our lives!*

We did locate a little sports clubhouse behind the parking lot where there were some toilets. None of the sinks in the bathroom worked, of course. The President had banned all public restrooms from dispensing tap water years ago. It was part of his campaign to crack down on "illegals taking all of our natural resources."

So I counted out five dollars for Ernie and five for me so we could each get a twelve-ounce bottle of water from a vending machine in the hall. I swear, I would've paid a hundred. That water was incredible. As I lifted the bottle to my lips, I felt the back of my throat leap up to grab the liquid coming down. I shelled out another ten for us each to buy more, and then Ernie begged me to buy a bag of corn chips and some gum.

"We don't have enough to buy junk," I told him.

"How much do we have?"

I didn't actually know how much was left of Mami's money after buying those bus tickets, but I wasn't about to pull out all the little wads of cash she'd tucked away and take inventory here.

"I know it's not healthy," Ernie said. "But I promise I'll eat better once we get there."

I didn't know if *there* meant Sister Lottie's to him, but I was so grateful that he believed we could get anywhere that I handed him five more dollars without argument. Then I bought us two more bottles of water for the road and steered us out the side exit.

The soccer game was just ending, and there were people trickling out of the church to their cars. I told Ernie to walk calmly and follow me as we made our way out of this town, out of this alternate reality where Sunday morning church bells and neon yellow soccer shorts were the loudest and brightest things to encounter.

Nobody in this town knew how loud we could wail, thinking of our mami being ripped away.

Nobody in this town knew how bright the sun burned as we ran through fields, or how dark it got as we collapsed in the trees at night.

Nobody in this town knew us—which I guess was all we could hope for as we walked toward a sign for Route 1.

"How much farther do you think we have until New York City?" Ernie asked as he sucked on a corn chip. I showed him the line on Mami's map again. It was a few inches long. I didn't dare tell him that by my calculations, that translated into about two hundred more miles of walking. Instead, I tried turning it into a little math game.

"Okay, let's say we walk two miles every hour. How many miles will we walk in eight hours?"

"Huh?"

He had just started multiplication this year at Southboro Elementary, and he usually loved word problems. Only, the words had never been so personal before.

"Okay, I have a better one. We started out with twelve hundred dollars. Then we bought three tickets for a hundred dollars each, which equals . . . ?"

"Three hundred."

"Great. Also, six bottles of water, corn chips, and gum which rounds up to about thirty-five dollars."

"Why are we doing this?" Ernie whined.

To see how much money we had left. But also, just to

occupy his brain because I knew, any minute now, he was going to tell me he was too tired to go on, and honestly, I was too.

"How about . . . how many pieces of gum are in that pack?" I asked.

"Twelve."

"Great. So, if we divide it by two, we get . . . ?"

"No," he told me. "This is the opposite of fun."

So, as we walked along the outskirts of this town, I did the calculations by myself. We had about $865 left to get us to Sister Lottie's, which was in Queens. At this rate, that would take us about two more weeks on foot to get to her. Two more weeks, with two bottles of water and six sticks of gum apiece, would be—

"Vali!" Ernie said. "Look! A bus! Can we get on it? Please, please?"

"But we don't even know where it's going. We don't have—"

"It says Route 1 South. We want to go south. *Please.*" His breath was so hot and sour. His face streaked with mud and tears.

"Just for a little bit," I said, my resolve wearing away. "It's too dangerous."

"Yeah, okay, thank you!" Ernie was giddy. He started sprinting toward a bus stop up ahead, dragging me along behind him. "Two passengers going south!" he announced as we boarded. "We're going to see cousins!" he added, with a look back at me for approval.

There was an error on the machine. It started beeping, calling too much attention to us.

"No. Sorry," I said to the machine's screen. "Two passengers going to the final stop."

"Is that machine acting up?" said an older man with a silvery beard standing behind us.

"What?" I yelped. "Oh no, not at all!" I couldn't tell if my voice was twenty octaves too high and shaky or if that was all in my head. I remembered that fanny-packed woman in Southboro complaining about her machine malfunction, and I couldn't get out of here fast enough. But I was stuck. The bearded man was still standing behind me, ready to board the bus, smiling.

"We just need to go south. We're visiting cousins, and they told us to get on Route 1, but I forgot what stop we have to get off at."

"The last stop before it goes east isn't 'til Connecticut," the man offered.

"Thanks!" I eked out.

I fed seventy dollars into the machine and grabbed our tickets, forgetting even to zip up my backpack as I pushed Ernie down the aisle.

There was an automatic scanner at our seats. We stuck out our wrists, and I puffed up my chest with fake confidence. The scanner clicked. The click of acceptance. A few minutes later, the bus pulled out onto the road. Ernie leaned into my shoulder and gave a full-body sigh.

"Thank you," he murmured.

Maybe this was a slightly blessed day after all.

It took only about twenty minutes for my panic to set in, though. I felt like everyone on this bus was out to get us. There was only a handful of them, but their eyes ran up and down our bodies; their silent faces made me shudder. I realized we had to look beyond horrible. Ernie's pants were still stained and smelling like pee. I reeked from that dumpster where we'd hidden that first day. Whenever someone walked down the aisle toward our seats, I ran through the self-defense techniques Mami had taught me years before:

Scream.

Knee them in the balls.

Scratch out their eyes.

I didn't know whether screaming was actually even part of the plan anymore, since it just drew attention. I started sifting through our backpacks so I could have Mami's knife close at hand if needed. As the bus edged onto the highway and sped past more white New England towns, I felt a thorny heat fill my body. Ernie and I were so naked and exposed in here, just waiting for someone to yank us to the ground or out the door.

"What's wrong? You look mad," Ernie whispered.

"I'm fine," I muttered, swimming in a cold sweat.

"¿Hablas español?" asked a woman behind us. I whipped my head around so quickly, I heard it crack. The woman looked innocent enough. She was small and squat, with deep creases lining her forehead. She also had a sleeping baby asleep on her lap.

Ernie must have remembered the rule about not talking to strangers, because he stared straight ahead and squeezed my hand. I wanted to do the same, but I also remembered what Mami always said about loving all creatures and looking after each other, and there was something so hungry and frightened in this woman's hazel eyes.

"Sí," I answered.

The woman's face lit up. "¡Ay!" she said loudly. "¿Sabes hasta donde llega el bus?"

"Um . . . no."

The woman was already stepping out of her row and scooting into the last seat in ours. She started talking quickly in Spanish as if we were old pals who'd just reunited. I felt like she was the only one on the bus talking this loudly, and I needed to get away from her before we became a spectacle. Love all creatures and help each other out, but not if it meant Ernie and I were going to get picked up by the next DF officer disguised as a passenger. Maybe I was being paranoid. Maybe I wasn't paranoid enough. I didn't know whether anybody was watching us, or everybody was watching us, or maybe nobody was watching us. It didn't matter, though. My heart was thumping wildly; I couldn't even hear what our new neighbor was saying.

"We have to get off," I mumbled to Ernie.

"What? Why?"

"Just . . . we have to."

"No," he moaned. I picked up his bag, Mami's bag, and mine, looped an elbow through his, and stood up.

"Sorry," I told the woman with the baby. "The next stop is ours."

The next stop didn't happen for a good forty-five minutes, but I stood while Ernie sat by the back door. We were ready to jump off at any second. When the bus announced that we were about to pull into a town called Arborton, Connecticut, I gave a big, plastic smile.

"Arborton! That's us!" I announced. The bus had barely come to a stop when I grabbed Ernie and pulled him off.

"What's wrong with you? Why did you do that?" he stormed.

"Shut up!" I marched him past the charging station here. There was a little roadside mall with a liquor store, an off-track betting house, and some place that called itself the Arborton Motel, but the door said **ADULTS ONLY**. Behind that, we found a parking lot that was being excavated and a crumpled fence leading out into some bedraggled-looking trees.

"Let's just . . . keep walking. It's safer," I told Ernie.

"But are we even in New York yet?"

"Almost," I lied.

"How close?" he pounced.

"Close. I mean . . . I don't know."

"What *do* you know?" he screamed.

"I know . . . a lot!" I yelled back. The last thing I wanted to do was make a scene, but I was angry too now. Because I knew some things—I knew algebra, Spanish, English. I knew how to type with one hand and recite the preamble to the American Constitution and how to play the guitar, or at least the chords C, G, and E. But what I didn't know was everything else.

I didn't know how long or how dangerous or how impossible this trek would be. I didn't know whether Mami was being detained or deported, or something so much worse I couldn't even imagine what it could be. I didn't know why her chip stopped working and mine kept going, or when mine would stop too. I didn't know how many days Ernie and I could survive on cracker crumbs, when thirst could become dangerous, or whether there were DF officers waiting to leap out of the next tree we passed.

I wanted to tell my little brother that I was lost and weak with longing too. That I was motherless, fatherless, homeless, groundless, and being actively hunted right now. Plus, somehow, I was in charge of his safety, which felt impossible.

But I didn't. I couldn't. It wouldn't help either of us, really. I looked at Ernie, slumping against one of those bedraggled trees, and just took him in my arms so he could cry. Letting him rage against my shoulder.

When we'd both caught our breath, I told him, "I know this for sure: Mami must be so proud of you."

That night, I used $38.93 of Mami's funds to go to a roadside diner and get us each a bowl of vegetable soup with oyster crackers, a plate of bacon and hash browns, and two glasses of water. Every time the waitress wasn't looking, I put more crackers and jelly packets into my backpack for later. Every time she was looking, I put on my most confident grin. There were only a few other customers in the place. An older couple at the counter ate pieces of pie with huge dollops of whipped cream. A girl who looked maybe a year or two older than me was crying into her milkshake while someone who looked like her mom lectured her.

None of them knew how lucky they were. None of them even blinked when the TV over the coffee maker flickered on and the anthem played after the National News was done. They all just put their hands to their hearts and repeated the words in sync with the music. Not even pausing to think what they were doing to us.

A few hours later, I found us a spot to sleep behind an apartment building nearby. It smelled like beer and vomit, and two guys got into a fight just a few feet away from us about batting averages. But they were too drunk to notice or care that under the doorway next to them were two broken children, aching for their parents, wondering if they'd make it until morning.

As long and as painful as the days were, the nights stretched on five times as long. I was on guard again, hovering over Ernie with Mami's knife in my fist. Fighting to keep my head up instead of bobbing into unconsciousness. Hearing everything . . .

Hearing Ernie's stomach gurgling.

Hearing my pulse banging against my skin.

Hearing the creaks and sighs of the trees.

Hearing the sky howl. Or maybe it was ravenous dogs.

Hearing the footsteps of rats and mice, squirrels and roaches. Skittering and scurrying between our legs.

Hearing probably a thousand different nocturnal creatures roaming the earth, hunting and gathering. The buzz of insects, the whir of cars, the *taca taca* of helicopter wings.

Praying for a bird's call or a factory bell to pull in the dawn.

✖

WE TREKKED LIKE this for ten days. Ten days of walking, limping, crying, looking for water, looking for food. We walked until our heels were shredding and our legs spasmed in pain. Whenever Ernie told me he couldn't go any farther, I made up more tales about how great it was in New York City. I told him it was a city built on an island and it had soft pretzels as big as his face. There were huge bridges and statues, skyscrapers so ginormous that they literally scraped the sky.

"And Mami will find us there?" Ernie asked.

It killed me to continue lying to him like this, but I didn't know how else to keep him going.

"That's . . . the plan," I mumbled.

As the sun went down each evening, I started searching for an alley or park bench that was empty and shadowy enough to call home. One night, we stuffed ourselves inside an abandoned tunnel filled with sewage. Another night, we hid behind a landfill covered in pigeons. The worst night was when we saw two DF officers stumble out of a bar and beat a man mercilessly on the sidewalk. Ernie and I hid behind a car just a few yards away, too scared to move, but were forced to hear every punch, kick, and scream. The next night was our best night. We were somewhere in the Hudson Valley by then, and I found a public library with its back doors unlocked. We crept in and rolled around on the carpet. Pulling books off the shelves in the children's reading nook and tearing through their pages about magic and wizards, good guys versus bad guys.

Ernie was so excited. He found a book about a superhero dog who lived in New York City and saved everyone from a monster made of slime.

"That's gonna be us," he said proudly. "We're gonna get to New York City, and find Sister Lottie, and save Mami from the bad guys."

"Yes. Yes, we are," I said.

Because I didn't have the heart to tell him that these were all just made-up stories.

It wasn't like that in the real world.

CHAPTER II

Mami's blue line looked so short and direct on the map, but it nearly killed us.

We were on day ten of walking, weeping, and if we were lucky, finding an overpriced, unattended rest stop with water before we crumpled by whatever desolate place looked like it could shelter us for a few hours of sleep.

And yet that blue line had also gotten us out of the scrub on the side of the highway, into more tree-lined streets now.

"Is that New York City? Is that New York City?"

Ernie's constant questions were driving me a little nuts. I knew it was my fault, since I'd built up this place to be the answer to all of our needs and hungers. Still, at a certain point I stopped even trying to answer him. Until he pointed up ahead to a bunch of tall buildings that looked like they were built with an inch of air in between. The skyline was clogged with huge lumps of flaking brick fighting for space.

"You know what? You might be right." I went to turn on

my phone just to check the GPS, but even the screen blinking awake scared me too much, so I turned it off again. "It's okay!" I said with fake cheer. "We'll figure it out for ourselves."

Without a word, we both broke into a staggering sort of jog. The sidewalks and streets started getting more and more crowded. There were mounds of garbage and pay-by-the-ounce water fountains. All the storefronts had loud neon displays, promising everything for ten dollars or less. People zoomed past us, yelling to stay on the left so they could pass on the right. Or maybe it was stay on the right so they could pass on the left. Everything and everyone was moving so fast and loud.

I tried to figure out exactly where we were in the city. The buildings all started to run together, a jumble of lights and LED screens, countless projections and advertisements for whitening your teeth. No wonder Mami thought that we could find some kind of safety in this city, or at least be overlooked. There were too many other attractions to bother with two wandering kids. That was my hope, anyway.

"C'mon!"

We ducked into a ten dollars or less store, and I picked out three more bottles of water, some granola bars, and bananas. The man behind the counter had a nose so sharp it looked like a beak. As we paid for our food with a few crumpled dollar bills, I could feel his squinty eyes boring holes through me.

"You know, they're doing that system upgrade to all the chips any day now," he said.

"Yeah!" I pushed out a grin. "Thank God. We need to . . . do that."

"Definitely," the man said, nodding his approval.

I put our food in my backpack. "Anyway, thanks!"

As we left the store, I heard the plastic frame of the door smack against the jamb. It sounded just like that door they'd hung on Uncle Jimi's after they'd taken him away. I wondered what the system upgrade was going to mean for my chip, but I knew it couldn't be good.

"Okay, so New York City. Where's Sister Lottie?" Ernie asked, jolting me back onto the street.

"Well, New York City is big," I explained, keeping my voice low. "We need to get to Queens."

I wanted to pull out Mami's map, but it felt dangerous to be walking around looking so obviously like tourists. We found an electronic transit map a few blocks away. On the display it said that it was May 29th, 2:43 P.M., and it was already ninety-two degrees. There were plenty of people huddled in front of the screen, waiting for the updates on which train was arriving when. Then, almost in unison, everyone except for Ernie and me tore up a set of stairs behind us as a train whooshed overhead on a set of suspended tracks.

"Please, can we get on it, please?" Ernie begged. I wanted to tell him absolutely no, but even the thought of sitting down made me swoon a little.

"Okay, but if anyone stares at us for too long . . ."

Ernie grabbed my hand before I could even finish that thought and pulled me toward the staircase too. There was a metal scaffolding over it that read **WAKEFIELD/241 STREET**, with a number two next to it. We scrambled up the stairs to a platform with a line of ticket machines and automated wrist scanners on either side.

I tugged Ernie back toward me. "Wait," I said.

"What?"

"It looks like we take this to Times Square and then we need to transfer to the seven."

"Transfer to the seven," he repeated.

"But if anything happens along the way—"

"Stop, Vali," he cut me off. "C'mon. We made it this far. We need to find Sister Lottie and Mami."

I let Ernie pay for two tickets from our thinning funds, and he stuck his wrist out for the scanner, staring at me until I did the same.

Click.

Click.

It was only a matter of time, though. System upgrade any day now. Somewhere, somehow . . .

When the next train came, it was so packed that I made Ernie stand nose to nose with me. He smelled like turned milk, or maybe that was me. I tried to just focus on breathing and keeping our gaze locked. There were cameras positioned every few feet along the subway walls, each no bigger than a walnut but clicking constantly. I wondered what kind of data they were recording, whether there was someone watching us in real time. Maybe even searching for a particular face.

There were girls in plaid skirts and navy cardigans, matching from the zippers on their backpacks to their high-pitched chatter. There were men in tailored suits and women with blood-red nail polish. Everyone had some sort of device plugged into their ears. Some wore glasses that were obviously projecting images, because they laughed and jabbed at the air in front of them. It was up to the rest of us to anticipate and get out of the way.

Ernie and I blended in much better on this train than we did anywhere in Southboro, though. There were so many different kinds of people here, so many different languages being spoken. I could pick out bits of Spanish, French, and Arabic. No complete sentences, though. I wondered if any of them were talking about needing to find their mamis or papis. Everybody was reaching across each other to grab a pole or the edge of a seat. How many of these exposed wrists were bulging with counterfeit chips?

I let my eyes roam over to the people sitting silently in their seats. They were even more curious to me. It was late afternoon, and these people looked glazed, their jaws set like weathered stone. There was a National News feed scrolling across the smart ceiling of the train. I hadn't seen a screen for almost two weeks, and the glare of it made me wince. The headlines were all the same bullshit I remembered—the

President was almighty; the trade war with China was a great success; most importantly, America was prepared to combat the most "colossal, overwhelming humanitarian problem of the rampant illegal invasion."

What were these people watching the news feed thinking? Did they know what any of this meant? Did they think that if they just kept their mouths shut and stared straight ahead, this would all go away?

I must have dozed off for a little while. I didn't mean to, but once we got seats, the gentle rocking and hum of the train car lulled me into a trance. The next thing I knew, Ernie was in my ear, his whisper so close I could feel little flecks of his saliva hitting the side of my neck.

"Vali, wake up! Wake up!"

"Huh?" I'd slept long and hard enough to even drool on my chin. So had Ernie, I guess. When I got my eyes to focus out the train window, I saw that we were zooming toward a station with bright tiles and pictures of some glittering carousel.

"Is this Queens?" Ernie yammered. "This must be Queens, right?"

"It's Clark Street," muttered a man seated next to us.

"Clark Street," I said to Ernie, trying to regain some sense of control. "But first we need to transfer at Times Square."

"Good luck with that. You missed it by a long shot." The man pushed past us as the train slowed down and the recording about doors opening came on.

"Let's get off," Ernie insisted. He shoved me toward the

train doors, and we tumbled off at the next stop. We were both stumbling like old people as the tide of commuters swept us up the stairs and out into the afternoon sunlight. There were people hawking flowers, phones, coffee, and salvation. Ernie counted five ice cream trucks in the space of one block, and I gave him five dollars mostly because I was so overwhelmed and confused.

We walked down a steep hill toward a sludgy-looking stretch of water, with Ernie slurping at his red, white, and blue ice pop and me anxious to find any sort of sign that could point us in the right direction.

"Are we still in New York City?" Ernie asked.

"Yeah," I said uncertainly. "I mean, we have to be, right?"

Ernie was too distracted by all the sights now, though. Especially when we got to the bottom of the hill and he spotted that giant bridge and the carousel beneath. It really was a magnificent carousel inside a huge clear enclosure. The painted horses and gilded carriages dipped and twirled to a tinny soundtrack of circus music. The children on top of each seat squealing with delight.

"You're right, Vali! New York City is magic!" Ernie was on a mission now. Dragging me toward this fantastical place, weaving us through the oncoming crowd.

He didn't even ask for my permission. Just marched me up to the carousel's turnstile behind a little girl dressed up like a ballerina with a purple sequined tutu and a crown that said PRINCESS!

"You go. I'll watch," I told him.

I paid ten dollars for his ticket and watched my little brother bounding onto the ride as soon as they let him, without so much as a glance back. The music started up again, and the horses began bobbing. Ernie was thrilled, screaming at me from atop his sky-blue stallion—chest proud, skinny arms raised above his head. He looked like such a sweet, innocent *kid* up there as a breeze ruffled his dirty hair.

I stared at those horses, wishing they could just throw off their chains and gallop into the sunset with me and Ernie on them. Or maybe my little brother would be better off without me, I thought. His chip was real. If I was out of the picture, he could ride this carousel as much and as long as he wanted, until someone took him home and gave him love, shelter, and lasting protection. If that even existed in this world.

I studied a little subway map display by the carousel, and my heart hurt. According to this map, we had not only missed our transfer at Times Square, we were in an entirely different neighborhood, or "borough" as they called them in New York. We'd have to backtrack and take at least two more trains to make it to Queens, and with the sky getting darker, I didn't think it'd be possible to knock on Sister Lottie's door today.

As the day faded, I paid for Ernie to go on that ride again and again. Yes, maybe it was a waste of Mami's hard-earned money, but I had to think she'd be okay with it.

While Ernie was on that carousel, nobody could touch him.

While Ernie was on that carousel, the night was full of twinkling lights instead of hunger and fear.

While Ernie was on that carousel, anything was possible, even blue stallions and mermaid-covered carriages.

So I let my little brother spin, over and over again, suspended in this crazy loop-di-loop. His face frozen into a goofy, dirt-stained grin. He was so deliriously happy, I had to blink away tears as he floated by.

CHAPTER 12

It took us most of the next morning to make our way to Sister Lottie's. When we did eventually get to the Eighty-Second Street stop in Queens, I thought I'd fallen backward in time. There were long-necked lampposts, old stone gargoyles on the buildings, and bright oranges, greens, and reds in the shop windows. It smelled like delicious warm dough and sizzling plantains. On the corner of Eighty-First Street and Thirty-Seventh Avenue was a small stone church with a red wooden door and a pot of wilting lilies on its one step. Engraved into the stone archway were the words ST. AUGUSTINE.

"This is it . . . I guess," I told Ernie. I just hoped Augustine was one of the saints who believed in helping the downtrodden. The front door was locked, but I could see a path worn into the dandelions along the side of the building. When we followed it, I found a narrow alley in the back and a set of steps leading down to a thick metal door. On the concrete base, next to a drainpipe, was a little porcelain statuette of la Virgen that looked exactly like Mami's.

Yes, all pictures or statues of la Virgen look pretty much the same, and maybe I was just seeing what I wanted to see, but I could swear this statue's head was tilted in exactly the same way as Mami's statue. She had the same little comma of a smile creeping up her cheek too. I stared at her for strength and courage as I knocked on that metal door.

Can I help you? came a woman's voice through a crackling speaker above us. I hadn't even noticed that it was there. Or that there was a little camera lens attached to it.

"Um . . . we were told . . ." I took Ernie's hand. "We need to find someone named Sister Lottie?"

Silence. An eternity of silence. I didn't know whether to run screaming or stand my ground. I begged la Virgen to give me a sign.

The door opened.

A rickety-looking old woman peeked out. Her milky skin was wrinkled with laugh lines and she had white wisps of hair flying in different directions. She waved a bony arm, ushering us in. "Yes, yes," she said. "This is me. Sister Lottie," she said with a thick German accent.

She led us down three stairs into a damp stone tunnel. As we followed her, she peppered us with questions, but never waited for us to answer.

"You are hungry? Of course. Thirsty? Yes! You must travel a long way to come here. Or maybe not so long?"

I could tell Ernie wanted to talk to her so badly and tell her all about our trip here, but I squeezed his arm to warn him, *Not yet*. I needed to be sure that this was really the Sister Lottie that Mami had sent us to meet. I didn't know how or when I'd be sure. Only that I needed us to tread lightly.

The tunnel led past a huge boiler room and into a large kitchen. There were two long aluminum tables pushed together in the middle of the floor, surrounded by maybe a dozen folding chairs, with people sitting in each one of them—sometimes even two to a seat. At the far end, by a refrigerator, there was a large bald man. He was holding up a tiny notebook, reading a poem aloud about the colors of the sun in Jamaica.

When the poem was over, everyone in the room clapped and cheered.

"That's Kelso," Sister Lottie told us. "He likes to give us some entertainment before lunch."

Kelso bowed deeply for his audience and waved up someone else to read next.

"Lakshmi, it's your turn!" he called. "You promised."

"No, no, no," said a young Indian woman with gorgeous black hair trailing down her back. An older woman next to her was pushing her toward the makeshift stage. "No, really!" Lakshmi laughed.

"Here, I save you," announced Sister Lottie. "We will take a pause to eat. And welcome . . ." She turned back to me and Ernie. "Agh! I didn't even ask you what is your names?"

Ernie stepped forward before I could stop him and said, "My name is Ernesto. But you can call me Ernie."

Ernie . . . I like that.

So sweet.

The murmurs of approval from the kitchen's crowd made him beam.

"And you?" Sister Lottie asked.

I thought of giving them my ID name; it felt not only dishonest but also probably useless at this point. Whenever the system upgrade happened, I was pretty sure the real Amelia Davis was going to demand her identity back from me.

"Her name's Vali," Ernie offered, seeing me lost in thought. "She's my big sister. And she's awesome." I didn't know what stunned me more—his sweet words and the fierce hug he gave me with it, or the smiles we got from this group of strangers.

"And you know our mami, Liliana," Ernie told Sister Lottie. "You're gonna help us find her!"

"Liliana . . . ?" Sister Lottie said, her smile drooping. I reached out to cover my little brother's mouth or at least give his hand a ferocious squeeze, so he knew to shut up. Sister Lottie either sensed my nervousness or wasn't sure herself how to respond. She stepped between the two of us and redirected our attention.

"Well, Ernesto-but-you-can-call-me-Ernie and Vali-awesome-big-sister, we are very happy to have you here," she said to the room. "Aren't we?"

The group mumbled different versions of *Yes!* and *Yay!*

Sister Lottie then made them each introduce themselves to us. "And say how you came here," she added, winking at me.

There was Esme, an older woman from Haiti who swore that she didn't know when her work visa expired. There was Mariana, who had skin the same color as mine except for a big swath of marbled scar tissue covering her forehead. She said she'd been in the United States for ten years and at Sister Lottie's for ten months, and she didn't want to say anything else but added that she was glad to meet us. Kelso was Jamaican and proud of it, but his wife had died and now he was "looking for citizenship and looking for love." Lakshmi came here as an au pair and was told to "wait in line" to renew her documents. But there never was any line.

One woman was pulled over for a speeding ticket even though she was driving twenty-five miles per hour. "Driving while undocumented," she declared. Another woman was robbed at gunpoint, and when she reported it to the police, they said to go home before they reported her to DF.

Eduardo just said, "Honduras. Happy to meet you. God bless!"

I felt my chest loosen a bit as each person spoke. They sounded so genuine, so vulnerable. I knew I should be on guard, but it would have been pretty ridiculous to suspect that Sister Lottie and this whole crew were imposters just waiting to pounce on us. Plus, I felt too weary and famished to come up with an escape plan. Especially when Sister Lottie then told us that lunch was served.

She pointed to a pile of chipped plates stacked on the Formica counter to our right and three large pots on a stove just past the sink. There were also two loaves of white bread, a tub of margarine, plastic cups, and bottles of soda. I heard Ernie gasp next to me.

"Come, come!" ordered Sister Lottie. She was old but feisty, flinging off the pot lids and spooning us out huge helpings of rice, black beans, and some creamy potato-looking thing.

"Thank you," I said.

"Thank you," Ernie echoed.

"Thank you so much," I said again.

"Enough! Now grab something to drink and sit down. We say grace when everyone's seated."

We ate and ate and ate. I couldn't stop shoveling food into my mouth. I think Ernie and I both could have eaten twenty servings, but I made us stop after thirds so we didn't seem too greedy. Esme kept saying Ernie needed more because he was a growing boy. Kelso was chatting on about how he used to prepare five-course meals, and did we know how to cook? I think they were amazed by having kids here. Sister Lottie hovered over us, making sure we knew there was always more.

After we'd stuffed ourselves silly, Sister Lottie took me and Ernie to her office, off the side of the kitchen. It was just big enough for a desk, a chair, and a broom closet. The floor was piled high with garbage bags full of clothing donations and canned goods.

"Why don't you pick out something fresh to wear, and I

can take your clothes home to wash them tonight," she offered. "We have a bathroom down the hall where you can wash up too. Water doesn't last for too long, of course . . ."

There were multiple stalls in the bathroom, which made me laugh and cry at once. I hadn't been in front of a clean toilet since we left home. The water in the sink was lukewarm and speckled with rust, but I didn't care. I felt like I was in a five-star hotel as I splashed it onto my face and let it drip down.

I peeled off the T-shirt and shorts I'd been wearing since Vermont and pulled on someone else's pink sweatpants, along with a lavender tank top. The pants were probably meant for a woman twice my height and they dragged along the ground when I walked. The shirt had a little ruffle along the bottom hem that made me giggle. It was so odd and girly to me.

When Ernie and I reappeared in the kitchen an hour later, Esme and Kelso applauded for us.

"Oh, so pretty! So handsome!" Esme cooed. Ernie loved the attention and showed her how he'd slicked back his hair like Mami taught him to do at home. He was decked out in a blue shirt with a white anchor on it. It looked so clean. *He* looked so clean.

"Is Mami coming here?" he asked. "Or are we gonna go get her?"

"We'll . . . we'll see," I stammered. "For today, we just need to rest."

"You know, I'm almost seventy years old, and I still miss my mom too," Esme admitted. "Isn't that something?"

"Yes," said Kelso. "The mamis. They are the world. They give us the world."

We spent a lot of the afternoon playing card games with Sister Lottie and Esme. They both were terrible at crazy eights. Or else they just chose to let Ernie win basically every round.

For dinner, we feasted again on leftover beans and rice and a tray of donated cinnamon rolls from a nearby bakery. I swear, Ernie gobbled up ten rolls before even coming up for air. By the time we washed and dried our plates, I was so drained I thought I might fall asleep standing up.

Then Sister Lottie, Kelso, and Eduardo folded up the aluminum tables and set out mattresses on the floor. There wasn't enough space for everyone here, so a few people headed upstairs to lie down on the church pews.

"We call this the penthouse," Sister Lottie told me and Ernie. "Follow me."

She took us up another flight of stone steps to the nave of the church. It was so much bigger and more decadent than I had imagined. The arched ceilings and stained-glass windows made everything feel echoey and cool.

"Here. You pick whichever spot looks comfiest to you," Sister Lottie said. A few women from downstairs were pulling out pillows and blankets from their bags in a corner. There was someone already snoring from one of the benches toward the back.

"How about here?" I said, pointing to a pew closest to the front. It just felt like there was a little more light there, and there were plenty of different statues of saints, with flickering electric candles to keep us company.

Sister Lottie brought us two winter coats to use as pillows and a few sleeping bags without working zippers.

"And now you sleep tight, and I see you in the morning, okay?"

"Okay . . ." answered Ernie in a mournful tone. "And you'll be here when we wake up?"

I knew exactly how he felt. I hadn't expected to be this sad saying good night to our host, but I was.

"Of course I will," answered Sister Lottie. "Would you like to say a prayer before you close your eyes?"

"Yes, please," said Ernie.

"Sure," I agreed.

I didn't know what to say, though. I knew I should confess to someone that I'd lied to Ernie about Mami being here. But more importantly, I wanted to tell God and la Virgen and all the saints of the rosary that you could not ask for a more pious, perfect disciple than my mother, Liliana. And to please, *please* watch over her, wherever she was.

"What would you like to offer up?" asked Sister Lottie.

"How about, please protect Mami, and thank you for the miracle of beans and rice," said Ernie.

Sister Lottie chuckled.

"Also, thank you for bringing us here to Sister Lottie and for her awesome generosity. Oh, and those rolls," I added.

"This is beautiful," said Sister Lottie. "Thank you for these wonderful children. May they rest easy and feel safe and secure here."

And together Ernie and I said, "En el nombre del Padre, del Hijo, y del Espíritu Santo. Amen."

CHAPTER 13

It was glorious to sleep with a roof over our heads, even if it was on a hard wooden bench. I would have probably slept all day if Sister Lottie hadn't woken me up.

"Okay now. Good morning!" she sang.

I was so startled to wake up there that I yelped in her face. She just rubbed one of her ears and gave me a crinkly smile, unfazed.

"Maybe you don't remember. I'm Sister Charlotte-Anne, but you can call me Lottie," she said, sticking out a bony hand for me to shake. "You came here to St. Augustine's last night with your–"

"My brother!" I scoured the pews, but he was gone. "Where's my brother? Where's my brother!"

Sister Lottie held up a palm to stop me before I completely spun out with worry. "Yes. He is Ernesto-but-you-can-call-me-Ernie. He is in the kitchen, eating some breakfast," she told me. "I think he tried to wake you before, but you know, the body needs rest."

"I'm so sorry. I'll be out of here in two seconds."

"No two seconds. You take your time," Sister Lottie said. "But first, I would like to ask you a question here."

"Yes?" I felt a ripple of panic charge through me. Even though she seemed incredibly kind, there was still a part of me that was terrified she'd threaten to scan me.

"It is okay," Sister Lottie assured me. "I just . . . I hear your little brother say that I am going to bring you to your mami, and I don't know . . ."

"Oh, yeah. Uhhh . . . sorry. That's my fault. I just needed to get him here, you know. We had to walk . . . a lot . . . every day, and I didn't know what else to say. Before they took my mami away, she told us to come here . . ."

"I see," said Sister Lottie. "Is your mami Liliana Ramirez?"

"Yes," I said.

"And she was . . . taken?"

I nodded.

"And you came here because I told your mom I'd help her."

I nodded again. Then I poured out our whole story, beginning with Papi getting deported. I couldn't hold it in anymore; it was just too much. I told Sister Lottie about the raids in our town and on the farm. I described that last horrific moment when we saw Mami pinned to the ground. I tried my hardest to speak in a clear, calm voice, but I was soon trembling and swiping away at tears. Sister Lottie squatted down so she could take my hands in hers and really digest every word I said, drawing me into her arms for a tight hug. She smelled like peppermint and coffee.

"I promise I'm going to help you. I will, I will," she said, her voice cracking. I was pretty sure she was crying too. When she released me, I felt relieved to have somebody else holding on to some of my sadness and fear. But also, so heavy, knowing she really had no answers for us.

In the kitchen, the mood was much livelier. There was a talkative group of people gathered around the folding tables speaking in all different languages, munching on sausage links and miniature waffles. Ernie waved me over to a spot at the far end of the table where he'd saved me not only a chair, but a plate piled high with breakfast.

"I hear you are good at math but not as good as this guy," Esme said to me as I walked over.

"Oh, really?" I asked Ernie, who was obviously charming the pants off anyone who would listen.

"What grade are you in, anyway?" Esme asked Ernie. Then, before he could answer, she jumped in with, "Let me guess—you're in university!"

Ernie laughed. He loved when people thought he was older than he actually was. He started telling Esme and Lakshmi about his second-grade class and how he was doing a project there on photosynthesis. Also, how most of the other students in his grade were still doing simple stuff, but he was multiplying with double digits. Still, he was scared for the end of this school year, because that was when they started the big standardized tests.

Esme and Lakshmi listened with rapt attention, nodding every now and then. But I felt crushed listening to Ernie go on and on. First of all, because I'd forgotten how much he loved to chat about his day with me or Mami back in Southboro. But what hurt even more was when he used phrases like "the end of this school year"—as if we were just taking a little break, going on an excursion to find our mami. As if everything could one day go back to normal and standardized tests would be the scariest thing to worry about again.

"Eat up! We have twenty more minutes to finish!" said Sister Lottie before ducking back into her office. "Remember, if you want to leave your belongings here for the day, label them carefully, and no food."

As I scarfed down some hot breakfast, Ernie explained to me that Sister Lottie had to lock the doors from nine in the morning until four thirty in the afternoon, while she taught classes and preschool groups in the church.

"What? Why?" I felt a quick flush of alarm fill my body at the thought of going back out on the streets again.

"*Monday, Monday,*" sang Esme in some tune only she could follow. Then she pointed to a clock above the refrigerator that had not only the time, but the date. Apparently in the real world, it was Monday, May 31. Which meant we'd been on the road for something like sixteen days already.

"What?" I said aloud, amazed by how long and how short it all felt.

"What what?" Ernie asked, clearing my plate.

"Nothing. Never mind."

When everyone put their plates away and had their things ready for the day, Sister Lottie led us up to the main church doors. She explained that we had to walk out a few minutes apart so it would look like we were just random parishioners finishing morning prayers. Kelso and Eduardo would leave first. Kelso waved and offered up a bright smile as he headed out the door. Eduardo trailed behind him with his head bowed. Lakshmi left a few minutes later, and then Esme. Sister Lottie was obviously saving us for last.

"Listen," she said when the church was empty except for us. "You don't have to go out if it feels like too much. But I will have to keep you hidden in my office—or, really, the broom closet. Until the afternoon."

"Um . . ." I didn't know what the streets of this neighborhood were like or what it would mean to wander around for hours. At the same time, I didn't know if my little brother could sit still in a closet for that long. Ernie's mind was already made up, though.

"Thanks, but we have to get out there and look for Mami. Right?"

I nodded, feeling Sister Lottie's eyes on me.

"Well, it's a lovely day out, and I packed you some snacks," she said, handing me a brown paper bag. "You know the rules—

don't talk to strangers, and don't talk to anyone you see from the church either, please. I'm sure you'll have a fun day. It's been very quiet around here."

As soon as we heard the metal door lock behind us, Ernie pounced on me with questions:

"Where do we go now? What do we do? Did Sister Lottie tell you where to find Mami?"

"Ernie, we just have to . . ."

I needed to come clean and tell him how both Sister Lottie and I had no idea where to find Mami.

"We just have to what? We just have to what?" Ernie was bouncing on his toes, so eager and earnest.

"We just have to . . . wait until it's safe," I said weakly. I was still too chickenshit to fess up.

"But when will we know?"

"Hold on."

I pulled out Mami's map again, as if it had some important new information for us. It looked like just a series of random lines and dots: the occasional hatch marks, which I guessed meant train lines, and blue blobs, which I supposed were rivers that were now long gone. Everyone, everything, disappearing.

Once again, I wondered why we were here. Not just outside this church or on this street, but in this world. In this new day, heading from one unknown to the next. The sunlight winked through a cluster of clouds like it knew a secret. Looking up, I felt this overwhelming need to cry.

"So?" asked Ernie.

I folded up the map and pasted on a smile. "Listen, it's complicated. I promise you I'm working on it. For now, let's just . . . look around."

I could tell Ernie was getting pissed with all my stalling and excuses, but maybe the possibility of Mami being close put him on his best behavior. He followed me around without protest for a few blocks as I tried to figure out what we could do all day without being too noticeable.

On the next corner, we saw one of the women who'd been at Sister Lottie's last night. She acted like she didn't know us, though. A few blocks later, we saw a playground filled with children swinging from monkey bars and chasing each other with toy guns. We spotted Eduardo in the parking lot of a grocery store called Snack 'N Save. He was pulling empty bottles and cans out of the trash and putting them in a grocery cart.

"What's he doing?" asked Ernie.

"If he finds enough, he can take them to a recycling machine and get some money," I answered. We watched Eduardo for a few minutes. Then we turned down a street that was lined with cafés and smelled like curry. We spent a while counting how many fire escapes there were on each building, then counting how many cracks there were in each block of sidewalk, then counting how many more minutes we had until the church clock said four thirty.

We were both getting impatient and frustrated—hungrier too. After three full meals from the church in his belly, Ernie was ravenous. I gave him most of the apples and bread that Sister Lottie had packed for us for the day, but he was still begging me to stop and buy another snack. I was too scared of there being scanners inside the Snack 'N Save, though, so I tried to distract him by circling back to that playground near St. Augustine's. It was mostly empty now, with just a few toddlers wandering in and out of a plastic playhouse and two Latina women pushing strollers near a bench.

"Go play," I told Ernie. In three seconds, he had bounded up the metal slide and hooked his legs around a monkey bar so he could dangle like a bat. Next, he found a partially deflated basketball and started dribbling it up and down the rubberized blacktop. One of the toddlers started chasing him, giggling uncontrollably.

"¡Cuidado!" called out one of the women behind me. Then she corrected herself: "Be careful!"

The women went back to chatting quietly with each other. Only somehow, their voices kept making their way over to me. My body started pulsing, tingling, as I heard them speaking Spanish, discussing how to get to California.

"Ay, ay, ay. La cosa está muy difícil."

"Pero en California no nos pueden joder. They want us there."

California. Could that be the one place in this upside-down world where I'd be welcome?

I was too scared to get any closer and draw attention, but I needed to hear every word, every detail.

"Lo único que sé . . . es que me tengo que ir. We have to go."

"How?"

"Coyote."

There was a prickly silence while that word reverberated through me: *coyote*.

Coyotes used to be for the people leaving behind their war-torn towns, their flooded homes, or their scorched farms in Central and South America. Hundreds of thousands of us had trusted coyotes with our lives. The coyotes were the bridge connecting the Americas from the south to the America of the north. If they actually did what they promised.

Those of us who'd traveled with coyotes had taken a drastic gamble. Most of us arrived. A lot of us didn't. The horror stories about coyotes swirled through my head now—coyotes stealing people's life savings, coyotes raping women and kidnapping children, coyotes brutally snuffing out so many people and so many dreams. Their hunger feeding on our fear.

"No tengo otra opción."

We didn't have any other options either.

"Renata . . ."

In a way, it was just like today. We were running from a country that wanted to destroy and exterminate us, to some sort of possible refuge. Only now, instead of going north, we were fleeing west for the hope of protection.

"Tú tampoco tienes otra opción. If it's not today, it'll be tomorrow."

"Alma, help! Alma! Alma!" the toddler in the sandbox whined. Alma ran over and swooped him into her arms. It was clear he was crying because he'd gotten sand in his mouth and he didn't like the way it felt. I wondered if that little boy would even remember Alma's face if she was one day just gone.

"Tut tut tut," she clucked as she cradled him. He flailed and kicked, but she just kept peppering him with kisses.

"No! I wanna go hooooome!"

"Okay, we go," Alma told him. I watched her say goodbye to her friend Renata. "Talk later," she said.

"I hope so," replied Renata.

Because who knew if there would be a later.

"Do we have to go too?" Ernie called.

"No. Not yet."

I felt a new urgent certainty. This must have been Mami's plan. And if it wasn't, it was now ours. I would not leave this park before I figured out how to get us to California. Before I could talk myself out of it, I stepped toward Renata.

"Disculpa, ¿Qué hora es?"

"Son las cuatro."

"Pretty day, cierto?"

"Sí . . ." She was getting suspicious. Her round face hardening as she rocked the navy stroller back and forth, pretending to be very interested in anything but me.

I didn't know how to get her to trust me, so I just blurted out, "I need a coyote."

She shot up from the bench.

"I don't know what you're talking about," she said in English. Her voice tight and clipped.

"Por favor," I begged. "They took our mami."

The woman's gaze seared through me. I pointed at Ernie kicking the basketball, and she studied him too. Trying to add it up and see if my story could equal the truth.

"They?" she said.

"The DF. Te lo juro." I held a shaky hand to my heart to prove I really meant it.

"It's dangerous," she warned. "Five thousand dollars each."

"Each?" I felt light-headed. Between the two of us, Ernie and I had maybe six hundred dollars left from Mami's savings. "Will they let us get on a payment plan?" I tried.

"No." The woman looked edgy, like she wanted to end this conversation as soon as possible. It was as if she'd given away too much and was now regretting what she'd told me. She packed up her diaper bag and shushed the baby in the stroller, even though it was sleeping soundly. Then she called the toddler who was still in the plastic playhouse and picked him up in her one free arm. The wheels of her stroller clicked on the rocky path as I tried to thank her.

"Be careful" was the last thing she said as she walked away.

✖

WHEN ERNIE AND I got back to St. Augustine's later that day, Sister Lottie gave us a big toothy smile and asked how our day went as if we were just coming home from school. She even offered us a cool glass of milk and some cookies, which we both wolfed down. I wanted to ask her about the possibility of finding a coyote, but I didn't dare in front of Ernie. He was already looking less ruddy and refreshed than this morning. That night, while we sat around a table with plates of manicotti and thick bread, he was quieter, pensive.

"I just don't get it," he said as we got ready for bed that night. "How long are we staying here? And why is Sister Lottie not doing anything?"

"Well, she's giving us food and a place to stay," I reminded him.

"Right. But when are we gonna find Mami and go to California?"

"Soon," I said. I was running out of lies and time.

✖

THE NEXT MORNING, Ernie asked if soon was now.

"Almost," I said. "But I have a fun idea for today. Wanna hear?"

I told him we were going to go canning just like Eduardo, so we could make some money too.

"Can we use the money to help get Mami back?" Ernie asked.

"Probably," I said. "Let's aim for fifty bucks, okay?"

"Why fifty?" Ernie asked.

"Because this is gonna help. I swear."

Not that fifty dollars was going to pay off a coyote or was even a feasible goal, but at least it was a number. That day, we collected enough cans to make seven dollars and thirty-five cents total. The next day, we made it up to nine dollars and ten cents. Ernie was unimpressed, though. He just kept muttering about everything taking too long and how I was making him do all this work when all he wanted was to go get Mami.

By Thursday afternoon, when we came back to the church, Sister Lottie must have seen how exhausted and defeated we both felt. She asked Ernie if he would help her make cookies in the kitchen and offered her office bathroom to me so I could wash my hair in the sink. Smelling those cookies in the oven and feeling the hot water on my scalp was miraculous. Only, as I tied my wet hair back into a ponytail, I started shivering from the cool air and couldn't stop. Soon, I was trembling and weeping. Everything just felt too painful, too impossible.

I couldn't lie my way past all of Ernie's questions anymore. I needed to tell him the truth. Mami wasn't here. Mami was detained, maybe deported. We couldn't just collect cans and live in a church indefinitely, either. Maybe we'd find a coyote, or maybe we'd just have to set out on our own again at night. Even with overcrowded streets and mounds of garbage to sift through, it felt too nerve-racking being out in broad daylight. I saw more and more cameras mounted on street poles and more storefront awnings coming down.

"You ready?" I asked Ernie on our fourth day of collecting cans. "I think today's the day we get to at least twenty dollars."

"Woo hoo," Ernie said dully.

As we went to pick up an empty grocery cart from the Snack 'N Save for canning, I saw two gray sedans parked next to each other by the entrance to the store, **DEPORTATION FORCE** emblazoned across the side of the cars. As soon as I heard the first screams coming from the store, I grabbed Ernie and turned around. Down the block, two more DF officers were running toward us. I panicked. I shoved Ernie around the corner and we tore off. The all-too-familiar terror burned through me, clawing at my lungs so I could barely breathe. We ran back to the church and pounded on the metal door by the statue of la Virgen.

"I'm so sorry, Sister Lottie," I whispered into the door frame. "But they're here! They're gonna get us!"

Sister Lottie didn't say a word. She just opened the metal door and took us directly to her office. She put us in her broom closet and made us swear to complete silence before locking us in. We heard the stampede of little feet as the preschoolers came in upstairs and started singing their songs about the alphabet. Then there was someone leading a service and promising redemption. And then—

There was pounding on the metal door at the back of the church.

"Open up! Open up right now! We have been authorized by the government to search the premises!"

"You can search all you want outside," Sister Lottie shouted back. "But this is a holy house of worship, and I am not required to open this door!"

More pounding. They sounded like they were kicking too. Or maybe using the butts of their guns against the thick metal.

"Article five in the Thirty-First Amendment clearly states—"

"Alien Registration Act of 2032!" one of the officers shouted back.

"The DF may arrest suspects without a warrant. They may also enter private property without a warrant!" added another. They'd memorized every Presidential proclamation.

Ernie had his head buried into my shoulder; his nails were digging into me so hard I thought they'd draw blood. But Sister Lottie was unmoving. She started quoting verses from the Bible about all of God's creatures being holy while the officers beat the door over and over again. Then, after three harrowing minutes that felt more like three hundred, the DF left. Vowing to come back and "clean up this shithole."

Everything was pulsing, throbbing, as Sister Lottie opened our broom closet door, and we both tumbled out.

"I'm sorry, I'm sorry. It's all my fault. I ran when I saw

them. My chip's working. I just wasn't thinking. And now they know . . ."

"Shhh . . . shhh," she soothed. Ernie and I both clutched her. Panting and sobbing. "It's going to be okay," she said with a heavy frown.

"Those are the people who took Mami!" Ernie wailed. "We have to go after them and get Mami back."

"No," I said in a low voice. "We need to leave."

"What?" he squeaked.

I didn't know how to say any of this, but I had wrestled with these words in so many different ways since we arrived at St. Augustine's, and now I had no choice but to just let them out.

"We can't stay here now. They're gonna take us—or at least me—too."

Ernie's eyes were anxious and glassy.

"What about Mami?"

"She's not here, Ernie. I . . . I . . . I . . . don't know where she is. Neither does Sister Lottie."

He gaped at both of us, trying to figure out what was going on.

"But . . . but . . ." he said.

"I didn't mean to lie to you. I didn't mean to hurt you. We just needed to get here, and telling you Mami was here was the only way . . ."

I tried to pull him in for a hug, but he just kept looking at me, caught under this glaze of hurt and confusion. Then he started screaming in my face, tearing at my shirt. His face a ragged mess as he told me what a horrible, lying traitor I was.

I didn't stop him. Sister Lottie was the one who pulled him off of me. Taking him in her arms and just letting him dissolve. I was so grateful she was here to witness my confession, even if she couldn't absolve me.

"I didn't mean to," I told them both again. "I didn't know what to do."

Sister Lottie rocked my little brother as he cried into her chest. I wanted to touch him, to hug him, but I knew he didn't want anything to do with me. Sister Lottie was able to give him the peace I could not.

I couldn't look at Ernie as I told him what my plan was.

"A lady told me about a coyote who could get us to California. Our Tía Luna lives there," I explained.

Sister Lottie's eyes were glittering now too.

"Ay, the coyotes," she whispered. "Yes, this was your mother's plan too."

"It was?" I practically jumped to the ceiling. "Did you hear that, Ernie? This is what Mami was going to do too!" I felt this new hint of hope growing inside me. Even if it was buried under layers of guilt and terror, it was there. It was Mami leading us to safety.

"Can you help us do that?" I asked Sister Lottie. "Please?"

"Yes." She was measuring her words carefully. "But you must know, many people are trying to get to California now. The coyotes can do . . . whatever they want to do. And now I hear that when you get closer to California, the DF get more and more . . ."

She didn't even attempt to fill in the blanks there.

"I don't know what else to do, though," I whimpered. "A woman told me it costs five thousand dollars for each of us."

"Yes. I will find the money. If this is really what you want to do, I will find someone to take you there. But only if you're sure . . ."

Sister Lottie's words hung heavy in the air.

California meant possibility. California meant freedom. California meant Tía Luna and walking outside without fear. But California also meant leaving Mami. It meant giving her up to the Deportation Force. It meant never seeing her again.

Ernie looked at me through his tears, waiting for my answer. I couldn't speak. The words were thrashing around inside me, trapped. Slowly, shamefully, I nodded yes.

Yes, because I believed Mami would want it this way.

Yes, because Ernie needed a big sister, and a future.

Yes, because staying here any longer was impossible.

A low, crying howl came out of Ernie. His pain hit me harder and deeper than anything I had felt in my life. And yet I kept nodding.

We were all just doing the best we could. Trying to survive.

CHAPTER 14

I did not say thank you. I did not say goodbye either.

A few hours later, when Sister Lottie woke me and Ernie at three in the morning and walked us ten blocks to a parked truck with its headlights off, I did not say anything at all. At the time, I felt too numb—it had cost Sister Lottie ten thousand dollars to get us a spot on this coyote's truck. There was no way I'd ever be able to repay her or thank her enough.

So I hugged her and turned away. And I will always regret that.

The coyote looked like just an average guy. After building him up in my head, I didn't know what to expect, but he could have easily passed as an older brother or uncle. He was a little taller than me with wavy black hair. I was careful not to make eye contact or say anything, though. He took the payment from Sister Lottie. Then he unlocked the back of the truck and lifted up the corrugated metal door with a crash.

"What you waiting for?" he said in my ear. Then he watched me and Ernie scramble in and slammed down the door behind us.

As soon as he did, I fell into the dim, humid cargo space, colliding with something warm and fleshy.

"Oof," I heard in the dark.

"Sorry," I whispered. I tried to turn around but rammed into another passenger.

"Ay!"

"Sorry," I said again.

I had no idea how many people were already in here. The stench was beyond putrid. It was a mixture of gasoline and sweaty armpits and something that was tangy and sharp. I tried to breathe through my mouth instead of my nose, but that just made me queasier. It felt like the smells were climbing up my nostrils, clinging inside my eyelids.

"Vali, what is that?" I heard Ernie whisper. There was just a sliver of light leaking under the back door, so I didn't know what he was talking about.

"Carne," came a voice next to me.

"What?" stammered Ernie. My stomach lurched, and I gagged a little. Now my eyes were adjusting to this nightmare whether I wanted them to or not. In the space of just a few cubic feet, there were over a dozen bodies pressed together. More if I counted the cow carcasses hanging from the ceiling. Which I refused to do. I didn't know which was scarier—the butchered animals swinging side to side or the hungry faces in between.

We were all just pieces of meat, really. Some of us with loss and shame weighing us down. The rest dismembered and frozen. All of us, beasts of prey.

I found a spot for Ernie and myself against a wall that was slippery and hot. There were two skinned calves dangling in front of us, swaying on their hooks.

"You okay?" I murmured, squeezing his hand tight.

"I want Mami."

I did too. Now more than ever, as I felt the driver shift gears and peel out onto the road.

I was afraid of making eye contact with anyone around us, though I knew they wouldn't be in here unless they were terrified and grasping for help too. It was silent for a long time; just the occasional sigh or passed whisper. We must have been on the road for hours before someone started talking. Then slowly, people made quiet introductions and started asking me and Ernie questions:

"Where did you get on? Did you see any DF nearby?" That was from Lydia and Kyrie, two girls around my age sitting on a milk crate together.

"How bad is it out there? You think we did the right thing?" That was from a man named Roman, who was holding on to a frail woman. I guessed she was his mom.

The only answer I could give him was "Bad. Yes."

Two other passengers sort of nodded but didn't want to give their names. One was rocking forward and back in a corner, with a shawl draped over him, chanting what sounded like a prayer. The other was a large, muscular man who kept standing, then sitting, cracking his knuckles and clearing his throat as if he was about to make an important announcement. But in the end, saying nothing.

"Hi! I'm Tomas! I'm four years old. What's your name?" said a little boy. I mumbled my name and nudged Ernie to do the same. "Do you like sports? I like sports," Tomas prattled on. "My favorite foods are spaghetti and ice cream, and I've already been to five different states. Where are you from?"

Ernie and I didn't say a word.

"Where do you come from?" Tomas repeated. "I'm from the United States of America, which is really good, right, Mami?" he went on. His mother was just next to him on the floor, breastfeeding an infant under her sweatshirt. "*Right, Mami?*"

Tomas's voice was getting louder and louder as he rattled on. Or maybe it wasn't that he was louder; it was that the truck had stopped moving.

"Shhhhh," demanded the large man cracking his knuckles.

I had no idea why we'd stopped, where we were, or how to get this boy to be quieter.

"What's going on?" asked Kyrie.

"Are we supposed to be stopped?" added Lydia.

"Shut up!" the large man ordered.

There was a lot of whispering in multiple languages. Some Spanish, some Creole. Lots of languages I couldn't name, but the current of fear was palpable. We heard the driver's door open and shut, and footsteps retreating. Followed by an unnerving quiet. Everyone held their breath.

"It's okay," came a raspy voice from behind one of the carcasses. "I don't hear anybody else out there. I think he just stopped to pee."

"Ooh, ooh, Mami!" Tomas said, now hopping up and down. "Tengo que hacer pee pee," he pleaded.

The rest of the truck tried to ignore him, while his mom drew him closer. But Tomas wasn't having any of it.

"¡Tengo que hacer pee pee!" he repeated, raising his volume again. The man with the knuckles was steaming now, blowing air out of his nostrils like a dragon.

"Shut him up!" he rumbled. "When we're stopped, there is *no talking*. You get it?"

"But I have to make—"

"Sssssshut up!"

I heard Tomas's mom whispering rapidly in Spanish. She offered Tomas a diaper, but he insisted he was "un niño grande" now. So she explained that even niños grandes wore diapers if there was an emergency, and otherwise, he'd have to hold it in, but most importantly, he had to be quieter before he got us in trouble.

"What kind of trouble?" Tomas squealed. "I did pee pee in my pants! It's wet all over!"

"Please," whispered the praying man.

"¡Silencio!" muttered someone else.

"Shut him up, or I will shut him up for you," said the big

man. His voice rumbled as if he was a human volcano. "I will *not* let you fuck this up, kid."

Even though he whispered, his words felt like daggers stabbing at this dank, disgusting air. A dozen pairs of eyes glittered with fright, watching Tomas wriggling and his mom begging him to please sit down and hush.

"Por favor," she whispered. "Tomas. No puedes hablar." Her voice was so thin and desperate.

"Pssst! Tomas!" I tried. "What if we play super ninjas?" Super ninjas was the trick Mami used to try to get Ernie quiet on nights when he was too wound up to sleep.

"Super ninjas?" Tomas's eyes were wide and glimmering. He crept toward me to hear more.

"Super ninjas means you have to be completely silent," I told Tomas now. He stood in front of me, squinting. Sizing me up.

"Or even better, we could play super ninja *soccer*." I unzipped Ernie's backpack and reached in for his lime green soccer ball. When Ernie had first gotten it, the green checkers glowed in the dark. I prayed they had enough glow left to enchant this boy too.

"What do you think?" I whispered.

Tomas nodded with a big, sneaky grin. He took the ball from me and gazed at those green checkers, getting lost in them, at least for this moment. Then he sat down a few feet away from me and rolled the ball across the floor of the truck. When I took it in my hands again, it was already slick with some disgusting goo—probably sweat, urine, and cow's blood. But I couldn't let that stop me. As I rolled the ball back to Tomas, I saw his mom inhale deeply and wipe her eyes with the sleeve of her oversized sweatshirt. Volcanoman gave me a dirty look and then said nothing more. I felt a flush of relief as our super ninja soccer game continued, and Ernie joined in too.

As soon as our driver came back and the truck started moving again, Tomas kicked the ball over to me and said, "Wait. Do super ninjas really play soccer?"

His mom and I both laughed a little at that.

"No. They play fútbol," said Ernie. "¿Te gusta?"

"Sí. Soy muy bueno," Tomas said proudly.

From then on, the two of them were tireless, passing the ball back and forth across those four square feet of space on the floor. I took a break from the game to collect myself and breathe. I was so grateful for both of those boys and their innocence. I just hoped one day Ernie could play soccer on a real field again and that some way, somehow, Mami could be there to cheer him on.

We were in that truck for hours. Days, even. At least, that's what it felt like. There was no way to officially mark time besides staring at that slim edge of light under the back doors of the truck. Lydia tried to turn on her phone, but as she did, everyone jumped in with some version of

No! Too dangerous.

They track through GPS.

¡Guardarlo!

She apologized and turned it off immediately, tucking it away.

After a while, snippets of hushed conversations started bubbling up here and there.

"No, you know what I miss? Loroco."

"Yeah, yeah. Even more, pepesca."

There were a bunch of different discussions about food. Even though we were in the most wretched-smelling place in the world, I could almost taste some of the meals people were describing.

"When I get outta here, I'm gonna have five bowls of cereal, a bowl of plátanos, a bowl of ajiaco, ten gallons of ice water, and strawberry ice cream for dessert," Ernie chimed in.

Tomas clapped gleefully.

"I'm gonna have *a hundred* bowls of ice cream. Then mangos. Then more ice cream, then . . . Mami, I'm so hungry!"

People passed around bits of bread or fruit that they'd brought along. Sister Lottie had given me and Ernie a grocery bag full of snacks for our journey. I offered up some of our apples and crackers to the group. I kept the granola bars and water bottles for me and Ernie, though.

At some point, I heard a loud snoring coming from behind me. Volcanoman had dozed off, I guess. Which probably made everyone feel a little more at ease. Then I must have fallen asleep too. Falling into dreams about soccer and cows and Mami trapped behind a window, just out of reach. I was explaining to her that we would meet up by a palm tree and have crackers when—

The truck's brakes screeched, and we lurched to a stop.

This time the cab door opened and slammed shut right away. There were deep male voices. Muffled at first, by the driver's side of the cab. Then, getting louder and louder, making their way around to the back of the truck.

"Shhhh!" spat Volcanoman, even though none of us inside were talking. Ernie turned his head toward me, his eyes begging me to tell him this was nothing again—just a stop sign, or a preplanned pit stop. I wanted so badly to nod my head and smile. But all I could do was clench his hand, hard.

I heard our driver going on and on about meat.

"Yeah, flanks, ground, chopped. They want everything there yesterday, ya know? Pain in my ass."

The other voice that spoke was lower. Garbled and indistinct. It was demanding to see something.

"No, I get it," our driver answered. "It's a lot to *track*."

There was something horrifying about the way he uttered that word. It sent a shock of electricity up my spine; it gathered in my chest and swirled like a tornado. Without a sound, all of us in the truck started scooting away from the corrugated metal of the back door. We were crouching behind the thawing carcasses, even hugging the thick flanks.

They won't get Ernie. His chip is real, I kept repeating in my head. I had to hold on to that thought and use it as a life vest.

I wrapped my arms around Ernie's middle too and forced him to face the cab of the truck, so if anything happened out there, my body could be his shield.

The back door of the truck screeched open. Metal grating against metal. I felt a rush of cool air hit my ankles. The creep of daylight tumbling in because somehow the world was still turning. Somehow there was sunrise and sunset and—

Prrrow!

The sound of a gunshot pierced through the world. It cracked open the truck, the door, the sky.

Prrrow! Prrrow!

Tomas was howling. The baby was wailing. I could feel a scream about to erupt from me, but there wasn't enough air between the crackle of fire and the rest of the world. I pulled Ernie into my chest so hard I could feel his pulse inside my ribs.

"I love you," I moaned into Ernie's sweaty neck. "I love you! I love you! I love you!"

Ernie would survive. He would find Mami. Tell her that I tried. That I was a good sister after all.

"I love you too!" Ernie cried.

A split second turned into an eternity as I tried to figure out who or what had been shot.

Ernie was still here. I was still here. Looking around now, I saw that the truck was filled with a burnt-smelling haze. It was blood and flesh, and terror. The sunlight pouring in stung my eyes. I blinked and coughed. All around me, people were inching toward the open door now. Toward the edge of the truck's bed.

And there,

on the ground below,

was a DF officer.

He was dressed in a gray button-down shirt and matching pants, both with the proud yellow letters announcing his authority. He had thick jowls, a clean shave, tightly cropped hair that was the color of sand.

And a tide of blood leaking out of his neck. Just next to his collar.

CHAPTER 15

I had never seen someone killed before. Never choked back the acrid smoke or felt the tremor of a bullet firing, pulling everything around and inside me into a vacuum. The before and after of that moment was so clear and irreversible. And now there was a dead man in front of us on a clear, open-skied morning. We were witnesses to a murder. A murder on the side of a one-lane highway, surrounded by stumps of trees and yellowing, deadened fields. Where nobody—or possibly everybody—could see us.

I couldn't decide which was more terrifying—the corpse lying at our feet, oozing into the hot asphalt, or our driver standing over him with a gun still in his hand. Surveying his kill.

Our driver's name was Jorge. At least that's what he told us. He also explained that this was not part of his job description. He'd been paid to transport us from New York City to "some shithole town" in Oklahoma. Then, apparently, a guy named BJ was going to take us west.

"But I saved you, see?" Jorge said, pointing a meaty finger at us.

"Thank you," said someone in our stunned crowd.

"Yeah, thanks," a few more of us whispered.

"Mami, Mami, is he gonna shoot us too?" cried Tomas. His mother held him into her side as she bounced her screaming baby.

"Fucking shit," said Jorge. "This really fucks up my plan." He nudged the dead man with his foot. "I can't . . . They're gonna come looking for him . . . so . . ." He paused to glance at us all before declaring, "I guess this means *adiós, amigos!*"

"Wait! Where you going?" asked Volcanoman. "We already paid you."

Now that I was seeing this man in the daylight, he didn't look so much like a volcano anymore. He was large, yes, and hulking. He had dark skin, a square jaw, and a shaved head. But his broad shoulders sagged forward and his lips trembled as he spoke. Like the rest of us, he seemed frightened and exhausted.

"Sorry, no can do. I gotta go," said Jorge. He stepped over the dead body and peered into the cargo hold of the truck. "Everybody, grab your stuff!"

¿Por qué?

What?

"No, no, no, no, no," Volcanoman said. "I gave you my life savings. I need to get to California. We *all* do."

Jorge either didn't hear, didn't care, or both. He was looking at his phone now, pressing buttons.

"It's for your own good," he said. "They gotta have his coordinates, and when they come sniffing around for him, you don't wanna be stuck with me, right?"

"But can't you at least drive us somewhere . . . else?" I mustered.

Jorge gave me a sneering smile. "You're cute, hon. Listen, next stop was gonna be . . ." He checked his phone again for the specifics. "I dunno. Some place called Scutter, Oklahoma? Looks like it's about sixty miles southwest of here."

"Sixty?" Lydia cried.

"Yep," Jorge answered. "When you get there, ask for BJ."

"Get where? We need an address," said someone else.

"Good point, good point." He went back to his phone to verify. "Yeah. Looks like BJ is on Thistlebrook Street. Number seventeen. Good luck."

We all just stood there watching as he tapped away on his phone. When we didn't move, he added, "C'mon! Get your stuff outta the truck, or I'm gonna take it with me."

We had no choice. Or if we did, I couldn't figure out what it was. None of us could.

"What if we just left the body here and kept going?" Volcanoman suggested.

"Nuh-uh," Jorge said. He started pulling our things out and throwing them onto the road.

"Why not?" asked Roman.

"Because I'm *done!*" roared Jorge, lifting his gun in the air. We all knew what that gun was capable of and started scrambling to retrieve our things. Tomas was shrieking now as he clung to Ernie's soccer ball.

"It's okay, buddy," offered another guy from our group. I hadn't noticed him before. He looked to be maybe seventeen or eighteen. Tall, thin, with a mess of jet-black hair and a sprinkling of stubble on his chin. He also had the saddest-looking brown eyes. "We're gonna make it. Together."

Tomas buried his head in his mom's sweatshirt again, unconvinced.

"Yeah. Let's go," I agreed. Not because I had any sort of plan, but because Jorge was circling all of us with his gun raised, and that boy's eyes were unnerving me, and we needed some way out of this desolate place—*now*.

"But where? How . . . ?" Volcanoman stammered.

Jorge started emptying out the cargo hold now. He picked up whatever bags and belongings he found and tossed them onto the ground.

"C'mon!" Jorge barked. "I saved your fuckin' asses. Now go!"

I made sure that Ernie and I had both our backpacks plus Mami's. Then I climbed back into the truck and got Tomas and his family their stuff. Jorge barely waited for the last bag to come out of the hold before jumping in and pulling the door down, locking it from the inside. Then he must've opened up the panel between the back and the front cab, because the next thing we heard was him revving the engine from the driver's seat. We all went around to the side of the truck.

"C'mon, man. What the hell?" Volcanoman bellowed.

The truck's gears made a high-pitched whine as the engine got louder. Then, maybe as a peace offering, Jorge rolled down his window and shouted, "Fastest way down to Scutter is Route Forty-Four, but be careful of flooding!"

As he careened back onto the road, we all ran after him. The spinning tires kicked up clods of gravel and dirt, flinging them in our faces. Volcanoman was cursing and flapping his burly arms as if he was trying to fly. But it wasn't going to work. We were all grounded, stranded on the side of the road with sixty miles ahead of us and no clue where or how to begin.

People started fanning out in different directions. A few went back and huddled around the dead DF officer. A few more around the officer's gray sedan. Tomas came up to Ernie with his red-rimmed eyes and asked if we were still going to go to "Cally-forna."

Ernie shrugged and looked at me.

"Are we?"

"Yes," I answered. "I just need to . . ."

I shook my head, trying to clear some space. But there was none. I was staring down the bleakest road I'd ever seen. On either side of it were huge swaths of bare dirt and ditches. There were upended trees with roots splaying out, their trunks split open in jagged seams. Everything swarmed with biting flies. I led Ernie over to a felled branch in the brush and sat us both down.

"Fuckin' hell!" Volcanoman stormed. He was pacing up and down the length of the dead man, vowing to hunt Jorge down and kill him with his bare hands. That was not going to get us out of here, though. "Shit. My phone's dead," he said.

"If everybody's okay with it, I can check where we are," I said, pulling out my cell. At least I could offer the group something.

There were a few nods. "Just be quick," Roman warned.

According to my GPS, we were now somewhere in southern Missouri. I plugged in *17 Thistlebrook Street, Scutter, Oklahoma*, and got a twisty route with *61 miles* written on the bottom.

"Let's take the DF car and go," said Lydia.

"Are you *crazy?*" boomed Volcanoman. "That's the first thing they're gonna look for!"

I had to agree. Taking the DF car sounded like a horrible idea to me. But both Lydia and Kyrie were already climbing into the front seats, fiddling with the voice-activated ignition. A few other people from the truck climbed into the back seat with their things too.

"Didn't you say you were a hacker or something?" one of the girls said to Roman. He nodded and shrugged, heading over to the car.

"I can probably get access to the source code responsible for the engine. But then you still need his fingerprint to unlock the steering wheel," he reported. At least, that was what I thought he said. He spoke very quickly, rattling off computer gibberish. The part I did understand him saying was "I really don't think this is a good idea."

The two girls ignored his warnings. They started debating who should drag the dead man over to the car for his fingerprint. Someone in the back seat said they should just chop off the dead man's finger and bring it along.

"Um, NO," I said. So loud and firm that I stunned even myself. All eyes were on me now as I stood up. "I mean, I want to get to California, but this doesn't seem like the way to do it."

"Exactly," said the guy with the sad eyes.

"He's DF," I continued. "People are gonna be looking for him and his car really soon. We have to leave it here and get to Route Forty-Four."

"Yes! Thank you," said Volcanoman, which felt slightly reassuring, though he still intimidated me. Particularly when he followed that up with "So, how do we do that? What's the plan?"

I didn't have a plan. All I had was a map, a phone that could've very well been beaming my coordinates out to the DF, and a mission that seemed more and more untenable each second—to keep my brother safe and to get to California. I opened up Mami's map again just to feel like I had some authority or insight. I checked my phone one more time to look at that curvy route to Thistlebrook Street, then powered it off.

"Scutter is around here." I pointed it out on my map to anyone who wanted to look. "So, we need to walk southwest."

When I said the word *walk*, Ernie shot me a pained, pleading look. But I had to ignore it. There was no other way, as far as I could tell. Roman and his mother were sitting on a rock, sipping water. The man in the prayer shawl had started wandering into the woods. The people in the car were still arguing about how to chop off the DF officer's finger, and his body was just baking in the sun on the road a few feet away from us. I couldn't wait any more for someone else to make a decision.

"Let's go," I ordered.

"Sounds good," said Volcanoman.

"I have a compass, if that helps," said the guy with sad eyes. "I'm Malakas."

"Mami, Mami, ¿podemos ir con ellos, por favor?" Tomas begged. His mom was leaning against a tree, breastfeeding again. She was tinier than me, with a dark bun pulling her brown skin tight and a sweatshirt that read PENN STATE NITTANY LIONS. It was big enough to fit her and her entire family. I wondered how old this woman was. How she'd come here with two children on her own and where she hoped to find safety.

"No sé," she mumbled.

"Perdón," I said, squatting down next to her. "Mi nombre es Valentina. Soy de Colombia. ¿Y tú?"

"De Guatemala," she said. "Mi nombre es Rosa."

I explained to her in Spanish that we were going to walk to where we were supposed to get dropped off. From there we'd get another ride to California. We had to leave now and use back roads because the DF would be coming to look for the dead officer any minute. Rosa nodded, expressionless. Without another word, she picked up her bags and reached for Tomas's hand, while the baby continued to suck. Malakas offered to take one of her bags, but she refused. I could feel her sunken sadness rolling off in waves.

Volcanoman strapped on his backpack and yelled, "Good luck!" to the crew fumbling around the DF car.

"Yeah, be safe," I said over my shoulder. I held on to Ernie even tighter, so he wouldn't look back.

And so Rosa and her kids, Volcanoman, Malakas, Ernie, and I headed out. The sun was still lifting from the east, and I could feel it blazing on the back of my neck. The winds were much stronger here too, churning up lots of twigs and leaves, lashing us in our faces.

"Isn't Missouri known for its tornadoes?" asked Volcanoman.

"Is it?" replied Malakas.

"Missouri is my new state!" declared Tomas, and I could see that even Volcanoman grinned at that.

Ernie and Tomas started running a few feet in front, picking out walking sticks and "magic rocks" for all of us. Then they wanted to play follow the leader. And then they were both too exhausted to move another inch, but I made them continue anyway.

It was ridiculously slow going. I knew it didn't help any that I made us travel near the woods and in the shadows for safety.

We also had very few food supplies, and I could feel the clouds rolling in, bringing with them a humid, heavy mist.

But we were moving. Forward, I hoped. It was all treacherous. All unknown.

Only, for the first time, I was choosing the path, knowing that I knew nothing about what lay ahead.

And in this fucked-up world, that somehow gave me strength.

CHAPTER 16

The sun was gone, and the winds were throwing a sharp, needly rain at us now. We hadn't traveled far from where Jorge left us, but already the skies were churning with thick, ominous clouds in every direction.

"Did you hear?" muttered Volcanoman bitterly. "The President says climate change is our fault too."

The farther south we went, the grimmer it got out there. All of southern Missouri was completely trashed. It looked like a series of tornadoes had ripped through recently. Or else one continuous funnel, spinning from town to town, sucking up clothes, toys, furniture, and livestock. Hurling them as far and as fast as it could. Everywhere we went, there was an obstacle course of swampy ravines, gnarled electrical wires, and what looked and smelled like an overturned septic tank to wade through. We walked by entire mobile homes tipped off their blocks and lying on the ground, doors yawning open. There were flattened cars and strollers; a street sign stuck in the roof of a cabin like a spear. A trail of shattered glass leading from one door to another. Like some glittering runway carpet, to the greatest spectacle on earth.

I remembered Mami telling me that nature was a fierce miracle, that we had to respect and tend to it, trusting in the calm after every storm. I wanted to have that kind of faith as we trudged through this apocalyptic landscape, but I was definitely struggling. We all were. It was the beginning of June, but the rain had me chilled. Then it stopped suddenly, and I got so hot I felt like I was suffocating.

At one point in the afternoon, Ernie and Tomas spotted a red tricycle stuck in a mangled camping tent. They tore at the tent cloth, trying to pry the tricycle free. When they did, Ernie had Tomas sit on the handlebars and gave him a little ride.

"¡No, mi'jo!" Rosa said.

"¿Por qué no?" Tomas cried with a crushed look on his face.

I didn't know why she was stopping the boys from riding, actually. It sounded like a brilliant idea to me. If only there were enough wheels for all of us. I started scouring through the piles of furniture and lifting up pieces of aluminum siding.

"It's all right," Volcanoman said. "I'll run alongside them for a little while. Make sure they're okay." I was warming to Volcanoman. He never did apologize to Tomas for getting so mad in the truck, but I could definitely understand how his anger was just fear in disguise. Since we'd been on foot, he'd been all about helping out. Malakas was really sweet to the boys too, telling them that they were warriors and that these magic rocks were keeping us all safe. I got teary when he said that—wishing so much it could be true.

We wound up taking turns on that tricycle. We biked, ran, or walked for the entire day, only pausing when the baby was hungry or one of us got stuck in a bog or ditch. As the day started dissolving, we staked out a place for us to sleep. It wasn't so much a shelter as it was a flimsy crawl space between the splintering bottom frame of another upturned RV and the cinder blocks that once held it off the ground. The RV was pitched at a precarious angle too—the roof crushed and now resting on a tree trunk. The two right wheels stuck up like the legs on some roadkill, and through the opening another cold drizzle fell on us.

"You okay?" I asked Ernie. He nodded, though I could tell he was far from it. He was bone-tired and ravenous. I dug through our backpacks and offered up the rest of our food from Sister Lottie to the group. Volcanoman had some stale bread to split, Malakas some apples, and Tomas stuck his hand out with a cracked cherry lollipop that had been in his pocket since they left their home.

Rosa looked so weak and depleted from traveling and feeding her baby that I told Tomas to give that lollipop to his mami. She kept saying, *No, No, No,* but as soon as he held the pink orb of candy up to her thin lips, I could actually see her body tremble with relief.

By the time the rain stopped completely, night had

descended. All that was left up above was a canopy of creaking tree limbs and a handful of stars peeking through. The whole group gave a collective sigh—wringing out wet shirts and hair, finding a spot of dry cloth on our backpacks to lay our heads if that was even possible. I pulled Ernie toward me and made a pillow out of his soccer ball. Rubbing the back of his neck and hopefully easing him into some layer of unconscious. Soon enough, I heard the hum of multiple snores.

I also saw an icy blue light coming from something just under my right arm.

Or rather, my right *wrist*.

I gasped.

"You too, huh?" said a soft voice in the dark. It was Malakas.

"What? No!" I snapped, tucking my wrist into my body as if I could erase or hide it.

"It's okay," he said with a vague kind of calm. "I mean, it's not okay, but . . . if it helps, mine just started glowing too."

He flipped over his right hand to reveal the inside of his wrist for me. That ice-blue light was glowing from under his skin too. It was no bigger than a grain of rice. The exact size of a microchip.

I looked down at the inside of my own wrist again just to be sure. There it was—the same speck of eerie light in between my veins. Marking me.

"Do you think this is . . . the *system upgrade*?" I asked, my voice shaky.

"Yeah, must be," said Malakas. "Who knows how long

we have before they find us now. I bet they have all our info lit up on some gigantic screen, mapped out like a giant constellation."

There was so much more I wanted to say, or scream. I didn't know where or how to start, though. Everything in me was stinging from holding back so much rage and fear. I felt like a giant exposed nerve.

I checked Ernie's right wrist, but it wasn't lit up. Neither was Tomas's, as far as I could see. I was not about to snoop around Volcanoman's body even if he was sleeping. I did see the glow of Rosa's wrist, though, reflecting off her baby's cheek as she held her tight.

"Should I wake her up and tell her? I wonder how long until it stops glowing like that?" I whispered to Malakas.

"Nah, don't wake her up. What's the point?" he offered.

I shook my arm as hard as I could, trying to snuff out that glowing spot. When that didn't work, I pulled my arm under my soggy shirt. Cradling my right wrist as if it was broken.

It was. *I* was broken.

"Hey, I'm sorry," he said quietly. "I didn't mean to make it worse for you."

"You didn't."

"Where'd you get yours, anyway?" he asked.

I paused, instinctively scared of saying too much. But what could this guy do to me, really? He was just as doomed as I was.

"California," I told him.

"Ah, our only hope."

"Maybe," I said. "Have you talked to anyone there?"

"I . . . don't know anyone there."

"Oh . . ." I felt sorry for him. His voice sounded so hollow.

"I just don't know where else to go at this point," he said.

"Where are you from?"

"The Philippines, but I don't know if anyone's left there either."

"What do you mean?" I asked, already scared to hear his answer.

He told me he was born in a place called northern Luzon, where there was incredible poverty and so many typhoons that he and his mom lived in a roofless shack for the first five years of his life. When Malakas turned six, Luzon was hit with a deadly string of cyclones and storms that buried his elementary school in a mudslide. The waters became contaminated, and his mother got so sick she couldn't even swallow rice. She begged a childhood friend to help get Malakas to America. One steamy October morning, Malakas's mother put him on an airplane with a single suitcase, a fake visa, and a promise.

"She told me to look at the moon, you know? And she would look at it too, and then we would be, kind of, together." He chuckled. "It's stupid, I know."

"No, it's not." I could barely get the words out of my mouth.

"It's just . . ." He sighed. "Anyway, I got to New York—that's where my lola, my grandma, lives." He corrected himself. "Lived."

187

He lived with his lola in Brooklyn for the next ten years. Malakas told me about how kind and smart his lola was, how she worked three jobs and cared for Malakas. He went to school. He played basketball and won a science fair with his report on space exploration. He was grateful that he got to talk to his mom all the time on phone.

"Until . . . yeah, she died."

I could already feel the urge to cry swelling in my chest as he told me about getting his counterfeit chip in the back of a nail salon and, that very same night, hearing that his town in Luzon had been washed away, obliterated. His mom, his home, everything he knew of home, gone. He kept on going to school, because that's what his mom would have wanted him to do. His lola knew he loved astronomy, so she fought for him to go to some fancy high school for "supernova nerds." He studied so hard, wanting to make her proud.

"But in the end, it doesn't matter how smart you are, does it?" he said. "It doesn't matter how kind or generous or pretty or rich you are . . ."

And then, a couple of weeks ago, Malakas came back from basketball practice one day, and his home was completely trashed. The windows shattered. His lola was gone. He packed the only belongings he had left—his favorite book about the stars, his binoculars. And he started running.

I heard Malakas catch his breath, fighting back his tears. He exhaled sharply and pressed his hands over his eyes. It looked like he was trying to reset his heart—or at least his brain.

"Wouldn't it be great if this was just another star?" he said, sticking his glowing wrist up above us. "There are so many of them out there in the universe that we'll never see, because they're invisible to the naked eye."

Malakas said maybe that was why he loved the stars so much—because they were always there, watching over him.

I didn't know where I'd heard that fact about hidden stars before, but it felt familiar, almost comforting.

"If only we were invisible too," I murmured.

"Yeah," Malakas replied. "If only."

CHAPTER 17

As soon as Ernie started stirring the next morning, I showed him my glowing chip and told him what I thought it meant.

Ernie nodded.

"But yours is fine," I assured him.

"Okay," he said. His eyes were dull and circled in a bruised-looking exhaustion.

"That's a good thing."

"If you say so."

"It is. It is!" I was practically shouting at him now. Ernie scrunched his face up into a tight scowl. I went to give him a hug, and he just sort of sat there, like a rag doll, in my arms. He was getting smaller and smaller as the days went on, gloomier too. I wondered if he was scared of losing me, or if he still resented me for leaving Mami at that bus station and, really, every moment since then. I wondered if he'd ever be silly or free enough to put toothpaste in his hair again.

"So what do we do now?" Ernie asked, staring at my glowing wrist.

"We . . . keep going," I said, tucking my arm into my side, as if that could protect or conceal us in any way. "We're gonna get to the safe house and then California."

"Okay," he answered in a monotone.

✖

CALL IT FAITH. Call it fate. Call it delirium or dizzy stubbornness. It took us another four and a half days of trekking through more ransacked towns and destroyed farms, but we did arrive on Thistlebrook Street in Scutter, Oklahoma.

It had no right being called a street, actually. It was more like a few feet of asphalt that sloped down into some trampled cattails and a barbed wire fence that had been strung between two metal poles. On the other side of the fence were a gully of dirt, rocks, and a once-blue-but-now-burned-out sedan. As we got closer, I saw there was also a low-slung ranch house. It was mostly obscured behind a sagging elm tree. Its yellow siding was spattered with mud, and there were pieces of warped plywood covering what I guessed were once windows.

Above the front door there was a single, bare lightbulb illuminating the number seventeen.

Seventeen Thistlebrook Street wasn't a traditional haunted house like in those old movies with the skeletons peeking out of attics and bats flying around. There was no caution tape or ghosts flitting between the shadows, moaning, *BEWARE*. But even before we stepped inside, I knew this place was going to be horrible. My skin felt like it was on fire as I lifted my arm to knock on the door. When there was no answer, Malakas suggested we go around to the back. I couldn't find any other entrance, though. Just more boarded windows, a bunch of wide tire tracks gutting the ground, and piles of garbage bags surrounded with flies.

"Are we sure he told us seventeen?" Volcanoman asked. He sounded like he already wanted to get out of here. "I mean, we could try walking a little farther and see if—"

But we'd been sniffed out.

From inside the house, we heard the scrape of some furniture being dragged across the floor. Then someone said, "Holy shit. I think it's Jorge's cargo."

There was the clicking sound of dead bolts being pushed apart. A hidden side door opened and we saw a man's face appear behind the barrel of a pistol. He was dressed in all black and had chalk-white skin. His deep-set eyes peered out from under his forehead. He also had a thin goatee, a black bandana on his head, and a cigarette, dripping ash from between his front teeth.

He waved his gun to usher us inside and barked, "Hurry up. Get in!"

I stepped through the door first, reaching back to lead Ernie inside. Malakas came next with Tomas in his arms. Then Rosa, the baby, and Volcanoman.

There was nothing safe about this safe house. Cigarette-breath was already closing the door and dead-bolting it again. He told us that his name was Ronny and that he was sick and tired of cleaning up after everyone's shit. He raged about how Jorge had really fucked up this time, killing that DF officer. Then Ronny walked away, muttering how everyone was going to have to pay for this mistake.

The inside of the house was revolting. There was a fog of cigarette smoke, body odor, and what smelled like human waste hanging over us. The only light was from a fluorescent camping lantern that was sitting on a three-legged table in the middle of the room, which must have once been a kitchen. The sink and stove were covered in stacks of cigarette cartons. There was a refrigerator that had been unplugged, and the door dangled off its hinge. From inside it, I heard what had to be tiny rodent feet scurrying.

Ronny's friend BJ came into the room next. He was the opposite of Ronny—short and squat, ruddy-cheeked, wearing red nylon basketball shorts that dripped almost to his ankles and a yellow shirt with some angry mascot spread across his chest. BJ was talking nonstop and cackling in between his words as if he was on speed. Which he might've been.

"How many we got tonight? Oh hello, ladies." He crossed his arms over his big belly and peered at me and Rosa, inspecting us. He even held the camping lantern up between us to get a better glimpse of our bodies. I'd seen Mami do this with cattle back on the farm in Vermont, sizing up the cows' flanks and humming softly if she was pleased with what she saw. BJ didn't hum, though. He just got closer and closer, staring us down and clucking his tongue. Then he put both of his clammy hands on my shoulders and said, "Mi casa es su casa. Capiche?"

Malakas stepped in between us. He and BJ stared at each other. Suddenly, BJ roared like a tiger, and Rosa's baby burst into tears.

"Whoa, whoa, whoa." BJ laughed.

Ronny rushed back in from the shadowy hallway, gun cocked and ready again. "You better shut that thing up!" he thundered. "BJ, this is why I told you I don't do babies! This is fuckin' crazy, man. I'm done!"

"Slow your roll, Ron. Slow. Your. Roll." BJ's teeth gleamed, and he winked at me as if we were in on some great secret. I tried to smile politely, but Ronny saw the exchange and smacked his hand against the kitchen wall. BJ cackled again.

"It's not funny, asshole," spat Ronny. "None of this is funny. We got too many spics clogging up the toilet. We haven't even gotten paid yet."

Ronny pulled off his bandana and ran his gigantic hands over his bald head. He started opening up empty cigarette cartons, shaking them to see if there were any extras, and tossing them onto the floor.

"Don't even have enough for a cig," he grunted, the anger boiling inside of him.

"C'mon, Ron. We're gonna get paid. I promise," BJ said. "And we got some nice fresh meat . . ." Here he winked at me again, and I willed myself to stand up straight, even though the room felt like it was spinning.

Malakas spoke up. "Look, man, we're just trying to get to California. You don't need to—"

"Oh, I see! You want her for yourself," said BJ, tipping his head my way. "I don't mind sharing, bro."

"No one's sharing anything," said Malakas. "We're just looking for a way to get to—"

"What the fuck's your problem?" shouted Ronny.

I appreciated Malakas sticking up for me, but I just wanted everyone to go back to their corners. We still needed one of these guys to drive us the rest of the way to California.

Volcanoman stepped in then. "Sorry, man, I just think we're all really tired. Been traveling for days now."

"Shut the fuck up!" Ronny commanded, blasting the whole room with his venom. BJ chuckled, and slithered in front of me and Malakas. When he spoke now, his face was just inches from ours.

"Hey, I get it. You're tired. You're hungry. You just wanna place to lay down for the night. Maybe grab a hot meal. Am I right?"

"Not a fuckin' Holiday Inn," came Ronny's voice behind him.

"Ronny, why don't you take a load off? You been working too hard. I got this."

"I'm good," Ronny spat.

"Or go get us some . . . party supplies, why don'cha?

Y'know, the ones that come in forty-ounce bottles and smell like sex?" I could feel BJ's eyes still fixed on me as he spoke, but I ignored it as best I could. Forcing myself to stare at one of those empty cigarette cartons while Malakas gripped my hand tighter and tighter. "C'mon, Ron. I promise, we're gonna have a fun night."

BJ pulled a few twenty-dollar bills out of his shorts waistband and flapped them in front of my face before handing them to his buddy. Ronny took the money and grunted.

"This is bullshit." He stormed out of the kitchen and down the hall. "You know that? Bullshit!"

We heard him open what must've been the front door on the opposite side of the house, slam it shut, and lock it from the outside.

"Sorry 'bout that," BJ said. "That time of the month, y'know? Here, lemme show you all around." He shoved me and Malakas down the hall, and we had no choice but to walk. The others followed. "See? I'm the only one with any manners around here," he snickered.

"I wanna go!" I heard Tomas whimper behind us.

"Todo va estar bien," Rosa told him. "Ya casi nos vamos."

"You're not leaving anywhere, mamacita. Y'all stuck with us until we say so. Can't have you out there blabbing 'bout what we got goin' on in here, you know what I mean?" said BJ.

"Vali?" Ernie asked. His voice sounded so small, trembling on the edge of tears.

"I'm right here," I said. I tried to swivel around and take his hand or at least reassure him with a fake smile, but BJ locked his arm around my shoulder so I couldn't turn.

"Come out, come out, wherever you are!" he sang as he started flinging open doors on either side of the hall. In one room, there were two glassy-eyed women in oversize T-shirts huddled in a corner. They were tied to an empty bed frame with a rope.

Ernie gasped. "Why are they like that?" he pleaded.

I didn't know how to answer him, but BJ did.

"You know how if you get in trouble at school, you have to go to the principal's office?"

Ernie nodded and looked only at the floor. I could tell he deeply regretted asking.

"Well, these girls have been very, very naughty. And for their punishment, they have to sit here and think about how to be nicer. How to make me *feel* better. Right, girls?" BJ said. His voice reminded me of toxic sludge, oozing toward us.

The women looked up and blinked in slow motion, as if they'd been sedated. I had to think of them as bodies or even dolls—anything but living, breathing people. It was just too horrifying otherwise. One of them started to nod, but got too tired and closed her eyes instead. BJ laughed again as he closed the door. He was looking right at me now.

I looked at the floor.

"People are always coming here, asking for my help. You're pretty lucky I took you in, wouldn't ya say?" He pinched my glowing wrist and spun me around so he could show it to the whole group. "Right? Don'tcha think she owes me a little something for keeping you all safe?"

"Nope. We're leaving," said Malakas. He pulled me toward him.

In the same breath, BJ drew a gun from his waistband and placed the barrel right on the side of Malakas's head. We all froze in fear, listening to BJ cock the gun. Then he held up Malakas's glowing chip as Exhibit B.

"Really, tough guy?" BJ taunted. "And where exactly are you gonna go? It's a nationwide upgrade, so the DF is just collecting its data right now and sending out the troops. The only reason why you haven't been caught yet is 'cuz the officers around here know me. They like me. Or, at least, they like what I have to offer."

Again, BJ leered at me and then at Rosa. Her baby was fussing, and she was trying to shield Tomas's eyes from that gun.

"It's okay. It's all right," I said with fake optimism. "We don't need to go anywhere. We're fine right here!"

BJ smiled. "Atta girl," he said, staring at Malakas.

"Okay" was all Malakas could mutter. BJ lowered the gun.

"Do you think we could just find a place to feed the baby?" I asked.

"Of course, of course. What was I thinking? You all get settled in the kitchen. Make yourselves at home. Don't worry—I'll come lookin' for you in a bit."

As we turned to head back down the hall, I felt BJ's meaty palm on my ass. I couldn't turn around or let out a peep. I couldn't let Ernie see how terrified I was or have Malakas try to step in again on my behalf. My whole body was convulsing, my skin throbbing as I tried to walk back to the kitchen without losing my shit. I knew BJ was probably still watching me. I wanted to rip his eyes out of their sockets and tear the flesh off of his face, but instead I just kept walking.

When I got to the kitchen, I hugged Ernie so tight.

"Why were they tied up? Are they gonna tie us up too?" he whimpered.

"It's okay. We're okay. It's okay," I babbled. These were good words to say, even if I couldn't believe them myself.

"When are we gonna be in California?" Ernie moaned. "I don't wanna be here. I wanna go hooooome." He was eight years old, after all. Starving, overtired, and whether he could process it or not, completely traumatized.

"Soon, Ernie, soon." I took him in my arms. "I'm sorry I brought you here. I'm sorry . . . for all of it."

I didn't know if he accepted my apology or not, if he ever could accept the fact that we left Mami behind. But he did hold on to me tight, and for that I was so grateful. We huddled like that for at least an hour, until the room was so dark, even the lantern couldn't give us more than a small circle of light. Then Malakas and I made a little bunker for all of us behind the trash cans, spreading out our backpacks in a semicircle.

"I promise," Malakas told me. "I won't let them touch you. I won't let them . . ."

He trailed off into a gaping silence that felt so helpless. I didn't know how he could protect me—from BJ, from Ronny, from anything. I wanted to push him away and say, *Leave me alone, I can take care of myself!* But that felt impossible too.

Rosa was already crouching down in a corner of the kitchen, behind two overflowing trash cans. She was urging her boy onto her lap and was trying to feed the baby without lifting her shirt too much.

"Do you think the DF are really sending out troops?" I asked Malakas.

"I dunno. But we need to get out of here."

We both stared in silence at Rosa's glowing wrist and then at our own. I guess weighing which felt more treacherous—the monsters inside this house or out. I didn't know how, but the government had obviously found me. They'd entered me in their database, and they would not let go until I was hunted down and captured.

"We have to find a way to get these chips out," I told Malakas.

"I wish," he said.

"Seriously."

It was the handle of Mami's kitchen knife that gave me the idea for how to do it.

I was rummaging through our stuff, trying to find another granola bar or apple slice to feed Ernie, but coming up short. When my hand found Mami's knife, I knew what needed to be done. I put Ernie's green soccer ball on the floor, and told him and Tomas to lay their heads down on it, side by side. When I was sure they both were asleep, I pulled out the knife, wiped it off, and handed it to Malakas. I pulled out my flashlight and stuck out my right arm so he could see the lump of icy blue just under my skin.

"You get mine out, and I'll get yours," I told him.

It wasn't a request so much as an order.

"But—" started Malakas. His eyes flashed with fear.

"Just do it," I insisted, thrusting my arm closer to his face. Willing my voice to stay steady. It was the only way, as far as I could see.

Malakas took my wrist in his hand, though he still looked too horrified to follow through.

"Please," I begged him. "*Do it.*"

The blade was a lot duller than I'd imagined. Malakas started poking and prodding, wincing for me with each touch.

"It's okay," I assured him. "I can take it."

He changed his grip and tried digging the blade in at a new angle. That didn't work either, though. He was just making these little scrapes along my skin that made me more anxious.

At some point, it was too excruciating to watch Malakas sigh and fumble anymore. I grasped his hand and forced the blade down, piercing my skin with a distinct *pop!*

We both gasped.

There was blood pooling everywhere, dripping down my arm in streams. I mopped at it with the edge of my T-shirt, but the cloth was soon soaked through.

"It doesn't hurt," I told him, even though the pain was

searing through my body now. "Keep going. Please. Just get it out."

It felt like he was slicing my veins, splitting me open. I had to look down to make sure my wrist was still attached to the rest of my body. Which it was. Only seeing that knife worming its way through my skin, as he tried to carve out the chip . . . the blood-soaked shirt below . . .

I tasted bile in the back of my throat and saw the room turn upside down.

And then everything went black.

CHAPTER 18

When I came to, it was still night. I heard the sputtering of an engine outside and twigs snapping underneath tires.

"What's going on?" Ernie whispered. I tried to answer him, but I was still so disoriented. Everything was dark and dank, reeking of blood. My right arm was stiff and firing out burning shock waves of pain.

"It's okay," I mumbled.

Only now there was someone kicking the front door of the house, smashing their heel so powerfully, the walls shook.

"Open up!" raged Ronny.

"What's the secret password?" teased BJ in the hall.

"Just open the door, you ass!"

Malakas was awake now too. As my eyes adjusted to the cool slate of this room, I saw that we had matching bandages around our right wrists. He must have managed to take out his own chip too. I wanted to thank him, to ask him if he was okay, but there were too many angry voices and boot steps charging down the hall.

"What's up, Lochland?" said BJ.

"Whatchu got?" grunted a voice I didn't recognize.

"Two new ones. Hot as fuck. Both Mexican, I think," BJ reported.

"Sounds good. Bring them to my room," the stranger said.

"Yes, sir!"

Ronny and BJ stomped toward the kitchen, and I tried to scramble to my feet. My first instinct was to grab Ernie and rip off the plywood over the kitchen window so we could jump through and run. But my right arm was like a dead weight, pulling me back down to the floor. I was soaked in blood and so dizzy now that I tipped over one of the garbage cans in front of us.

Malakas pointed to the cabinets under the kitchen sink. I grabbed Ernie's quivering hand and got us inside one of them. The space was probably three feet by three feet, and I was crunched so tight, my top two teeth broke through the skin of my knee. But it was dark, which I had to hope meant we were safe.

"Let's go!" ordered Ronny in the kitchen.

I pressed my hand over Ernie's mouth and told him to just breathe. Which was harder than it sounded with mice scampering over our feet and a stench so fierce, it was impossible not to gag.

"Get up!" BJ shouted.

"Please," Rosa cried. "Please no. My babies!"

"Where are you taking her?" asked Volcanoman.

"Shut the fuck up!" Ronny spat.

The image of Mami being taken by an officer into a dark alley shook inside me. I felt the same crushing guilt paralyzing me. There I was, hiding in a cupboard, letting it happen, just like I did with Mami. There was a loud crash, the shattering of glass.

"Stop!" said Malakas.

The thump of fists meeting skin meeting groans. Ernie's eyes were right in front of mine, bright with fear. I felt his lips quivering under my palm. I wanted to plug his ears, his eyes, his head and heart and mind from taking in all of this. But I couldn't protect him from anything anymore.

The baby was bawling.

"Mami! Mami!" cried Tomas.

"Shut the fuck up!" Ronny blazed.

"Todo va estar bien." Rosa wept. "I come back soon!"

Then there were more doors slamming, more shrieking. The sound of a body thrashing as it was dragged across the linoleum floor. Rosa begging for mercy. If not from humans, then from God.

Ernie clung to me. His tears were burning hot. Stinging me even through my shirt.

"Mami! Mami! Where you go?" wailed Tomas.

I couldn't take it anymore. I crawled out of the cupboard and pawed my way through the maze of trash on the floor until

I got both of Rosa's children into my arms. Then Ernie draped his body around us too as we all gasped and sobbed.

"It's okay," I tried to tell them. "We'll get your mami back. She'll be right back, I promise."

I knew I had no right making that kind of promise to them, but I couldn't let anyone else be orphaned. I couldn't let another mom get ripped apart from her children. I clung to those kids as much as they did to me. Desperate to put us all back together.

Ernie was the one who noticed Malakas first. He was knocked out, sprawled on the floor under the three-legged table, shaking his head slowly from side to side and moaning.

"Malakas?" I whispered.

Malakas sat up dazed when he heard me.

"Are you okay?" I asked, though he clearly was not.

"Where's Rosa?" Ernie whined.

And then, from the other room, a shot.

Prrrow.

This time, I recognized the sound right away.

I knew that bitter smell, that manic trembling as saliva flooded my mouth.

Prrrow prrrow.

I heard another body hitting the floor.

"What the fuck?" Ronny squealed.

"Shut up!" boomed Volcanoman.

"Please," sniveled BJ, "I didn't mean—"

Another smack, and he stopped talking. There were bodies fumbling, doors opening and closing, weeping, whispering. Then, quiet. Even Rosa's children grew hushed as we waited to see what would happen.

"Can we leave?" came Ernie's muffled voice.

"Not yet," I mumbled.

I didn't know how to trust that it was over. I didn't know who had fired that gun and whether he was heading toward the kitchen next. The dead air was terrifying. My heart was made of static electricity, raw and ready to burst into flames.

We heard more doors opening. The sounds of so many frantic footsteps stumbling down the hall. People tripping over each other, knocking into walls.

"Go! Run!" Volcanoman yelled.

"Tomas! Lupe!" Rosa wept. She came rushing at us in the kitchen. She pulled her children from my arms and smothered them in kisses.

"C'mon. This way," said Malakas. He got the plywood off the kitchen window and started ushering people through. In the mottled dawn light, I could see that one of his eyes was swollen and purple, his bottom lip split open.

"Are you . . . okay?" I asked again.

Malakas wouldn't answer me. He just guided Ernie toward the window. Rosa and her kids went next, with Tomas still holding on to Ernie's soccer ball.

"What about . . . ?" I looked around the kitchen. There was garbage everywhere. The refrigerator was still dangling open, its scuttling mice nowhere to be seen. I inched over to look down the hallway for anyone else left behind. But all I saw was a dark tide of blood seeping across the floorboards.

I felt like I was going to throw up. The tangy stench of blood filling my nostrils, smothering me.

"Come on," Malakas said, reaching for me. "We have to get out of here."

We climbed out of the plywood opening into the thin light of morning. I saw those two glassy-eyed women from one of the bedrooms running away through a line of straggling trees. And Volcanoman rushing toward us, slick with sweat and tears.

"Okay," he told us, his whole body twitching. "The DF's dead. BJ and Ronny are gone. But we gotta get out of here before more DF show up."

"Are we all here?" I asked.

"Tomaaaaas!" Rosa was flitting back and forth across the field, clutching her baby and shouting for her son. "Tomas! Tomas!"

Ernie, Volcanoman, Malakas, and I all joined her in the field, looking for Tomas.

"I come out and tell him wait, but he runs," Rosa told us. "He is here. And then he is running. Tomas! He was scared. So, he run. *Tomas?*"

Her words were getting more and more shrill and discombobulated. She lurched from one tree to another, searching. Pulling back leaves and branches, kicking over rocks. We all were now.

"I tell him wait for us . . ." she repeated. Replaying the same scene again and again. Only never getting to the end.

Tomas, Tomas, Tomas!

We were all scouring the trampled field, calling out his name. Then we ducked through a patch of woods, fanning out in a modest V formation.

Tomas! Tomas!

"Tomas! You wanna play fútbol?" Ernie squeaked. His voice so trembly and terrified that I felt myself come undone. I just wanted to grab Ernie and run as far as we could in any direction. To put as much distance as possible between us and this moment. Between us and the growing army of people who wanted us exterminated.

"Tomas," I yelled. "It's okay. You can come out now. It's—shit!"

I had stepped into a deep puddle. The water seeping up my pants leg. Actually, it was more than a puddle. As I tried to turn around, my foot sank lower and lower into a marshy, mucky pond. It seemed to stretch out and wind through yards and yards of drooping trees. The only break in the landscape a small, bright buoy. Lime green.

"Ernie, is that your soccer ball?"

Bobbing up and down. And next to it, a tiny, floating sneaker.

✖

I DOVE IN. The water smacking me in the face, filling up all the shrieking spaces in my brain. Only it could never fill up all of it. There was too much pain ripping through me. Ripping through this world. Ripping children from their parents and drowning them in grief. I pushed through the tangles of seaweed and bounced between rocks, and . . .

There he was.

Sweet little Tomas. He was too light to sink and too pale to be alive and too far gone, gone, gone. His arm wrapped around a rotting log.

The howls that came out of Rosa's mouth were unbearable. Her face twisted into a wild, bottomless hole. I had once seen pigs being slaughtered on McAuley's farm where Mami worked. Their bodies gutted right in front of us. Rosa's piercing agony sounded infinitely worse. She pumped Tomas's chest and blew air into his body, but it was clear there was no point. Then she collapsed onto her little boy's body, with the baby still strapped to her chest between them, screaming.

I pulled Ernie in to me and tried to shield his face. It was too horrible. Too unbelievable.

But I couldn't stop him from hearing Rosa's cries or smelling that wretched swamp.

I couldn't make any of this untrue.

CHAPTER 19

Malakas tried to put a baseball hat on Rosa's head. The sun was strong, I guess, and he wanted to protect her from the glare. It felt like such a pitiful, useless thing to do, though, considering she was holding the bloated, purplish corpse of her four-year-old son in her lap. And yet, when the hat fell off because Rosa was shuddering so much, all of us leaned in to put it back on her head. Over and over again, we did this futile activity. Watching the hat slip off, then wordlessly taking turns to place it back.

That was all we could do.

Rosa's body was too tiny to hold all that grief inside. Her pain rippled out in a huge vortex, sucking us all into her misery. I felt breathless. Like her agony was going to eat up whatever was left of this algae-caked pond and shriveled land, this deceitfully sunny sky. I almost wanted it to. I wanted to project Rosa's face out into the ether like an enormous hologram. So the entire planet and all the constellations would have to know her tragedy. They would have to look at her hunched body, holding her squirming baby and her dead son on her knees. Her eyes like two dark pebbles. Feeling everything yet showing nothing.

I couldn't watch her anymore. I had to do something, anything. I got on my knees and started trying to paw through the dirt to dig a grave for little Tomas. The pain in my right wrist was staggering. My whole arm was swollen and hot, turning all kinds of angry reds.

"Why are you doing that?" wept Ernie.

"Just . . . help me," I told him.

I couldn't tell if Ernie knew what I was doing or not, but he joined me on the ground—his face still a dripping storm cloud as we pulled apart clumps of soggy scrub and weeds. If we hit a large rock or a knot of roots, we dug in deeper and scraped even harder. I just needed to keep on tearing away at this ground. To feel something sharp or cold or dirty. Anything besides this obliterating death.

When we'd finished the little grave, I put my arms out to carry Tomas over to it. Rosa wouldn't let him go, though. She wrapped herself tighter around both her children and turned her head away from me.

"I wanna say something," I announced. Surprising myself as much as anyone else. Back in Southboro, if I had to give a presentation at school or something, I felt nauseous. But there was no room for those feelings now. There was only this fierce need rising up from my lungs.

"I learned this in Spanish. And . . ."

I started singing an old song my mami used to sing. I didn't know why exactly, but it came out of me before I could think about it or try to stop myself.

Intentaron enterrarnos. No sabían que éramos semillas.
No sabían, no sabían, no sabían que éramos semillas.
They tried to bury us, but they didn't know
  we were seeds.
They didn't know, they didn't know, they didn't know
  we were seeds.

I heard Ernie pick up the words under me, his voice tripping over his tears. When the song was over, he stepped forward and stood over his dead friend. He took his beloved lime green soccer ball and laid it at Rosa's feet. Then he dove into my arms, racked with sobs.

One by one, we paid tribute to sweet Tomas in whatever way we knew how. Malakas recited a prayer in Tagalog. Then he took out of his bag a string of rosary beads and broke the thread with his teeth, laying the broken chain on Tomas's unmoving chest.

Volcanoman sprinkled some dirt on Tomas's bloated feet. Then, he started pursing his lips and squinching his eyes. Working so hard to hold back his emotions, though he lost that battle. I lost it too. Somehow, watching Volcanoman quake was the hardest. His wide frame convulsing, like a mountain about to unleash an avalanche. I felt my eyes fill up with all those angry, desperate tears I'd been holding back for days, and I just let them rush down my face, hot and fast. Licking them away from my lips and knowing there would always be more.

"He run," Rosa wailed. "He run to be away from them . . ."

As her voice drifted off, I heard a high-pitched buzzing noise. Malakas must have heard it too. He took a pair of binoculars out of his pack and peered up beyond a far-off line of lopsided trees. The sunlight shifted as a bank of gauzy clouds moved in from the east. Only, they were moving too fast to be actual clouds. The buzzing sound was getting louder as they approached us.

"Drones," Malakas announced, inspecting the horizon.

"Shit," said Volcanoman.

"Looks like they're still probably about eight to ten miles away, but—"

"We gotta go," said Volcanoman.

I tapped Rosa on the shoulder. It was just the lightest of touches, and yet she swooned forward. I was scared she'd crack into a thousand pieces.

"No," she said. Still looking out at that pond. "I do not go."

"You can't stay here," said Volcanoman.

"I stay with Tomas," she declared.

"No, no, no. If you want, I can carry him on my back. You just have to get up now." Volcanoman reached out for the dead boy, but Rosa stopped him with her palm.

"You go," she said. "I. Stay. With. Tomas."

There was not a scrap of self-pity in her voice. She was grounded and sure of what she wanted. As if speaking not only for herself, but for every mother who'd ever lost a child before her. She rocked back and forth with both her children in her lap. The baby still drinking from her breast.

"What about the baby?" I asked.

"Mi bebé," Rosa muttered. Tipping her head to one side so she could inspect her child from a different angle. "Yes, mi Guadalupe," she told me.

I wanted to shake Rosa, plead with her to just trust us. But there was no guarantee of anything.

"Guadalupe needs you," I tried. "What if you come with us? We'll get you somewhere safe and . . ." I had no right telling her we could fix this or make her whole again. Especially as the drones' humming was getting louder and louder.

"We don't have a lot of time," said Malakas. He put down his binoculars, reached into his backpack again, and took out two of those large foil blankets the government gave out to people at the border as they threw them in detention.

"Everyone, cover up," Malakas said. "It hides your body heat, so it messes up the thermal cameras in the drones . . . I hope, anyway."

I wrapped one of the foil blankets over Rosa and her kids.

The drones kept moving in closer. I could even see them edging over those trees in a looming, whirring shadow. Could feel their hum crawling up inside my skin. The sky was closing in and squeezing us in its vicious, buzzing grip.

"I'm sorry," Volcanoman mumbled. "I don't want to say this, but . . . I think we should go."

"Yeah. He's right," Malakas said. "Even with the blankets, it's just too dangerous for us to stay."

"GO!" Rosa said. Her mouth forming a perfect circle. She was clear and purposeful as she pulled off her foil blanket and lifted her face to the sky. Just like my mami on the floor of that bus station, giving us the safety she no longer had.

She was not a martyr. She was a mother.

Volcanoman motioned for us to follow him away from the pond. We couldn't wait any longer. As I was turning to go, I felt something icy clamp down on my left ankle. I gasped and looked down. It was Rosa's hand.

"Please, Vali," she said. Her glistening eyes found mine. "Please do not forget him."

"No, I won't."

"His name is Tomas Roberto Mejia. He is a good boy. He laughs and makes jokes, and he runs so, so fast."

I nodded to show her that I understood. "I won't ever forget him. I promise."

She drew Tomas in to her chest again and rocked her whole family over that open grave. Closing her eyes and covering their heads with kisses, as if she was in a warm nursery trying to get her children to sleep. Singing them a song or telling them a story that ended in happily ever after.

And even though there could never be a happily ever after

in this world for them, I saw them bound together by a love that transcended life or death.

A love that would carry them from this place into whatever happened next.

A love that would hold them, protect them, even as that flock of drones swooped in overhead.

They were bigger than I'd ever seen before—bright metallic gray orbs with arms that extended down. They looked like giant, menacing spiders. Malakas, Volcanoman, Ernie, and I ran to a pile of rotting wood that was probably once a barn. As we hid there, under our foil blanket, I lifted it just enough to see one of the drones lowering itself until it was directly over Rosa and her family. Then it spat out a thick wire netting that covered and trapped them.

No sabían, no sabían, no sabían que éramos semillas . . .

I kept singing, while they lifted Rosa, Tomas, and Guadalupe out of the mucky marsh.

Streaking away through the sky.

CHAPTER 20

We ran all day, driven by the image of Tomas's blue lips and the metal netting that scooped Rosa's family into the sky. There was nothing else to do, nothing else to say. We could only communicate in gasps and tears. Ernie was limping, his feet covered with blisters. My right wrist was throbbing and tingling. All of our mouths were dry and cracked.

We were just so weak.

For "dinner" I was able to find a few edible-looking berries, and we chewed on the cleanest bark we could find just so our stomachs would stop gnawing on themselves. For "dessert" Malakas said we should suck on some rocks to help stave off dehydration. We found a ditch to serve as shelter for the night and slumped down, panting and groaning. All of our phones were out of battery power by now. Ernie clung to me as I tried to figure out where we were on Mami's map. Her blue ballpoint line couldn't help us anymore—it had ended way back in New York City. There were no other clues to follow except for those hatch marks starting somewhere in northern Texas. But where we were in relation to them, I had no idea.

"I guess we're somewhere . . . between here and here?" I said, pointing to a stretch of pastel pink that was below Scutter, Oklahoma. Malakas had a compass to give us at least a little sense of direction. He also scoped the landscape with his binoculars and assured us that there were no more drones.

Volcanoman couldn't offer anything, though. He just kept weeping.

"I'm sorry," he cried. He was breathless and huge, and his shirt was covered in blood. It was the blood of that DF officer he'd shot just this morning. "I swear, I never . . . I never . . . I just . . . I saw that guy going for Rosa and something snapped. I had to stop him. It was too . . . familiar."

I didn't know which stunned me more—the actual words Volcanoman was saying or the soft, vulnerable tone he had now as he cried for Rosa, Tomas, Guadalupe, and some personal grief I could only guess at. He'd cracked open that spiky armor of anger and was looking at us with no pretense. It was beautiful and horrible and mesmerizing to hear him speak like this. He started describing to us how he had loved growing up in Rio de Janeiro. He loved his neighborhood. Loved his friends. Loved his family. Volcanoman had two older sisters who doted on him and taught him how to dance the samba. But one of the sisters had a boyfriend who wound up being in a gang. She tried to break up with him, and he came to Volcanoman's house with two friends. Each one of them with a gun in their waistband.

Volcanoman was almost babbling now, his words tumbling over each other.

"They grabbed Juliana by the hair. They were swinging her around like a toy. Then my mom came in and tried to stop them. They shot Mom in the stomach . . . but I couldn't . . . move. There was so much blood. So much screaming."

Ernie whimpered.

His mother and sister miraculously survived. He couldn't believe it. "I thought they both were going to die that day—especially my mom. I thought I would never see her again, and the thought of her not knowing who I really was made me so sad. More sad than I had ever been . . ."

When she'd recovered, Volcanoman told his mom that he was gay. "I remember when I said it, she smiled a big, toothy smile. She held my face in her hands and told me how perfect I was. But to be gay in Brazil at that time . . . it was *not easy*. So, my mom . . ."

He stifled a hiccupy sob as we waited for him to fill in the blanks. I could already guess that she was dead from the ache in his voice, though.

"She knew I wouldn't survive there," Volcanoman murmured. "She did so much, just so I could get here."

She sold practically all of their belongings so she could pay a man to smuggle Volcanoman over to the US. When he got here, he was a teenager, being shuffled around in New York City between foster care families.

"Finally I got a job," he went on. "I washed dishes and started saving every cent."

The raids started soon after that. Volcanoman tried to use whatever money he had to buy a fake chip, but the man doing the procedure took his money and cut open Volcanoman using dirty tools. He got a horrible infection and spent the rest of everything he had paying for medicine at clinics that promised not to report him.

He was soon homeless on the streets of New York. He spent days and nights riding the subway trains up and down through the different boroughs, just wandering. He lived on the train, he said. Eating on the train, sleeping on the train, even hanging off the back of the train when they came up from underground so he could catch a ray of sun or a drop of rain.

"My lola and I rode the trains a lot," said Malakas. "Mostly on the weekends when she didn't have to work. She wanted me to see every part of New York City."

He and Volcanoman started talking about all the crazy things they saw on the subway system. It almost felt like a practical joke or a riddle—that they could have been traveling right next to each other and have never known it. They could have even jostled for the same seat, never dreaming that they'd one day be huddled together under some rocks in the wilderness. Praying they would survive.

"Actually, that's how I found out about these silver blankets," Malakas explained. "I loved taking the train up to Morningside Heights to look at the stars. Lola bought these so we could stay out late at night, even if it got cold."

I closed my eyes and tried to imagine those cool nights, the trains zipping up and down through cities, mountains, space, time. Taking us somewhere—anywhere—safe.

Instead, I had a vision of my own memories with trains. Or really, a very specific train—la Bestia. La Bestia was the freight train that ran through Mexico and helped deliver people fleeing the droughts, famines, wars, and poverty of Latin America. I remembered baking in the sun on the roof of la Bestia with Mami and Papi. We were up there for days after we left Colombia. I was terrified on those trains, because people could attack us at any moment. Falling asleep could kill you too. There was no way to really secure yourself onto the hot metal roof. Sometimes people would doze off, and the next thing we knew, they were tumbling off.

La Bestia was cruel, but it also gave us hope. Mami, Papi, and I rode on top of it through most of Mexico. When we arrived in the United States and saw that sprawling slope of palm trees in San Diego and the garden that was built just for butterflies, Papi shouted, ¡Dios bendiga la Bestia!

"Wait! What if—the train!" I blurted out.

"The train?" Volcanoman asked.

Malakas looked at us both uncertainly while Ernie tugged on my sleeve.

"Are we gonna get in a train?" he asked. "Please say yes. Please, please, please say yes." He showed me his hot, blistered feet again to make his point even more.

"Not *in* a train. *On* a train," I clarified.

Malakas's eyes widened as he realized what I was saying.

"There must be a California-bound train around here, right? Look at this map. I think this means there's train tracks around here," I said, pointing to those hatch marks.

Malakas, Volcanoman, and Ernie leaned in to see what I was talking about. Using Ernie's pinky as our "ruler," we guesstimated that we had to walk about twenty miles southwest to meet up with the closest tracks.

"Twenty?" Ernie repeated mournfully.

"Yep," I told him. "But that's better than sixty. Or two hundred." We had already come so far. We had already lost so much. I couldn't let him give up now.

I thought of Rosa tipping her head up to the sky and Mami mouthing the word *GO!*

"We can do it," I told my little brother. "We have to go."

CHAPTER 21

A word problem.
Because at one point in my life, these were just words, and not my reality.

> If four people are standing on the side of a desolate, scorched field with no food, no water, and no idea of whether they'll ever be reunited with their families again, and a driverless freight train is approaching them at approximately fifty miles per hour, how fast and how far do they have to jump in order to get on without killing themselves?

No matter how many times we went over the probable speed of the train and the trajectory of its route, I knew I couldn't feel truly prepared. There was nothing predictable or solvable about this equation. We had walked another twenty miles, studying Mami's map and Malakas's compass to direct us toward the nearest tracks. It looked like if we made it on—*when* we made it on—we could take a train all the way to the Verde Valley, close to the California border.

At least, that was the hope.

We spent another full day hiding, rummaging through the occasional trash can for food, just trying to regain some strength and decipher the trains' schedules. Most of them were driverless and electric-powered, but ironically delivering coal up and down the plains, dropping off their goods at a series of extraction silos. It was too risky to climb on a train at an actual stop, of course. But if we made our move close enough to a silo, it would have to be slowing down for the approach.

And so, the next morning, the four of us stood by a dusty embankment leading up to some train tracks about three miles away from a gleaming silo. It looked like we really only had ten seconds when the train would be decelerating, and it still would be clipping along at a fast pace.

"You ready, little man?" Malakas asked Ernie. Ernie nodded. He looked equal parts terrified and excited. Volcanoman, on the other hand, looked just plain terrified. He kept telling us that he wasn't strong enough and that there had to be another way. He offered to walk solo, if we could give him a meeting spot. Maybe he could just follow the train tracks and catch up to us near the next extraction station.

"Hey, I don't want to do this either," I admitted. "But we have another *thousand miles* to go. The DF could be anywhere;

my arm feels like it's gonna fall off. And I don't know about you, but I can't live on scraps and berries much longer."

"But I . . . I . . ."

"You got this," I said, looking him straight in the eye.

✖

A MEMORY.

Because those felt so precious and were just as real as this present moment or any possible future.

I was standing on top of a high ledge of rock, overlooking the Pacific Ocean. Papi was already in the frigid water, cheering me on, and Mami was on the sand, nursing a hungry baby Ernie.

"You can do this, mi'ja! Jump!" Papi yelled. I wanted to prove him right and be his brave little girl, but the water looked like it was moving farther and farther away. My vision was blurry, and I was shaking so uncontrollably that at the last minute, I chickened out.

Running back to Mami and Ernie on the sand, I felt a flush of hot shame sweep through my body. Papi charged up from the water, dripping wet.

"What happened to my brave Valentina?" he asked.

I buried my head in a towel, too disappointed in myself to speak.

"No la presiones, Juan-Pablo," Mami said.

"What are you talking about? Ella puede. ¡Ella es valiente!"

"She's trying to impress you!" Mami shot back, as if I wasn't right next to her, crumpled in self-pity. "Déjala en paz."

"Lo siento," Papi said, his voice softening. "We try again next time, ¿bueno? Sigues siendo mi Valentina valiente."

Only there was no next time. At least, not with my papi. A month later, he was locked in a detention center and I was on the phone with him, begging him to tell me when we could all go back to the beach again.

"Pronto, mi'ja. Pronto."

"Because I'm practicing my jumps," I told him. "I'm gonna do it next time."

✖

"HERE IT COMES," announced Malakas. "Put your backpacks on . . ."

The air felt so close and charged. My vision was blurry. I was shaking uncontrollably. But there was no way I could chicken out here. As I waited for that train to barrel toward us, I decided that both of my parents were right. It was too much pressure, and I was very brave.

"On my count," Malakas said. "Twenty, nineteen, eighteen—"

"Wait!" cried Ernie. "What if I don't get far enough? What if everyone gets on except me? What if the train smushes us or there's DF inside and they climb out through the windows? What if . . . ?"

227

All valid questions that I couldn't even try to answer. The only thing I could tell my little brother with any confidence was this:

"If I get on and you don't, I will jump off, and I will—"

"Three, two, one, here we go!"

And then we did the only thing we could do—jump. I felt that sick sensation of everything in my body puckering and tightening. Malakas was a little ahead of us. Ernie was right next to me. We were on the verge of everything, leaping into life or death. I clamped on to my brother's arm and hurtled us both forward. Clawing at the train's blistering hot exterior.

Thunk.

My nose whacked into the siding, and I bit down so hard on my tongue that my mouth immediately pooled with blood. But besides that, I was alive. And so was Ernie. Gazing up at me with a look of windblown triumph. We both had our hands wedged into air vents and our knees tucked into our torsos.

"You good?" called Malakas.

"Yeah!" I answered. My right wrist still felt like it was splintering open, but I willed myself to breathe through the pain.

The side of the train was so much slicker than I'd anticipated. My feet kept slipping and sliding under me, like I was on some crazy treadmill. Ernie was doing great, though, scaling the side of the car just a few feet away from me now. His long, spindly legs were made for this kind of Spider-Man move.

I got my left foot onto a metal seam. From there, I was able to hoist myself up with my right knee and elbow. I rolled onto the roof and felt my eyes puddle with relief. But there was no time to bask in the moment. Volcanoman was still dangling off the side of the train, cursing and struggling.

"This is . . . too much," Volcanoman screamed.

"You got this!" Malakas shouted.

"No, I don't," Volcanoman panicked. "I don't got it."

Both of his hands were gripping an air vent, knuckles white and clenched like claws. He was flailing wildly. Screaming, "I can't! I can't!"

"Yes you can!" I yelled back at him.

"No!"

I told Ernie to lock his arms around my stomach and then had Malakas do the same around Ernie's. Together, the three of us made a human pulley—tugging and hoisting until Volcanoman flopped onto the roof like a beached whale. He was gasping for air and stuttering out some sort of apology or thank-you.

"I didn't . . . I couldn't . . . You all . . ."

He kept telling us how much we meant to him. I couldn't understand much of what he was saying, though, because I was so busy sobbing, caught between terror and amazement.

Ernie was the one who managed to get out, "Damn, we are awesome."

And the four of us were actually able to laugh.

We tied Malakas's rope around the metal grates on top of the train and tethered each of us on tight. I was in between Ernie and Malakas, jerking and jostling into them both. The first few times I knocked into Malakas, I apologized. After a while, though, I stopped. There was no point to saying sorry. This was all so far beyond our control.

If I could just forget about everything possibly lurking all around us. Or even down below. The plains rolled out in front of us in a zigzag patchwork of browns and grays. The only specks of color were from rows of genetically modified corn—their leaves too green and perfectly shaped, their stalks too thick, with neon yellow tassels on top.

I couldn't tell what hurt more, my physical body or my aching heart. I heard it pounding in my chest, my ears, my neck, even behind my eyes. I had this overwhelming feeling that even though the sky was clear of drones now, it was just waiting to close in and crush us in a single blow.

"Oooh, it's fun with your eyes closed," Ernie said. I wanted to tell him that this wasn't a game, that we had to be on guard for everything and anything. And yet he looked so peaceful with his eyes closed and his head tilting to the side. A quiet grin crept across his lips.

As I closed my eyes, I had to admit it did feel a little magical. It was almost like a roller coaster at first, whipping and spinning me into some new dimension. I remembered that roller coaster I rode with Mami years ago, back in San Diego. It twisted and turned, tunneling toward some crazy loop-di-loop through fake mountains and enchanted forests. Fairies and lollipops as big as the sky. It made me believe in princesses and magic beanstalks and a giant mouse who could talk.

I thought of that girl in the Mickey Mouse shirt at the border, and my pulse started racing again. Only now, up here, it wasn't so much that hunted feeling. It was more a sense of momentum. She was so brave, so deliberate. I had to wonder, when she was blown to bits, was it all hot, searing pain? Or could it have felt like a release? Weightless and airborne and free?

Some way, somehow, I wanted to tell that girl that she had given me courage and purpose. That her fifteen steps were not in vain. I didn't know for sure if we would make it to California. But I did know that her face was giving me some version of hope.

✖

AS THE SUN started sinking and the sky got cooler, we were still here. The winds were picking up now. I held Ernie tight and felt the air rushing at me, wiping away every moment before now and emptying my brain.

Malakas offered me his shoulder to lean on, and I accepted wordlessly. His pulse was so close now I could hear it thumping in my ear.

Shwa shwa shwa. Steady, sturdy.

It was the closest I could get to feeling safe.

The train was silent and stealthy, winding through the hushed evening into night. Ernie scooted down to curl into my lap and was soon limp with sleep. I stared at his eyes—so much like Mami's, with their tall, arching lids and long, dark lashes. I wanted her to see him. She would be so proud.

I soon heard Volcanoman snoring on the other side of Ernie. There were thousands of stars winking at us and even a fingernail of moon. Malakas pulled out his binoculars and told me he was fine staying up to keep watch if I wanted to close my eyes too.

Which I tried to do, only, my mind wouldn't let me sleep.

There was just so much inside this night. So much fear and hope and confusion and relief bubbling up in my chest. I didn't know how to hold on to this many emotions at once. And still a thousand unanswered questions.

"Can I ask you something?" I said to Malakas.

"Sure."

"How long have you been doing this?"

"Doing . . . ?"

"Running."

Malakas paused. "Since they took my lola. But really, since I moved to the US," he said. "You?"

"Same, I guess." I told him how Mami and Ernie and I stayed up that last night we were all together in Vermont. Huddled under the blankets, letting Ernie ask over and over again, *Why? Why? Why?*

"Vermont. Is that where you're from?" Malakas said.

"No." I straightened my back and sat up proudly. "I'm from a town called Suárez, in Colombia."

"I've always wanted to go to Colombia."

"Really?"

"Yeah, I really wanna go to the Tatacoa Desert. You know, where they have those incredible meteor showers?"

"No, I've never heard of them," I admitted.

"I guess I'm kind of an astronomy nerd," Malakas said. "Anyways . . . what's Suárez like?"

I told him everything I remembered about my hometown in el Cauca. The lazy picnics along the Ovejas River. The bright green leaves forming a canopy overhead. The taste of fresh mango, so sweet it made me cry, and all the trips we took to Buga, so Mami could visit the big pink church and pray for miracles. I didn't know if I believed in miracles, but if I was there now, I'd beg for so many things: that Mami could be safe, Rosa and her kids too; that we could all get to California without the DF coming up with some new way to track us. I looked down at my throbbing wrist.

"Wait a second." I paused. "I never thanked you for taking out my chip."

Malakas picked up my right arm gingerly, and I tried not to wince. His looked equally swollen from what I could see in this light.

"Yeah, I don't think I want to be a surgeon," he said with a sad sort of chuckle.

"Yeah, me neither. But what *do* you want to be?"

"You mean, besides free?"

"Yeah."

Malakas started talking to me about astronomy again and how he wanted to study exoplanets and galaxy evolution.

"Whoa."

"I just love knowing there are all these other worlds out there. That humans aren't the center of the universe."

That definitely made sense to me. Even those DF officers and their drones were powerless against the sun and moon.

Neither of us said anything for a while after that. Instead, I felt Malakas take my hand in his. Holding on for a slow, deep breath. His fingers felt warm and comforting as he laced them through mine. We sat like that, in a well of silence, for a long time. It wasn't even a scary silence. Because what did we have to fear anymore?

I wondered what life would have been like if Malakas and I had met each other in a totally different context—like walking down the halls of some silly high school or bumping into each other in line for a concert. Maybe Malakas was thinking something like that too, because then he asked, "If you could go anywhere in the world, where would you go?"

"California," I answered without missing a beat. "What about you?"

"I've always wanted to go to the Galapagos Islands. Or to the International Space Station."

"Oooh, yeah." I hadn't thought about those possibilities. About truly having a choice to go anywhere or be anyone.

About life beyond all this madness. "Okay, wait, can I change my answer?"

"Sure."

"I want to go to the space station too. I mean, if you don't mind. We could probably carpool or something."

Malakas laughed. Then he lifted my hand to his mouth and kissed it lightly.

"Yeah," he said. "Let's do that."

CHAPTER 22

The sky didn't feel as magical the next day when we were baking in the morning sun. We ate the last of our food and finished the water we were all sharing. Then Malakas suggested that we all get under the foil blankets again for some sort of shade and protection. As Ernie and I sat together in our little silver cocoon, I felt like I was melting into a puddle.

We took turns being the lookout with Malakas's high-powered binoculars. It was hard for me to concentrate, though. The landscape was just so bleak. Another storm had obviously blasted through here—or maybe it was wildfires. As we wound our way southwest, I saw miles and miles of burned-out fields and pastures, toppled windmills, crushed ranch houses with their roofs blown off. In the background were rows of abandoned oil rigs lurking like forgotten dinosaurs.

I knew from checking Malakas's compass that we were

heading in the right direction. I wasn't sure how far we'd gotten, though. By the end of that second day, all I could say for sure was that it was getting drier and hotter, and even blinking was painful because I had so little moisture left in my body.

And yet at least I was still free.

✖

"SORRY TO WAKE you up. But you gotta see this," whispered Volcanoman. It was almost morning on our third day up here. He had been on watch duty for the past few hours and was now nodding at something on the horizon.

I took the binoculars from him and peered through. I couldn't tell what I was looking at, no matter how much I zoomed in. Everything was covered in a layer of soot, and as we sped through, we were stirring up more dust and debris.

"What do you think it is?" he asked.

"I'm . . . not sure."

At first, I thought I saw gigantic gray clouds hovering just above the ground to the east. Then I realized they weren't clouds at all. They were huge tents pitched in the middle of the desert. Each one was at least the size of a few football fields strung together.

"I think it has to do with the government," I told Volcanoman. I fiddled with some of the buttons on the binoculars and twisted the lens as far as it would go, feeling more and more urgent about figuring out what I was looking at.

I saw the letters painted on the side of a tent in bright yellow: **DEPORTATION FORCE**.

"No! Shit! No, no, no!"

"No what?" asked Ernie, waking up with a startle.

"What's going on?" said a confused Malakas.

Volcanoman tried to explain to them what we saw, though he was full of *ums* and *maybes*.

"Is it the DF?" asked Ernie.

"Let me see," said Malakas.

But I refused to let the binoculars go. My arms were shaking, and I could hear my pulse pounding in my ears as I leaned forward to glean more. I saw one of the tent flaps open. Inside, something glinted wildly, bouncing sunlight in all directions. I squinted from the glare and tried to focus again. Everything inside those tents seemed to be made of sparkling metal. There were columns or maybe bars. With the outline of people behind them.

"They're in cages!" I gasped.

Now I saw a line of hunched silhouettes emerging from another one of the tents. All of them stooped over, walking with the pained stagger of someone half dead. They were attached to each other with what looked like neck collars and leashes. Surrounded by armed DF officers.

"No!" I moaned. "What the . . . what are they doing?" I could feel my chest tightening with panic.

"Lemme see! C'mon, Vali!" Ernie tried to pry the binoculars from me, but there was no way I was letting go.

Now the DF officers started slicing the air with their batons. The chained figures were being beaten to the ground, one by one. Then one of the officers shot a rifle into the air, and the rest of the captives raised their arms in submission.

And there it was: a line of ice-blue, glowing chips on their wrists. Faint yet undeniable, even from this distance. That eerie light radiating through me and making me scream.

"What?" Ernie cried. "What are you seeing?"

"Vali!" Malakas said. "We need to know."

I was pulling my eyes away to hand him the binoculars when I saw her.

"Mami?" I screamed. "Mami!"

At least I thought it was her. I thought that I saw the shape of her face, her strong hands, her wide back. I thought I saw her hobbling in a line of chained immigrants. But then she was gone.

"Mami?" Ernie hollered. "Mami! Mami!" He tried to soothe himself by combing his hair with his fingers and rubbing his palms on his cheeks to give them color—doing all the things Mami used to do for him to get ready for an important event. All the while repeating, "Mami, Mami, Mami . . ."

"Calm down, Ernie." I took his frantic hands in mine. They were hot and trembly. "I think it was her, but maybe . . . it . . . wasn't."

"But you said you saw her!" he cried.

"I don't know. I just saw her for a second. I . . . I—"

"We have to find her. We have to go! Let's go! Let's go!" Ernie wailed.

Our train was already turning away from the tents to head further west. I started pulling at our rope tethers, desperate to untie us before the tents disappeared completely from view. Only, the ropes were so hot from days scorching up here on the train's metal roof, I kept fumbling. Even touching the fibers made my fingertips burn.

"What are you doing?" asked Malakas.

"You can't jump off in the middle of the desert," Volcanoman argued.

I wasn't asking for their permission, though. I kept yanking at those ropes, trying to block out their protests.

"Vali," said Malakas. "Look how far we are. You don't know what's going on in there. You can't just go walking through the desert because you think—"

"What if it *was* her?" I cut him off. "I mean, what if your lola's in there too? What if that's where they took Rosa and her baby? What if . . . ?"

"And what if it's not," Malakas said.

I stopped trying to untie the ropes. Those what-ifs were flooding every fold of my brain now. Filling me up and strangling me with all the horrible possibilities. As I dropped the ropes, I felt a helplessness that gutted me. If Mami was there, chained by the neck in some brutal camp, how could I leave her to wither and die? At the same time, if that wasn't her, how could I put my brother in this kind of danger by jumping off a train and heading toward the DF?

I couldn't be sure that was Mami. I couldn't be sure of anything. I was so desperate to talk to her, to ask for her guidance. If there was one saint or prophet I believed in fully, it was Liliana Ramirez. She could tell me the earth was flat, and I'd be the first one to agree. I remembered as a kid being so grateful when people told me I looked like her twin. I wanted so badly to be her.

She made me. I didn't want to exist without her.

No. I didn't know for sure that Mami was in one of those cages. But the what-ifs would not let me go. As the train veered westward, I knew whatever was going on in those cages would soon disappear from view.

I picked the ropes back up. "Please!" I begged Malakas and Volcanoman. "Help me with these ropes?"

Neither of them moved fast enough for me. And now Ernie had the binoculars in his hands, trying to make out exactly what was going on.

"Wait," I heard him say. "What are those trucks?"

"Tents," Volcanoman corrected him.

"No. Trucks." He pointed out into the desert.

Malakas grabbed the binoculars back just as the brakes on our train began stuttering and squeaking.

"Shit," he muttered. "We gotta untie ourselves. NOW! We gotta jump!"

"Jump?" said Volcanoman. "Fuck!"

I didn't need the binoculars to see which trucks Ernie had spotted now. They were tearing in from the east, kicking up huge swaths of dirt in their wake. The four of us ripped at those ropes, clawing and pulling until they came undone.

Everything was happening in slow motion and also spinning so fast that I felt like we would be thrown out of the earth's orbit at any moment. The train's gears were slowing; the DF sirens were screaming. The train was almost at a complete standstill.

"Jump NOW!" Malakas ordered.

There was no time for what-ifs anymore. I gripped Ernie's hand. And we leapt off, hands outstretched, together. Hurling ourselves into the air with our foil blanket flapping behind us. Maybe even in that moment, looking like some sort of giant, majestic bird, taking flight. Soaring above it all.

CHAPTER 23

The ground was coming toward my face, thwacking me in the shoulder and chest. All the wind flushed out of me as I gulped a mouthful of dirt and sputtered.

Ernie was crumpled on the ground next to me.

"You okay?" I wheezed.

He just moaned, rubbing the side of his head and clenching his eyes shut—I guess to push back the tears.

"C'mon! Run!" urged Malakas from a few feet away. His face was covered in dust, and his wrist bandage looked bloodier than before, but the important thing was he was here and he was alive. But where was Volcanoman?

✖

WE SCRAMBLED UP and broke into a run. It didn't matter which direction, we just needed to find some sort of covering and put distance between us and the officers on the train.

Ernie grabbed me. "But what about Volcanoman?"

We'd called him that since the meat truck, even though he'd proven to be such a good, kind guy. And now he was gone.

"I don't know," I whispered to Ernie. "Come on." I told Malakas to follow us, then yanked Ernie's arm so we slid down a rocky embankment. Each stone or root jabbed me in a new spot. We made it down into a thicket of some sort. That was probably the most painful part of all, because there were stinging nettles piercing our shins, our arms, our cheeks.

"Ow! Ow!" Ernie whimpered.

I wanted to cradle him in my arms and nurse all his wounds, but there were too many to count now, and I could still hear those DF officers on the other side of the embankment.

"*Shut up! Hands behind your back!* one of them bellowed.

"Fuck you!" Those were the last words we heard Volcanoman say.

I caught Malakas's eyes as they filled with tears. I pressed my lips together in a tight, trembling line. This is what I did when my papi was taken too—because I was just too scared that if I opened my mouth I would scream and shriek and tear up this whole world with my rage.

We felt the rocks and sand around us shaking, the topsoil skidding as a drone descended out of the sky. We knew exactly what it was now—it was just like the one that took Rosa and her family after Tomas's funeral. The mesh cage dropping from the sky and scooping up its prey.

As I shielded my little brother's eyes so he wouldn't have

to see that cage, I could feel his face, wet with tears. The drone snatched up Volcanoman and lifted back into the air. The DF officers enjoyed their moment of triumph.

Didn't even have a chip.

Smelled like trash.

"Where are they taking him?" Ernie whispered. I looked down at the ground beneath my feet. I couldn't tell him what I was really thinking. Maybe they would slit his throat. Maybe they would drop him in the desert. Or maybe he'd be put in one of those cages, chained by the neck, and beaten senseless.

I wanted to turn us around and make our way back to those cages so I could see if that was Mami for sure. Even without our chips, though, Malakas and I were clearly targets. The DF had just taken Volcanoman, and he didn't have a chip either. There was no way to know how the government was tracking us now.

I looked at my little brother tucked into my side. He was already so depleted and sad. Even if I was willing to risk it all and go back to possibly find Mami, that wouldn't be fair to him. Mami would never forgive me if I abandoned him in the desert, sacrificing myself for her.

Once again, our only option was to run. Just like Mami had said,

When they are coming for you, run. Run faster than them. Run smarter than them. Just run.

We sprinted through a maze of shriveled bushes and jagged rock, crouching under branches just long enough to catch our breath before running again. My legs felt numb. I knew they were moving. Only because they had to be. But I couldn't direct them or even decipher which foot was stepping down and which heel was lifting up. There had to be some sort of survival-mode adrenaline carrying me forward. My brain couldn't process anything specific, except for holding on to Ernie.

He was really struggling, swooning and staggering. Tripping over himself as if he was drunk. Then he started coughing and couldn't stop.

"Take a breath. Take a breath," I urged.

Easier said than done. The air was so thin and chalky. The ground so cracked and parched. There was a haze of soot and dust on everything—my skin, my hair, my thoughts. Even when we tried to alternate between running and walking, none of us could take in enough gulps of air. Somewhere in my head, I registered the sounds of our freight train speeding away along with those DF trucks, though. That's when I stopped running.

"So that's it?" Ernie cried. "He's just gone?"

My heart felt raw from the sting of those words, from the sting of longing and unknowing. It was just the three of us left now, with an endless stretch of desert ahead. And not a drop of water left in our backpacks.

"I think . . . we need to head that way, and I bet we find some cactus," I said, trying to sound confident, or at least semisure.

"That way" was west.

"That way" was the opposite direction from those tents

and cages and the remote possibility of rescuing Volcanoman, Rosa, Lola, and Mami.

The list of missing persons was getting longer and longer. But as I watched my little brother plodding next to me, I had to tell myself that this was the right decision. "That way" was the only way. And so we kept going.

The sun was getting so strong now that we decided to scramble from one clump of crackly-leaved bushes to the next. I didn't know if we were actually moving forward or if we were just stumbling in a circle. Sometimes the only cover we had was the shadow of a boulder. Then there were more terrifying stretches of land where we were completely open and exposed. The stubs of withered branches and burnt tree trunks poked out of the ground. Ernie found a trail of dead prairie dogs and wept miserably.

According to Mami's map and Malakas's compass, it looked like we were heading into the Verde Valley, though there was nothing *verde* about it. The most vegetation we could find were little knots of squat brown trees to hide under for a bit of shade. About an hour into our trek, I found a gnarled-looking cactus and tried cutting off a pad with Mami's kitchen knife. The spines kept digging into my hands. When I tried to peel back the skin to get some of the juicy meat out, there was barely anything there. I handed whatever I had to Ernie. He popped it into his mouth and tried to chew, but then had to spit it out immediately.

"Yuck," he rasped.

"Can I help you?" Malakas asked me, looking at my pin-cushioned hand. Before I could even answer, he started pulling the spines out of my hand one by one. I knew he was just being kind, but that hurt even more.

"Sorry," he said as I watched the little drops of blood bloom on my palms.

"Not your fault," I eked out.

I tried to cheer Ernie up by telling him we were on a grand adventure. The midday sun made everything shimmer; the earth was carved into these deep orange slabs of raw stone. These rocks had so many stories to share with us, I told Ernie. They'd been here through rain, fog, sleet, and hail. Through eons, epochs, lifetimes. They'd seen Native American celebrations, crusades and revolutions, first kisses and dying wishes.

I wondered how many people had walked this path or breathed in this air or even seen this stretch of horizon. Had the Apaches and the Yavapai tribes really coexisted here? (I had tried once to do a report for school about the Native American homelands and gotten a stern warning from my teacher "never to pull a stunt like that again.")

"Vali, please," Ernie moaned, breaking my reverie. "I need to stop for a sec."

"In a little bit," I told him. "We need to keep going." The longer we were in the desert, the easier it was for us to either get captured or become too dehydrated to move.

"Pleeeease," Ernie moaned. "I don't feel good."

His grunts and groans were coming from someplace rooted

248

inside. An ache so full and fierce, he couldn't even tell me where exactly it hurt. Whether it was the cactus I'd fed him or the endless walking, the sleepless nights or the leap from the train—this was all my fault. He was clearly getting weaker and weaker, and I had no idea how to help him. I tried to pretend he was just part of the soundscape—a bird chirping or a jackrabbit dodging through the brush. Not my little brother falling apart.

"Vali, please!"

"You're okay. You're okay," I kept telling him. It sounded like I didn't care, but that was because his agony was rattling me. The sky was getting dimmer and dimmer. Passing through whatever dusty colors were left for a sunset, sinking into a thick, dismal night. I kept lurching forward, hoping to outrun the dark, though I knew it was impossible. We didn't even know what we were running toward.

"Ernie!" Malakas screamed.

I spun around just in time to watch him crash to the ground, limp. His face was cavernous and pale.

"Ernie!" He wasn't moving. "C'mon, Ernie! Wake up!" When I tugged on his arm, it just flailed like wet yarn. "Ernie!"

I dropped to my knees and started touching his face, his neck, his shoulders, arms, legs. There was no blood as far as I could tell. But his skin was so hot and brittle. His face too still. I ran my hands over his thin frame until I located a tiny lump of pulse just under his ear. It was racing. He was unconscious, but still alive.

"Ernie!" I pleaded into his ear, shaking him by the shoulders.

I didn't want to. I just needed to knock all the missing pieces back together or wake him up or something. I was screaming and crying and demanding that he answer me now. He didn't have to do anything or go anywhere. He just had to open his eyes and let me know he was still here. "Ernie, wake up!"

Malakas searched the area and found another tuft of cactus, chopping it off at the bottom. I ripped into a leaf, feeling the pins tearing through my hands again. Digging my fingers into the top of the pad and peeling back the tough flesh to get to the juice. Squeezing Ernie's cheeks together, I got his lips open just enough to dribble some of the liquid into his mouth.

"Please," I said. "Just a little. Now swallow."

His back arched, and he started gagging. I rolled him onto his side so he wouldn't choke as he retched into the ground.

"Okay, okay." I wept, horrified but also relieved. My little brother's body was fighting so hard to stay alive. Its valves opening and shutting, his lungs pushing out carbon dioxide so he could gasp in some sips of new air. I even imagined his hot saliva pouring into the ground like magical molten lava. Splitting open the earth and forging a tunnel for us to climb through to someplace hidden and safe.

"It's okay," I told him, though clearly, it was not. "I got you. It's okay." I could feel the heat in his skin throbbing. His eyes opened and started roaming, searching. Like they were still running for someplace to call home.

"Vali, I can't . . ." he started to tell me. Then he stopped to vomit a little more.

"All right." I stroked his sweaty forehead. "You're okay." It felt cruel to be feeding him these lies. Every time I tried, he spat them back out onto the ground. I tried to just focus on Ernie's realness, his tiny, smooth nose and sprigs of eyelash. I loved him so much it hurt. The fear of losing him too was knocking on my rib cage until I shook.

"I'm sorry," I told him.

"It's okay," he whispered. His face was just inches from mine, yet his voice sounded so far away. His pupils were dilated; his lips, ashen.

"We need to find a place to rest," I told Malakas. He looked beyond exhausted and nodded in agreement.

I didn't want to stop, but it was clear we couldn't go any farther with Ernie as sick as he was. I didn't know where we were at this point or whether there was DF surrounding us, just waiting to attack. If they wanted to take us, they could have at us.

The only thing we could find that counted as some sort of shelter was a tangle of withered bushes. I carried Ernie over to it, and Malakas tucked him into a foil blanket. There was just enough room under the bush for Ernie to extend his full body with his head on my lap and his feet on Malakas's. We sat on either side of him, keeping guard. It barely felt like protection, but it would do for the night.

"You're okay," I kept telling my little brother. "You're going to get some sleep and feel a lot better in the morning."

His head was so hot now, he had to be feverish. I sucked in

some deep breaths and counted out loud. Trying to get Ernie to match his inhales and exhales to my voice. He was miserable, though, moaning and writhing. I put one of my filthy T-shirts under his head, as if that could help cushion his hurt. I tried to give him something hopeful to focus on.

"And then we're going to get to California and then . . ."

"And . . . then . . . what?" he mumbled. As if I was telling him a fairy tale, which most likely, I was.

"And then . . . and then we'll figure out where Mami is, and we'll all play fútbol together," I told him. Because he deserved every wonderful possibility, even if they were so far out of reach.

"Soccer," I heard him mumble as he spat up again.

"You're a good sister," Malakas told me.

"Yeah, right," I said bitterly.

I had to turn away now, my eyes pooling with tears. I wanted so badly to tell Malakas how scared and paralyzed I felt, but I couldn't even put it into words. I was terrified that if I did name all my ferocious fears, they would only get stronger. All I could really do was keep breathing, willing Ernie to do the same. There were so many voices in my head arguing for my attention. Screaming at me that I had to get us out of here.

But how? I asked the night sky. *Please don't let Ernie die. Please.*

The night didn't answer me. It couldn't make any promises. I heard a lonesome-sounding yowl in the distance and something slithering along the ground.

Este niño hermoso no quiere dormir...

I sang—both to help Ernie to sleep and to blot out this horrible night.

Cierra los ojitos y los vuelva abrir...

I tried to imagine Mami singing with me, through me. My tongue was so dry by now that it scraped against the insides of my teeth, but I kept on singing. It was movement and breath and sound.

Cierra los ojitos y vera que calma...

And slowly, painfully, Ernie's panting eased. His pulse grew steadier as he released into sleep.

CHAPTER 24

"You can do this," I told my little brother later that night. He was shivering under his drenched foil blanket, his own chattering teeth waking him up from a fevered dream. It didn't matter whether this was heat exhaustion or bad cactus; I just had to find a way to get fluids into him and cool him down. Watching him struggle like this was terrifying, but I couldn't let him hear the tremor in my voice.

"You have to," I repeated. "Because you are still alive, and I am still alive, and somewhere out there, Mami is still alive, waiting for us to find her and take her to California. You hear me?"

The heat was unbearable in our makeshift shelter. I took our flashlight and scuttled out of our hideout just far enough to find another stem of that thick cactus. I hacked at two giant leaf pads and brought them back to the bushes. Just that little trip left me breathless and dizzy. My skin was so itchy and tight, covered in a film of salt from all my dried sweat. Even my eyelids were cracking.

"Okay," I told Ernie. "Slowly now." Malakas helped me strip the leaves and squeeze the plant's juice onto Ernie's lips.

"Swallow," I instructed. I fed him some of the leaf's meat too, watching him chew and making sure it didn't come back up. I listened to his breath move in and out of his lungs. Felt his hot skin and tried to just appreciate and hold on to his aliveness. As he drifted back to sleep, I broke up the rest of the leaf into little chunks for Malakas and myself. It was actually kind of tasty—sticky but cool.

Still, I felt nauseous thinking about all the pain and loss I'd put Ernie through—Mami being pinned down in the bus station, Tomas drowning in that lake, Volcanoman being lifted into the air. Most of all, I felt racked with guilt thinking of him rubbing his cheeks to make them rosy for Mami. For the slimmest of hopes that we could find her and rescue her and flee together.

"Hey," Malakas said. "What are you thinking about?"

"I just . . . nothing. We need to find some more water," I told him.

I leaned out of the bushes with the binoculars and searched on the ground in front of me. As if the rocks or tree roots could give us some sort of sustenance. The sky was shifting from a cool navy to grayish pink. We'd made it to face another day. But all I saw ahead were unending stretches of dry dirt.

"I don't know what to do," I admitted.

"Let me try," Malakas offered.

He took the binoculars and ducked out. I saw him slink from one clutch of stubby trees to the next. Pulling through roots and sniffing at berries. Then he went down to a small rocky slope and I wanted to shout at him to stop and turn around, but my mouth was too dry to yell.

"It's okay," I told my sleeping brother. I knew I was actually saying it to convince myself. To shut out the jumble of emotions as I watched Malakas disappear. He wasn't gone, though. He couldn't be. The fear of being abandoned again walloped me so hard. I felt huge sobs racking and rocking me, pulling me apart and emptying me out. I couldn't even count how many losses I was mourning now—Mami, Papi, Kenna, Volcanoman, Rosa, Tomas. And what was the baby's name?

"Guadalupe," I whispered to myself, burying my head into Ernie's side. Feeling so lost and undone.

"Hey!" I heard Malakas whisper behind me. I must have cried myself into some sort of sleep. Honestly, I thought I was hallucinating, even as I felt his hand on my shoulder. "Vali, look!"

Maybe it *was* a hallucination. The most glorious, miraculous, life-sustaining vision of all time. Malakas had come back to our hideout with two gallon jugs of water and a big bag of trail mix.

"What the—"

"Can you believe this? C'mere!" He opened one of the jugs

256

of water and brought it to my lips. It was a little salty, and hot, but it was water! With the other jug, Malakas wet one of his hands and pressed it onto the back of my neck. The tingle of moisture made my whole body flush.

"How did you . . . Who . . . ?"

"There was a campsite with a fire pit. Nobody was there. Just two empty tents and some tire tracks."

"Someone could have seen you."

"Nah, we're good. I promise." Malakas dribbled some water into Ernie's mouth, and I watched as my brother blinked awake.

"Vali?" he rasped. His skin still felt overheated, but not as trembly. His eyes were steadier as he locked on mine.

"When are we gonna play soccer with Mami?" he asked.

"Fútbol," I told him. I saw the hint of a smile pass his lips and exhaled fully for the first time in hours.

Once Ernie had gulped down some more water and closed his eyes again, Malakas and I sat down with that bag of trail mix. At first, I was just shoveling the salty-sweet pieces into my mouth and chomping as fast as I could. But then I noticed Malakas gazing at an almond in his palm. rolling it over his dusty skin as if it was a rare diamond.

I remembered Mami saying the first time she put an almond in her mouth in the United States, she tucked it into her cheek for hours because she didn't want to miss out on any of its flavor. I was too starving and impatient to do that now, but I did reach into the bag and pull out another, marveling at its smooth skin and chewing it slowly until it turned into a delicious paste.

I couldn't remember the last real meal I'd had. Was it that manicotti at Sister Lottie's? By my calculations, Ernie and I had been running, walking, foraging, fleeing for more than a month now. And so far, this felt like one of the few moments when I could stop and see how far we'd come.

"Vali," said Malakas, "we gotta be close to California, right? I mean, it feels like this desert has to end soon."

The heat was closing in on us again. Malakas laid our backpacks over the strongest-looking branches of our shelter so we could get some sort of shade while we ate and scrunched together inside.

"I don't mean to make it more cramped in here," he apologized.

"No, I like it!" I blurted. My neck flushed with embarrassment. "I mean, thank you. I like . . . having you here."

"I like having *you* here," he said.

I dove into his chest for a long hug. I didn't even think about it; I just did it. Even though it was so stifling, and I knew I was being kind of forward, there wasn't time or space to worry about any of that anymore. At least Kenna would be proud of me. She always said I needed to be bolder and louder and that life was too short for shyness. I felt another sob catching in my throat as I pictured that last time I saw Kenna, charging up the hill away from Uncle Jimi's.

"What?" Malakas asked.

"I just don't understand . . . I don't understand how we're here and so many people are gone."

"I know." He sighed. "I used to be all about making plans for the future. Mapping the stars and dreaming about going to college. I imagined myself working at this research lab and making enough money that my lola could retire. I even told her to pick out her favorite wallpaper because I was gonna get her an apartment and she could decorate it however she wanted. I thought the chip would always protect me." He sort of scoffed at his own idea. "So stupid."

"No, it's not stupid . . ." I said. "I mean, I didn't even have a plan. My mami warned me all the time that we had to be careful and take care of each other. But I always just expected her to be there. And now . . ."

Malakas tucked his chin over my head.

"Yeah," he said. "I know . . ."

CHAPTER 25

We stayed in that scraggly hideout for three days and two nights. Or maybe it was three nights and two days. I didn't even try to measure time in sunrises and sunsets anymore. All that mattered to me was doling out enough water for each of us to stay alive and checking that Ernie's forehead was getting cooler.

When he regained enough strength to sit up, the first thing he asked was "Are there any more snacks?"

I laughed and cried and snotted all over myself when he said that. My little brother was back. I was so grateful to have him alive and talking in complete sentences, I squeezed him until he begged me to "chill out."

Malakas was wiping away tears too. He handed Ernie the rest of the trail mix and told him it was good to see him again.

"Where are we?" Ernie asked.

I explained as much as I could. Even with the map, the binoculars, and the compass, I couldn't tell where we were with certainty.

"If we're reading it right, I'd say about fifty miles to California."

"Fifty? That's awesome!" said Ernie. "Let's go!"

"Slow down, little man," Malakas said, making him drink some more water. "Let's give you a little more time."

We both agreed it would be better to wait in these bushes until dark to venture any closer. The heat was too vicious now for running, and hopefully nightfall would make us less visible. As the sun dipped and twilight set in, I felt Ernie's head for about the hundredth time.

"You sure you're ready?"

"Yep," he said.

We checked and rechecked our route and supplies. I wanted to get out of this place so badly, but at the same time, I was crippled with unknowing. Looking out of our shelter and up at that star-dappled sky, I felt an electricity and finality to this night. We were too close to do anything except push ahead.

How do we know when to leave? I had asked Mami. We were hiding in our Southboro apartment at the time, and I couldn't imagine life getting any worse.

No sé, she'd answered. *We just know when it is too dangerous to stay.*

That felt like a lifetime ago now, and yet it was still true. This was what Mami had been preparing us for all along. This was our last chance to find passage to California.

I was so busy gazing up and steeling my nerves for our next move that I didn't even pick up on the more immediate threat coming toward us on the ground.

I did feel Malakas's hand squeezing mine, though, as he muttered, "Oh shit."

"What?"

What started out as just a pin-sized light was getting bigger and brighter as it zoomed toward us. Within moments it took shape as a headlight on some sort of moped-looking thing with a figure hunched over the handlebars.

That's all I knew.

That's all I needed to know.

I shoved Ernie down so he was wedged tight under the branches again. Then I crawled out and picked up two hefty-looking rocks.

Malakas was out and on his feet now too. "Wait. Vali, what are you doing?"

I didn't try to answer him. I just handed him one of the rocks and pulled him into another knot of dried-out shrubs where we could hide.

"Where are you guys?" squeaked Ernie behind us.

"Shhh!" I whisper-shouted. I couldn't let Ernie or Malakas hear the panic burning inside me or try to talk me out of this half-baked scheme. "Just—don't let him get too close," I told Malakas.

I felt the headlight getting nearer, hotter. I heard the electric motor stuttering to a stop. The crunch of twigs underfoot.

I saw a shadow cutting through the headlight's beam, getting taller and wider.

I peeked through two branches and saw the moped's driver, just standing there, his back to us. His yellow DF letters so close now I could almost see the stitching. He took off his helmet and shook out his shaggy hair. Then he pulled out a pack of cigarettes from one of his pockets and lit up.

He was pretty short and scrawny. Or at least, that's what I told myself so I couldn't talk myself out of this plan. I didn't want to hurt this man; I really didn't. But I also couldn't let us get caught. So I did the only thing I could think of in that hot, hideous moment. I gripped the rock in my hand as tight as I could, lunged out from our hiding spot, and slammed the rock into the side of the officer's head. Not hard enough to kill him, I hoped. The sound of the impact was horrible, though. A dull cracking noise that jolted through me.

The officer toppled over and Malakas dashed out with his rope, binding his arms and legs together as I checked for his pulse. He was still alive. With a nasty cut along his forehead, but nothing fatal.

"Why did you do that to him?" asked Ernie, running up beside me.

"He's okay. Or . . . he will be," I told him. "We're too close now. We gotta do whatever it takes." I kissed my little brother's head, trying not to cry.

The officer was an older guy. He had a silver chain around his neck with a crucifix that reminded me of my mami's. The guilt and horror of what I'd just done was pressing in on my lungs as I stood there now. I felt wobbly.

"You okay?" asked Malakas.

"Yeah, I guess so."

"You did the right thing," he assured me.

Malakas picked up the officer's helmet and put it on my head. Then he opened the officer's backpack. Inside was a phone, a key fob, a handgun, and a gray DF T-shirt.

Seeing that shirt made it all real—his humanness measured against mine. I felt the man's pulse again. He was definitely out cold, but his breaths were coming faster. It was just a matter of time before he started to wake up and yell for help, so I had to gag him too. With his own shirt.

The officer's phone started buzzing and flashing.

Status update? a computerized voice asked. When we didn't respond, the phone repeated, *Officer. Status update!*

"We gotta get the hell out of here," Malakas said, taking the words out of my mouth. He packed up the officer's things and handed me his key fob.

"C'mon, Ernie. Let's go," I said.

"But . . . we're just gonna leave him here?" Ernie asked.

"We have to," said Malakas.

Ernie reached into my backpack and got out the last of our water. "He can have mine," he said, putting the water in the man's lap. I didn't know how he would be able to drink it, but I hugged Ernie hard and kissed his salty, chapped cheeks.

"That's a great idea, Ernie."

The three of us got on the moped with me in the driver's seat. Ernie wrapped his arms around me, and Malakas gripped on to Ernie. The engine started up easily. There was even a GPS map on the dashboard. As the display lit up, I clapped my hands with glee. The location dot came alive and started skimming forward.

"Whoa! Cool!" Ernie said in awe.

We were definitely in the Sonoran Desert. According to this GPS, we were more like eighty miles northeast of the border between Arizona and California, and we now had just a few hours before it would be dawn.

"Everybody, hold on!" I warned, pressing on the pedals.

It was treacherous on these roads—if we could even call them roads. Sometimes we were hobbling over broken boulders and craters. Other times we swerved into sandbanks. The moped's display map didn't tell us what we were headed toward in terms of terrain. I could barely make out the names of the towns we were passing through. I just gunned the motor and tried to shake off all the dirt and flies pummeling my face.

"You guys okay?" I screamed into the wind.

But even if Ernie or Malakas heard me, there was no time for them to respond. As we sped around another crest of red rock, I saw a figure in the distance, struggling to put up a tent in the blowing sand. It was a gray tent.

A DF checkpoint.

"No, no, no," I said over and over. In the split second before we got there, I thought of aiming the steering wheel straight at those lopsided tentpoles and taking the whole thing down. But we'd already been spotted. The officer dropped her tent and held up her rifle.

"Hold up!" she shouted. I pressed on the brakes and came to a slow stop in front of her. The two of us face-to-face.

The craziest part was that she was probably only a few months older than me, if that. She looked like that girl Maddie Fitz from Morrow Magnet High School, with the freckles and confident posture of someone who knows they belong. What had Maddie said with that smug look of hers?

Um, sad for who?

This officer was wearing her DF pants rolled up to the knees. I could see in our headlight that she had those red lace-up sneakers with the snaps on top that all the Morrow girls liked too. She was snapping bubble gum in her mouth. We had made it so far; we had fought so hard, and now it was all going to end with this girl who probably moaned about calculus homework just like me?

It was unbelievable. There was nothing distinguishing the two of us except where we were born. Through no fault or choice of our own, she was somehow the hunter and I was the prey.

She pressed her lips together, still pointing the rifle at us. Then she pulled out a flashlight and ran it over my body, looking me up and down in slow motion. I saw her take in my lopsided helmet and bloodstained clothes. The silence was excruciating as her eyes blazed through me. Ernie was shaking uncontrollably, his fingers squeezing my rib cage so tight I thought I would crack. And was that Malakas I heard breathing through his nostrils, trying to control the sheer terror of this moment?

Wordlessly, I stuck out my right wrist. I could feel the rustle of Ernie and Malakas doing the same thing behind me. I wanted to scream, *Ernie, go straight! Don't look back! Whatever happens to me and Malakas, we'll catch up to you in California!*

The officer looked horrified, even a little sick.

I looked down at my wrist to see what she was gaping at. The shred of shirt that Malakas had used for my bandage was once a light blue, but now it was covered in clouds of dried blood. There were fierce red streaks climbing up my arm from the wound site, weaving in and out of a huge yellow-green bruise.

She squinted at me, then back down at my wrist. Maybe it wasn't horror so much as pity that I saw in her eyes. "Name?" she asked.

"Um . . ."

There was no point in giving her a fake name anymore. I had no chip to either prove it true or false. So I told her who I was.

"Valentina González Ramirez. July twenty-second, two thousand sixteen."

"July what?" the girl said with a furrowed brow.

"Twenty-second."

"I'm the twenty-third," she said.

One day apart, but a lifetime of differences. She kept looking at me and taking deep breaths, her lower lip quivering. She lowered her rifle. Her freckles seemed to sag now as she whispered . . .

"Go."

I blinked at her. I couldn't process what she had just said. My mind didn't know what to do. Ernie was the one who had to snap me back into reality.

He whispered in my ear, "Vali, go. Go! Go! GO!"

I pressed on the throttle and we hurtled forward.

I didn't know why she'd let us go. I was half convinced that it was a hallucination. Except I could hear Ernie crying behind me, clinging to me and drenching my back with his tears. And now I was sobbing too. We all were. The rocks and sand sticking to our wet faces as we raced toward California again, twisting and veering through that desert wasteland for those last forty miles.

✖

WHEN THE DAWN started seeping in, the first thing I saw on the horizon was a single palm tree swaying far off in the distance. Its fronds were so long and spindly.

"Ernie! Malakas!" I laughed. "Look!"

I thought of Mami calling Ernie *Ernesto Palmero*. I remembered Papi lifting me over my head so I could touch the palm tree's scratchy coconut shells.

"How far now?" Ernie called.

The moped's screen said we were up in Yuma County, Arizona, with just a few miles to go. I pulled us over to get a better view. We all got off the bike, and Malakas took out the binoculars.

"What do you see?" Ernie asked. Malakas wouldn't answer.

"Are there a ton of checkpoints?" I added.

"No," he said. "There's some sort of . . . construction."

He handed me the binoculars, and I peered through. There were searchlights and camera poles looming, hydraulic lifts rising and stacking asphalt blocks. One on top of the other on top of the other.

"What is that?" Ernie asked.

It couldn't be the Great American Wall. This barrier wasn't five layers thick with steel and electrified fencing, tilted angles, and perched lasers. This thing was still under construction. With rows of gray trucks and bulldozers below, and cranes still lifting new sheets of metal to the top rung of scaffolding. The glaring fluorescent lights doused the whole mess in a skim-milk blue.

"It must be the new wall they're building around California."

The President had warned us. He was going to wall off California from the rest of the United States and anyone trying to get through would be subject to martial law.

Malakas took the binoculars back. "Holy shit, you're right," he said. "How the fuck do we get past it?"

269

"I dunno. Look."

Even without the binoculars now I could see clusters of small aircraft and drones up ahead in the lavender sky. Some of them were as small as birds. Others looked like they were probably the size of our moped, with metal pincers on the bottom. They danced around each other like some sort of drunken constellation. I tried to decipher if there was some pattern to their movements as they swelled in a buzzing, billowing hive.

"What are the drones doing?" Ernie asked. We watched as they dove toward the ground, depositing little cylinders into a line just a little way west of us.

"I don't know," Malakas responded. "But I'm scared it has to do with those." He pointed to the moped's screen. Every time a drone deposited something onto the ground, a red dot appeared on the display map.

We watched another red dot appear. And another.

"We gotta hide. In case the DF shows up," I said. We got back on the moped, and I drove just far enough to find another mass of big rocks we could crouch behind. Malakas put the foil blankets over us so our body heat couldn't be detected. I had no idea whether that would protect us or not anymore. We stayed there, passing those binoculars back and forth and sneaking out to watch for brief blips of time. Desperate to figure out what those drones were depositing and how we could get past them. Those red dots kept multiplying on the moped's screen, though. Malakas was right: every time a drone deposited something on the ground, another red dot blinked awake. As the sun got stronger and higher in the sky, we watched that sea of red take over almost the entire map.

Until we heard an explosion.

"What was that?" Ernie quivered in my arms.

"I don't know," I told him.

Malakas had the binoculars and was searching around the side of the rocks to make sense of it all.

"It looks like one of the drones dropped something that . . . exploded?"

I took the binoculars and saw a DF truck doused in flames. There were figures running around trying to put it out with fire extinguishers.

"Land mines?" I took a horrified guess. I flashed to that girl in the Mickey Mouse shirt, crossing the demilitarized zone and getting snuffed out in a blast of bright red. It was just barbaric and unthinkable enough to be true.

Ernie took the binoculars from me. "But then how can we . . . ?"

The three of us studied the moped's map again. One of the red dots had a black X through it now. I zoomed in to see if the screen could tell us more. It had only one answer for us now. It was a cool blue ribbon running up through Yuma County, labeled Colorado River.

It had no red dots in it.

It is the miracle, water, Mami had said.

"That's it!" My skin prickled in goose bumps even though I was sweating from the oppressive heat. "That's it! That's it!" I was shrieking now. Laughing. Crying. Pointing at that blue line with tears streaming down my face.

"That's where we can get across! In the water!"

CHAPTER 26

"Faster!" squealed Ernie.

"Slower!" urged Malakas.

I wanted so badly to steer us full throttle to the river's edge, but according to those red dots on our screen, we were heading straight toward a barrage of land mines. I thought of that girl with the Mickey Mouse shirt again. It had only taken her one misstep to be obliterated. Her face so serene as she walked.

Could she have known there were land mines underneath her?

Would she have stepped forward anyway?

I tried to weave the moped slowly, carefully. But I kept stopping and starting, lurching in and out of scrub and shadows. The three of us together were too heavy for this kind of riding; we kept listing to one side and almost tipped over several times. Tipping over had to be avoided at all costs, though. In this situation, it would be certain death.

At one point, I got so close to one of the red dots that I had to come to a complete stop. My heart was thrumming so loudly, I couldn't accelerate. I completely froze. My mind was screaming all kinds of orders, but my body refused to move. It wasn't until Ernie rubbed my back and whispered in my ear, "You got this, Vali," that my fingers began to move again. My breath started slowing down; my brain scrambled to refocus on getting us to the water.

"I'm okay. I'm okay," I repeated to Ernie and to myself.

The red dots began to cluster more and more. Driving was now becoming impossible, but we couldn't ditch the moped, because we needed the screen to guide us through this maze of land mines. We had no other choice but to walk the moped. Malakas and Ernie walked behind me, being careful to only step on the tires' tread marks in the dirt.

It was harrowing to go at this snail's pace. We were so vulnerable and exposed as we stumbled along. There was really nothing to cover or hide us anymore. I heard sirens cutting through the dry air now. The DF were racing toward us. Whether they'd found our tied-up officer in the desert or were tipped off by the woman who'd taken pity on us at that last checkpoint, we'd never know. It didn't matter anyway. As we got closer to the water, I could see the officers jumping out of their cars. At least they had to stop and start too, in order to avoid the land mines.

"Vali, watch out!" Malakas cried.

I was entirely focused on the screen on the moped and navigating us through the land mines. But now there were nets being dropped from up above. Pincers lowering a cylinder just a few yards ahead. Malakas pulled out our silver blankets again. This was our only weapon against the grotesque drones. If they couldn't detect our body heat, they couldn't trap us in their nets.

For a brief second, I glanced away from the road in front of me and saw a broadleaf plant just ahead of us, in the distance. Just like Mami had told us about back in Southboro. It was sucking the liquid from whatever source was closest. Finding a way to survive. We all needed that water to survive.

"We're almost there! We gotta hurry!"

There were three red dots between us and that blue line of water, between life and death.

I gaped at that moped's screen for one last time to commit it to memory. There was no way to bring the bike any farther. The DF mopeds behind us were getting louder and closer, sputtering and coughing up dust as they came bearing down on us. The buzz of the drones was inside my skin, catapulting me forward. Suddenly there was a loud bang. I knew the sound perfectly well by now. A bullet whizzed by my ear.

There was no more time to wait or strategize. There was nothing left except this moment.

This glorious moment when my foot sank into the wet sand and the three of us jumped into that river.

CHAPTER 27

It took five hundred eighty-three strokes for us to get across. Five hundred eighty-three—I know that for sure because I was counting with Ernie. Urging him to breathe and duck under the water's filmy surface. The gunshots were deafening, skimming the river's surface just a few feet from us. I pushed Ernie under the water and dove down to hold on to him. Flooding my mouth, my nose, my mind with this cool murkiness. When we came up for air again, the sky was swarming with drones. Some of them swooped so close now, I could see their blades whirring. They were dropping more of those metal nets that had taken Volcanoman, Rosa, Tomas, and Guadalupe.

But they would not take us too.

"How much farther?" Ernie gasped.

"You got this, little man," replied Malakas.

Ernie and I were not great swimmers. Vermont was not exactly the place to learn. But Malakas was sure and smooth, scooping out palmfuls of water and pulling Ernie along when he couldn't lift his arms anymore. Whether or not I had the skills to stay afloat, I felt like there was a greater current moving me forward. Maybe connected to the sun and moon or the magical weightlessness of everything floating, gliding, compelling us forward. Definitely connected to Mami and Papi and the girl in the Mickey Mouse T-shirt. Because we were all woven from the same thread. Braided together in an intricate pattern. It was only on land that humans could draw all these boundaries and build these gigantic walls.

"Vali, I'm scared!" cried Ernie. He was splashing a lot now, flailing.

"It's okay. It's okay." I grasped at whatever soccer lingo I could remember. "It's just like a breakaway," I told him. "Watch the goal. Charge ahead."

We swam back under again, wriggling through a maze of seaweed and brackish sludge. When we bobbed back up, there was a crowd of people gathering on the California side. A mad rush of bodies tearing into the water, yelling.

¡Tú puedes!

You're almost here!

"Go! Go! Swim faster!" Malakas screamed. He held Ernie by the ribs and told us both to suck in a deep breath. Then he counted to three, and we dove underwater as one. Forcing our bodies to tunnel down, down, down.

The voices and gunfire faded behind us.

The rage and fury melted into a warbly hum.

There was only the burbling sound of this amazing underwater universe now. This other existence where everything and everyone was suspended and free.

The fish swam in every direction, slipping in and out of the algae in their own natural rhythm. Basking in a watery beam of sunlight and then dipping into another pocket of darkness. I knew they had some sort of pecking order on the food chain, but at least it was based on primal urges and hungers. Not hatred and indoctrination. For them, the world was always moving, shifting, changing. Everything evolving, dazzling, and alive.

I remembered Mami telling me and Ernie the story of Genesis. The waters being here before even the earth or the sky. We were each born in a sac of water, she told us. We were made of water. I pictured Papi lifting me onto his shoulder at the beach, treading water below me as I stood on that rock ledge. I felt like they were both with us now. Holding us and guiding us. Washing away everything and everyone chasing us.

✖

I HAD JUST reached my palm forward for the five hundred and eighty-third time when I felt something soft and silty underfoot.

California.

Malakas was holding my hand. Pulling me back up. Ernie was being lifted out of the water—gasping, crying.

We were on the other side.

Call it a miracle. Call it a prayer answered. Call it the fight-or-flight rush of adrenaline that gives all creatures the chance to survive.

I call it

Sanctuary.

CHAPTER 28

This is not a dream.

I am here. Ernie is here. Malakas too.

The rescue team is wrapping huge blankets around us that smell like fabric softener. I'm bundled up in a girl's comforter that has pictures on it of some cartoon princess in a pink tutu and sparkly crown. Ernie is tucked into a navy blanket with pictures of rockets. Malakas gets brown and green stripes.

They bring us into a little shed and give us mugs of hot chocolate and crackers that crumble in our trembling fingers. There are so many different faces coming into the room, staring at us. So many sounds and smells, smiles and furrowed brows. Ernie is beaming, though. Malakas is telling everyone how brave my little brother is and how far he swam, how valiantly he fought.

They ask us questions in Spanish, English, Creole, Portuguese. They ask *Who? What? Where?* But not *Why?*

No one can really answer that.

✖

I tell them what I know. Or what I think I know. The words fly out of my mouth in no coherent order. I have so many things to say, and I don't know where to start.

"The DF took our mami. We were on a bus. Then we were in a truck and in the desert. They came to the house, and we all ran, but this little boy, Tomas . . . he didn't make it."

I know I'm not making any sense. I can't stop myself, though. I just spill out any detail I can latch on to as it comes to my lips.

"We wanted to get to California. Our Tía Luna lives here. But we don't know where they took Mami or Volcanoman, or Rosa and her babies." These threads of memory keep unraveling. I am unraveling. "Please help us find them." My eyes well with tears. I can't stop them. I don't want to stop them.

They promise me they will do their best to find our mami. They swear that we are safe and protected by the country of California now.

✖

THE CHILD REFUGEE Service League is here. They want to take us to a group home in San Bernardino, where we can bathe and sleep, but again I tell them that my Tía Luna lives close by. I'm not sure where, really. One of the counselors from the League gives me a phone to call her. I try all these different numbers until I remember them in the right order. Then, I hear Tía Luna's voice shrieking through the telephone:

"¡Vali! ¡Ernesto! ¡Mis amores! ¡Ya voy por ustedes!"

We are in a town just outside of Bond, California, which is east of Joshua Tree National Park. That means Tía Luna will have to drive an hour and a half to come get us. Malakas has to go to the group home, though. He doesn't have any relatives here. I don't want him to go, but he assures me it's okay; we will see each other soon.

"How soon?"

"Soon, soon," he says. "Call you later?"

"Sure," I answer.

Because that's what people do when they know or at least trust that there is such a thing as *later*.

But I don't know how to trust yet. I keep shaking as I sip my hot cocoa. I keep crying for all the people who didn't make it across the Colorado River with us. I keep feeling the water flooding my nose, my throat, my brain.

✖

TÍA LUNA IS here now. Her hair is so much shorter and spikier than I remember it. Her eyes are desperate and bloodshot as she rushes at us. I collapse into her arms with Ernie, the three of us sobbing and holding each other. There are so many things I want to say, but none of them mean anything now. I keep clamping on to Tía Luna tighter and tighter, trying to seal myself inside her shuddery breath. We are in her arms for so long, I feel like I may have melted into unconsciousness. Only this is not a dream. This is real.

We get into her silver hatchback. She opens the front door for me to sit in the passenger seat, but I'm scared of leaving Ernie alone in the back. Or maybe I just don't know how to sit still without holding him, so I get in the back seat too. We squeeze together in our blankets and let the wind from the open window smack us in the face.

Tía Luna looks and sounds so much like Mami, with her fast Spanish patter. Only, her eyes don't crinkle in the corners like Mami's and her fingernails are too clean. She's petite and bouncy, and she doesn't smell like onions. I know it's not her fault. It makes me miss Mami more, though. I can't find any words to say. There are just too many feelings rushing through me. The sunlight is so bright here it's blinding.

Tía Luna's home is nice enough. It's a one-room guest-house in someone else's backyard with a screen door that slaps against the frame so loud, I shiver. Ernie is already asleep by the time we get there, and Tía carries him into the house like a swaddled newborn, laying him on her bed and hovering over him.

I take a shower that feels miraculous—the hot water running down my face, my arms, my stomach. Tía Luna's bar of soap turns a grimy rust color from all the dirt and blood caked on my skin. My wrist throbs and burns. I stay under the spigot until my eyes start to close. Then Tía Luna tells me to take a clean towel and come have some rice and beans she just made.

The food is so warm, I start to cry.

A lot of things here make me cry.

Tía Luna says that's a good thing. That I need to feel it all and tell my story to everyone. Loudly. I don't know how to yet. I feel like I'm walking around with all of my nerve endings exposed. Even a gentle breeze makes me shudder.

I'm amazed by so many things too.

The majestic palm trees stretching their fronds out like ballerinas and the speckled woodpeckers who tap out their own Morse code. Lemons hanging from a tree outside Tía Luna's window like bright ornaments. The taste of a crisp lettuce leaf.

Yes, that is really the last thing I ever thought I'd appreciate. But after Ernie and I both stay in bed for almost twenty-four hours straight, Tía Luna makes us a huge meal of chicken, rice, beans, and salad so fresh, my mouth does somersaults. And then, of course, I start to cry again. Or rather, bawl so hard that I have snot and tears dripping down onto my plate of bright greens.

"I know, mi'ja. I know," whispers Tía Luna.

But how can she know, really?

There are not enough ways to name this aching knot in my throat. I still don't know how to trust that we are safe or even alive. I don't know how to explain that when I see a lettuce leaf, I also see the neon green soccer ball in Tomas's dead hands. I see a thick cactus pad and Ernie vomiting into the dust. Most of all, I see Mami begging me to eat my vegetables. When we lived in Southboro, we could only afford canned corn and the occasional wilted pepper that she bargained for at the farm. But she fried them up or stirred them into eggs so that Ernie and I would get more nutrients, whether we liked it or not. If I didn't eat my vegetables, she said, it would stunt my growth.

Which is a laugh. Because yes, I'm only five foot two, but that already makes me a full inch taller than Mami. Wherever she is.

I describe those tents in the desert to Tía Luna and tell her that however crazy it sounds, I think I saw Mami in one of them. Tía Luna shakes her head and blinks back tears. She tells me what she knows about those tents. She hasn't seen one up close, only pictures via satellite. But they are labor camps, and they are brutal. The President created the camps to have "illegals pay off their debt to America." This means no more deportations. Instead, the DF puts undocumented immigrants in cages and forces them work without pay and with no end in sight.

"What are they working on?"

"Nobody knows. No one's escaped yet, so we can only guess what's going on in there," she tells me.

"We have to help them."

Tía Luna nods and gives me the saddest excuse for a smile.

"We can't do that right now, mi'ja. It's just not safe," she says. "But hopefully . . . one day."

By *we*, I guess she means all the different action committees she's joined. The night after we get to Tía Luna's home, she hosts a meeting full of community organizers. They talk about all the things they want to do to help people in the Other 49—that's what everyone here calls the rest of the United States. All of the people at Tía's meeting are committed and logical about their work, and I'm grateful, but I also want to jump up and down and shout, *We have to DO something! NOW!*

One day is not enough of an action plan. *One day* is like wishing on a star. I don't know how to just sit here and wait for something to change. I feel itchy and impatient listening to all of these organizers pass around snacks and make agendas.

At least physically, I'm doing much better.

On our second day here, Tía Luna brings me and Ernie to the doctor, who gives me antibiotics for my arm because it's slightly infected. The doctor also tells me I'm very lucky I didn't cut into any of the nerves. I want to thank Malakas for that. I track down the number for his group home, and we get to talk that evening.

"How are you doing?" he asks me.

"Good, I guess. You?"

"Same . . ."

I ask him to describe the place where he's living. It's an

old house with bunk beds full of kids in each room. The age range is something like two to twenty-two. Everyone sort of walks around in a daze, wondering when or if they'll ever get reunited with family. They have a makeshift school in the basement where they read from donated textbooks. And a playground with just one swing.

"Wow. That sounds . . ."

Dismal, but I don't say that.

"What about you?" he asks. I tell him about Tía Luna's. About her meetings and plans and the smell of lemons in her backyard.

"I wish I could have you come stay here," I tell him.

It's tiny, though. She only has room for a table, a dresser, and a bed in this guesthouse. And to be honest, I haven't been able to sleep since I got here. I spend most of my nights either staring at the ceiling or pacing the floor because every time I try to close my eyes, I feel like I'm back in that river again. Only this time, instead of making it to shore, I'm gasping, grasping, drowning.

"We'll find a way to meet up soon," Malakas says.

I miss Malakas more than I thought I would. I miss who we were when we had a purpose, when we were fighting for our lives.

I'm not sure who we are to each other anymore.

I want to ask him if he still looks at the moon every night, like his mom taught him to do. I want to know if he's heard anything about his lola or whether he's been in touch with anyone in the Philippines. But I don't ask him any of those things. I'm too scared of touching those memories. Between the two of us, there's so much lost and broken. Woven into our bones and our matching worms of scar tissue. I want to know him in another time or place. Only, we're here now.

Which feels like the most magical, exciting, surreal, confusing place to be.

CHAPTER 29

The country of California is trying to gather information about what exactly is going on in the Other 49. They have created a database with thousands of people's names, telephone numbers, addresses, and personal stories of arrival. It's part of an effort to reunite families who've been torn apart. On our one-week anniversary of coming to California, Tía Luna takes me and Ernie on a four-hour trip to San Diego so we can answer a few questions about our journey and officially become part of the database.

My interviewer is nice enough. She has silky brown hair and ivory skin, an overeager smile and a little bit of a lisp. She tells me her name is Kelly and she just has a few questions to ask to help gather information. It won't hurt a bit.

Only, an hour later, we are still going over my country of origin.

"So, besides being born in Colombia, have you ever been outside the Other 49 before?"

"No."

"And while living in the Other 49, were you ever involved in a court hearing?"

"No."

"Were you ever placed in a detention center?"

"No."

"And, according to your account, you left Vermont on May fourth, which would mean you were traveling for . . . forty-seven days?"

Traveling? More like clawing, grasping, hiding, fleeing.

"Yes."

"Okay, so let's review all the addresses at which you resided, beginning with your arrival date."

"Okay. But what does this have to do with getting my mami back?"

Kelly pauses and bites her lip. I interrupted her flow. She was much happier clicking away at her keyboard than actually facing me and talking.

"I mean, is this . . ."

Necessary? Meaningful? Just an exercise in pretending we're doing something to help the people still trapped in the Other 49 when in fact we're doing nothing?

"I understand you have some questions too," Kelly says. She speaks slowly, and her smile isn't so eager anymore. "I really need to file this information into the Sanctuary database, though. So can we just . . . get back to it?"

"Yeah."

I don't understand what this Sanctuary database is. Her computer screen is pointed away from me, and she could be playing video games or sending emails for all I know. I just feel so useless and unprotected in this little room.

"Great. The first address at which you resided was . . . ?"

It's very sterile in here. Tía Luna told me this used to be a dentist's office. There's a desk and two folding chairs, a small window that doesn't open, and an air vent that puffs out warm, antiseptic-smelling air. The walls are a soft beige, and there are sleek silver filing cabinets lining the wall behind Kelly. There's also a wire bookcase with a few kids' books on them, a Batman figurine still in its plastic packaging, and a thousand-piece jigsaw puzzle that promises to look like a picture of a cat in a teacup. I don't know who would possibly stay here long enough to complete a thousand-piece jigsaw puzzle. This doesn't feel like a place where anyone would choose to linger.

Including Kelly. She's tapping her foot against the leg of her metal desk in a rapid patter. I guess reminding me that she's still waiting for an answer to her most recent question.

"Can you repeat that, please?"

"It's okay. Just skip it, and we'll come back to it later," she says.

"Okay, sorry."

I don't know why I am apologizing. This woman is taking all of this information from me but giving me nothing in return.

I don't want to come back to this later. I want to know who

is gathering these details about my life and who is going to analyze it and how this can ever translate into tracking down all the people still missing. How can my old street addresses stop those drones from scooping people up in nets or unlock those glinting cages in the desert? How can my court records make these drowning dreams go away?

After the interview is over, Tía Luna takes me and Ernie out to dinner at a steakhouse. I know she doesn't have much money and that it's hard for her to spend it on rib eyes and baked potatoes. So, I don't tell her that the smell of even cooked meat makes me think of crouching behind a butchered cow in a truck. Or that every ounce of water she leaves in her glass could save someone crawling across the Sonoran Desert.

When we get back to Tía Luna's in Cactus, I start writing letters to Mami, even though I have no place to send them.

Dear Mami, we made fresh guacamole today!

Dear Mami, we went to a nature preserve, and a bird pooped in my hair!

They are silly updates, just like I used to give to Papi when he was in the detention center and we couldn't say anything more. I hope and pray that Mami is in a detention center like Papi's—with a bathroom, a blanket, or even a lukewarm bowl of soup. Because the alternative is . . .

Those tents.

I make Tía Luna show me the satellite pictures of those tents, and they twist my insides into a fierce knot. There are

292

women, men, children, babies. They are chained together by the neck and being beaten with batons. I want to reach into those tents and pull every one of those prisoners out of there. I want to destroy all of these grainy photographs, erase their possibility. Only now those images are emblazoned on my brain. They are with me when I'm putting on clean socks in the morning, when I'm pouring myself a bowl of cereal, when I'm lying in bed, sandwiched between Ernie and Tía Luna at night. Sinking to the bottom of the Colorado River with me.

Tía Luna sends me and Ernie to school again. It's only five hours a day, and we get to wear whatever we like. Ernie joins the soccer team, of course, and stays out running and dribbling with flushed cheeks until nightfall, which makes me relieved.

I actually find school mildly interesting, but I don't feel like socializing much. I make one friend, named Isabel. She's from Honduras, and she kind of reminds me of Kenna—loud and skinny as a beanpole. When Isabel laughs, her mouth opens big enough to swallow the sun, but she is not Kenna. Kenna is somewhere in that hollow space in my chest. Clutching me with her echoing cries whenever I pause. And Mami is in the sounds of birds chirping outside my window in the morning. Volcanoman could be hiding behind the dumpster outside our school cafeteria . . .

"Am I going crazy? Are you seeing people too?" I ask Malakas one night on the phone. We talk every few days now, which is exciting, but also disorienting. His voice thrusts me back into this feeling of desperation that I'm scared will swallow me whole. But he's also the only one who seems to hear me and soothe me.

"Totally," he confesses. "I swear I saw my lola last week on a bus. I even went up to her and almost gave her a hug."

We both laugh and cry in the same breath.

"What was that about?" Tía Luna asks when I get off the phone.

"Oh . . . nothing." I don't know how to share these feelings with her. I don't think she'd get it even if I tried.

I don't mean to act ungrateful or obnoxious about our new life here. It is pretty amazing, having my tía and my brother and the smell of lemons drifting through 4512 North Alma Street—this place we now call home. Tía Luna has a tiny patch of garden that I love. A bush with big, waxy leaves, and some floppy stems by the front door that have lost whatever flowers they once had. I spend long weekend days gardening. Or, really, just digging.

I don't know what exactly I'm looking for as I kneel down and start pawing through the dirt. The stems pop off quickly, leaving short, stringy roots behind. The branches poke and scratch me as I try to burrow down. I pull out clumps of grass and weeds. Tear open knots of twisty, dry roots. When I hit a rock, I scrape even harder. My fingernails are soon caked in mud and my fingertips are shredding, but I keep going. I just need to feel something sharp or cold or dirty. It's just, I feel like I'm fragmented, displaced. Which I know sounds bizarre since

I've been literally fleeing and homeless for a month and a half. But now everyone expects me to stay here. To be content with this new life.

And I can't.

For July Fourth, Tía Luna helps organize a big gathering of Sanctuary activists at a convention center in Los Angeles. She drives us the four hours there, and we stay at a hotel. She tells me and Ernie that we can stay in and order hamburgers instead of going to the meeting if we want. But I'm curious to hear what they're going to say. Ernie shrugs and adds, "Sure. Why not?"

There is a huge slide presentation about the history of US independence and the different challenges that California faces as a newly forming country. Someone stands behind a podium and reads out all these numbers to us:

Since California seceded two months ago, fifteen thousand undocumented immigrants have crossed safely to Sanctuary. There are thought to be another ten million undocumented immigrants still unaccounted for in the Other 49. They don't know how many people are in the labor camps. Satellite images show ten new tents have been erected in the last two weeks, which could mean thousands of new captives. As far as they know, no one has been able to escape the camps, so the limited information they have hasn't been verified. The President's new wall around California is projected to be completed within the next year. It will be seven layers thick and fortified with 2,258 land mines; Alaska (the forty-ninth state) has chosen to align with the United States, but Hawaii (the fiftieth) has announced that it is in the process of trying to secede.

Everyone in the convention center starts applauding for Hawaii. For "the process of trying." I want to clap too, but it feels so ineffective. I know the hearts of these people are in the right place. They make up chants and slogans, mission statements and action plans. But I'm too raw and jumpy to celebrate any of this. Everyone who gets up to that podium is at least twenty years older than me. None of them have seen what it's actually like in the Other 49. None of them have heard the sky buzzing with drones or tried to bury a boy in front of his mother. Even the statistics they spout sound too simplistic. They don't tell the full story. They don't recognize that one of those numbers could be my mami.

"Pretty exciting, right?" Tía Luna asks as she drives us back to Cactus the next day.

"Yeah. Totally."

I want to do something real, but I don't know what I can do, at least not from here. I turn to Ernie to see what he'll say, but his eyes are at half-mast as he stares out the car window. I try to close my eyes too, but I know I won't be able to sleep. Whenever I do sink into any kind of unconsciousness, images of the river invade my dreams. My legs twitch, my heart clenches, my arms are trying to pull me through those waters again. I see Ernie and Malakas drowning in the darkness. I feel my mami pulling me down into the cold currents, her cries telling me I failed her. I failed Ernie. I failed Papi. I failed myself.

"Close your eyes, mi'ja," says Tía Luna from the driver's seat.

"I don't need to sleep," I tell her.

I need to be awake. I need to open my eyes wider than they've ever been before. I need to find my mami.

Tía nods and doesn't say anything, which is what adults do when they don't understand or believe kids. Only, she has no idea what I'm capable of.

CHAPTER 30

Mami was in my dream last night. It started off like so many other dreams I've had lately . . .

I jump into the Colorado River. The coldness of the water takes my breath away. I try to inhale, but I can't. I look for Ernie and I see him too far away. I try to call his name, but water rushes into my mouth. I see Ernie being chased by a DF officer. I look below, and I see Mami sinking. I swim to her. She's just out of reach. I desperately try to grab on to her fingers, her hair, her anything. But I can't. She keeps slipping away.

And this is where the dream differs from all the others. This time, right before Mami disappears into the murky deep, she turns to me and says, *Go back to the river.*

I wake up sweating and panting. My mind is racing. It's been twenty-eight days since we got to California, and it's been twenty-eight nights of me thrashing in the Colorado River. I am so exhausted and crushed by these dreams that I don't even feel relief when the morning comes anymore. Tía Luna wants me to go back to the doctor and tell her how I feel, maybe even get some medication to help me relax. But I don't need to relax. I need to *do* something.

And now I know what I need to do. I need to go back to the river and see what's there.

I call Malakas and ask him if he can come with me. It's also been twenty-eight days since I've seen him, which feels impossibly long. It will be a three-hour trip for him, but he doesn't even pause before saying yes.

"I promise I'll be back by dinnertime," I tell Ernie. We haven't been apart since we left Southboro, and I feel myself clinging to him as I say goodbye. He nods and waves from the door, but I can tell his face is set in a tight frown to keep from crying.

There's a rideshare that's going east.

"Where ya headed?" the driver asks me. He is an older white man with a salt-and-pepper beard. His eyes are gray too, but kind.

"Bond. Off Route Ten, please," I tell him.

"Mind me asking what's there?" the man asks.

"I'm . . . visiting a friend," I tell him.

Bond really is a nothing town. There's a diner and a convenience store, a few clumps of houses. Malakas and I spot each other by the rescue shed. This is where they first wrapped us in those comforters and told us we were safe and protected by the country of California. Malakas takes me in his arms now and I can tell he's already taller, because my chin only reaches his armpit. I feel my eyes welling up again, a raw tremor blooming inside me. Our bare wrists touch; both are scarred, but healing.

Does yours still hurt? I want to ask. But I cannot break the silence yet.

We walk toward the shoreline, which has a halo of fog just above it. We're heading into fall now, but it's still sweltering, around ninety degrees. Even so, I won't let go of Malakas's sweaty hand. Neither of us have said a word yet. I'm still not sure what to say. I sense how different we are from just a month ago.

We aren't fugitives, fleeing and fighting for our lives.

We aren't starving, dehydrated, or faint from pain.

We aren't pressed together inside a decaying log, crunched so tight, savoring the taste of a single almond.

I want to ask him, *Do you remember when . . . ?* or *Did we really . . . ?* because a lot of times since we arrived, I felt crazy. I'm not sure if my memories of those days we spent together are reliable. They feel so loud and demanding spinning through my brain. And now we're supposed to be on the other side of it all, with no obligations to each other or the world. We have roofs over our heads and food on our plates and the freedom to walk onto this beach to put our feet in the water. We can do what we want, for the most part.

And that doesn't feel right.

Not when there are so many people who are still missing—mothers, fathers, sisters, brothers, lolas, tías. I can't just make up this new life here when Tomas is bobbing in that marsh. When his mother and baby sister are being trapped like wild beasts in a net. I can't memorize algebra rules when people are being stuffed into meat trucks or chained together by the neck. When a girl in a Mickey Mouse T-shirt and ponytail gets blown into bits and Mami is being pinned to the ground, screaming, screaming.

✖

THERE'S A CRUMBLING rock wall where Malakas and I sit and put our things down. We stare out at the rolling waves, and I feel his hand find mine. A jolt of hope runs through me. We are on this precipice together.

"I don't know what it is," I tell him. "I just feel like I'm forever in that water. Like I can't get out of it."

"Hmmm," he says. He doesn't sound concerned, though. More like fascinated. "You know what my favorite thing about the water is?" he asks.

"What?"

"It always looks so random and unpredictable, right? But the moon is kind of directing it."

"You mean because of gravity?" I know vaguely what he's talking about from science classes in school.

"Yeah. The pull is so strong it makes the land swell too. I mean, we don't notice it most of the time because we're spinning and all. But it's happening, all the time. Everything is . . . happening."

Just like right now, someone is probably being beaten outside a cage in the desert. Right now, someone is strapping on his AK-47 or reciting the Pledge of Allegiance. Right now, someone is being born. All of it, continuous.

Malakas is still marveling at the river in front of us. He tells me more about how the moon pulls all the earth's water and the friction it has to overcome. He also winds into stories about the turquoise waters of the Luzon Strait near where he grew up. How the wave crests could get so high, they looked like foamy mountains. Still, he loved it so much. He spent every second he could in the water.

"My papi was like that too," I say. "I swear, he was part fish."

I tell Malakas that after my papi was deported to his death, I refused to go near the water for a long time. I just couldn't bring myself to be on the beach without him there too. But before we got on that plane to Vermont, Mami insisted we go say goodbye to the Pacific Ocean. It was a bright, sunny day, and Ernie was laughing and splashing in a small tidal pool.

Mami saw how troubled I was still. She took my hand and led me to the water, slowly, deliberately. We let the tide roll toward our toes, just tickling the tips of them. The ocean was frigid. I started shaking, overwhelmed by these thick, deep sobs. Because I missed my papi so much, but I also had this powerful sense that he was *part of* the water now. I could feel him rising with each crest. He was flowing with the current, crashing with the spray.

"That's beautiful," says Malakas.

"Thanks," I say. "It's just . . . how I felt."

And as I say those words, I sense it again. Papi is in that water. Mami is too.

I take off my sneakers now and step into the hot sand. Malakas does the same. It's only thirty or so steps to reach the water. I try not to count. I just want to let our feet sink into the rough grains without measuring the distance. As the water glides over our toes, it feels cool, but not cold. The water stretches for miles in so many directions—lapping at the shores of the Other 49, reaching toward the sky when it feels that pull, connecting us to maybe everyone we love.

"Do you . . . think about going back?" I ask.

Malakas chuckles softly. "Hmmm, to which part? The peaceful desert? The romantic views from the train?"

"No, I'm being serious," I tell him.

Maybe it's a gravitational thing, just like the tides being conducted by the moon. But I think it's more primal than that. I think it's the pull of Rosa, Tomas, Guadalupe, Volcanoman. It's the pull of Malakas's lola and my mami and papi. It's us, standing on this patch of land called Sanctuary, knowing we can't be free until they are free too.

"Yeah," Malakas says, squeezing my hand. "I do think about it. A lot."

We look out again at the water rolling in and out.

In and out.

Calling us back.

AUTHORS' NOTES

FROM PAOLA:

The idea for *Sanctuary* came to me during a very dark period of our nation's history. In the spring of 2018, the Trump administration began separating families at our southern border. In response to this horrific and shameful policy, I helped organize marches across the country to end family separation. Hundreds of thousands of people flooded the streets and demanded family separations halted. Our voices were so powerful the administration could not ignore us. Trump was forced to end his hateful policy. Our win was bittersweet. Advocates and activists were left to help families pick up the pieces after heartbreaking reunions. Children were traumatized, as were their parents. The Trump administration didn't stop its relentless pursuit of detainment, deportations, and continued family separations. I personally felt as if I was drowning in despair as I tried to fight back against all the injustices happening to my friends, my neighbors, and my community.

In my despair, I allowed myself to imagine the worst possible future for our country. I brought to life the fears of the thousands of undocumented immigrants I had interviewed over the past decade. I remembered the stories the mothers of the caravan told me as we walked through Mexico trying to reach the United States. I recalled the tears of mothers and fathers who had been deported without their children to countries that hunted them like prey. I stared into the darkness of our collective nightmares. I saw a future full of injustice. But what frightened me the most was that this imagined reality was an actual possibility.

As I peered into what our future could be, I asked myself, "How do we stop this from happening?" My answer was clear: Vali. Vali was born from the fire of the women I have been organizing with for years. These women have taught me that to be an activist is to be an eternal optimist. Activists believe change is possible even though everything around them tells them it is impossible. Activists fight, against the odds, for years, decades, and centuries. I believe what guides activists in their difficult pursuit of equity is a profound faith in the possibility of a just world and an unconditional love for their communities. It is these same principles of love and justice that guide my work as a storyteller. I tell the stories of immigrants because I am a proud immigrant. The stories I strive to tell are the love stories of mothers and their children.

In the beginning of *Sanctuary*, Vali is a teenager struggling to live a normal life. She is not naive to the world around her.

She is undocumented in America. She lives with the fear that her life can change at any moment. This constant fear has made Vali strong beyond her years. When her mother is finally taken by the Deportation Force, she has a choice to make. She can crumble or she can survive. Vali does what millions of immigrants have done before her. She forges a path out of nothing. Vali doesn't crumble because that is not an option for her, nor does she merely survive. Vali creates a beloved community. She fights back against injustice. She allows love to guide her. Over the course of the story, Vali transforms into a freedom fighter. She becomes the answer to our present.

One of my favorite quotes is "Art is not a mirror held up to reality, but a hammer with which to shape it."

Sanctuary is my hammer.

FROM ABBY:

I wanted this book to be dystopian. Maybe even an allegory. When Paola and I first started mapping out Vali's journey, I was excited to invent a new world on the page, one that could serve as a warning. But every time we wove in a new plot twist or finished a chapter, the breaking news alerts stole our ideas. Every time I thought we'd made this future too bleak or barbaric, the headlines proved us wrong.

During the year that Paola and I wrote this, we witnessed the Supreme Court ruling that the United States could turn away asylum seekers; Óscar Alberto Martinez and his twenty-three-month-old daughter, Angie Valeria, drowning in the Rio

Grande; the Amazon rain forest burning, Australia burning, California burning. And as I sat down to write this last note before publication, most of the globe was quarantined, desperate to stop the spread of a new and deadly pandemic.

This year has also generated astounding beauty and heroism. The coalitions of DACA recipients banding together and challenging the current administration; the Lastesis protests rippling across the globe; a sixteen-year-old global activist waking up our conscience; and each and every personal narrative from the caravan, as told by Paola Mendoza.

Meeting and collaborating with Paola has been one of the greatest honors of my life. Paola is a fierce visionary, leading the charge forward for all humans to be treated with the love and respect we each deserve. She ignites and inspires, making art and activism inseparable. She's taught me that we are all so intricately connected to and unaware of each other at the same time. We are vulnerable, powerful, and responsible for everything that happens on this earth.

We wrote this book together and it is not dystopian. It is not an allegory. It is just a few steps into "What if . . . ?" It's both bleak and hopeful; a call to arms. I am thrilled to bring this book into the world and see what happens.

Because it's about our human potential to love, or hate, or start a revolution.

THANK YOU

There are so many people to thank.

FROM PAOLA:
To my mom, I am eternally grateful to you for teaching me to be a proud immigrant. Your sacrifices and unconditional love guide everything I do.

To Mateo, your curiosity is the spark to my imagination.

To Michael Skolnik, I could not be the artist, activist, and mother I am without you by my side. I am because you are.

To my hermanas in the movement, Sarah Sophie Flicker, Nelini Stamp, Jenna Arnold, Becky Morrison, Alida Garcia, Linda Sarsour, Eisa Davis, Mona Chalabi, Linda Rivas, Jess Morales, Zakiyah Ansari, and Ginny Suss, fighting alongside you has been an honor of a lifetime. Each of you is in these pages. Vali was born of your fire.

To Jose Antonio Vargas, thank you for always picking

up the phone, for giving me guidance, and for loving me unconditionally. You make me better.

To Tony Choi Tolulope Aleshinloye, for reading an early draft and making sure I got it right.

To Abby Sher, for being my sister in art.

To the thousands of people who shared their immigrant stories with me, I celebrate you every day. I honor you at every moment. You are my inspiration.

FROM ABBY:

To all of my friends and family who read these pages: Brian Schwartz, Roger Rosen, and Katherine Dykstra.

To my dearest friends and writing gurus who helped talk me through to the truth: Joselin Linder, Gabra Zackman, Sara Moss, Samantha Karpel, Susan Shapiro, V. C. Chickering, Tara Benigno, Cynthia Kern, Sandra Sampayo, and Marvi Lacar.

To my amazing family, who kept my head connected to my heart: Jason, Sonya, Zev, Sam, Lucy, Peggy, Gene, CK, Elisabeth, Jon, and Antoinette.

To Semyon, who fed me dumplings and hope as he told me about his homeland.

And most of all, to Paola, who inspires me every single day to be loud, honest, and brave.

FROM BOTH OF US:

Thank you to our amazing editor Stacey Barney, Caitlin Tutterow, and Jen Klonsky at Putnam, for seeing this story so clearly and pushing us further. Thank you to Mollie Glick and Lola Bellier at CAA for believing in us right from the start. Thank you to Dana Ledl for our stunning cover art and to Maria Fazio for the beautiful book design.

And thank you to you, our treasured readers, for traveling this course with us, and finding *Sanctuary*.